PENGUIN

SUG

D1009605

A. S. Byatt was born in 1936 and educated at York and Newnham College, Cambridge. She has taught at the Central School of Art and Design, and from 1972 to 1983 was a lecturer in English and American literature at University College, London, becoming a senior lecturer in 1981. She has broadcast regularly on the BBC and contributed to *The Independent*, *Encounter* and *The Times Literary Supplement*, as well as many other newspapers and weeklies. She has also written critical studies of Iris Murdoch and Wordsworth and Coleridge, and edited George Eliot's *The Mill on the Floss* for Penguin Classics. Her highly acclaimed novels include *Shadow of a Sun*, *The Virgin in the Garden* (Penguin 1981), *The Game* (Penguin 1983) and *Still Life* (Penguin 1986), winner of the Silver Pen Award. Her most recent novel is *Possession: A Romance* (1990), which won the Booker Prize and the *Irish Times*/Aer Lingus International Fiction Prize, both in 1990. A. S. Byatt was awarded a CBE in 1989.

SUGAR

AND OTHER STORIES

A. S. Byatt

PENGUIN BOOKS

PENGUIN BOOKS

Published by the Penguin Group
Penguin Books Ltd, 27 Wrights Lane, London W8 5TZ, England
Penguin Books USA Inc., 375 Hudson Street, New York, New York 10014, USA
Penguin Books Australia Ltd, Ringwood, Victoria, Australia
Penguin Books Canada Ltd, 10 Alcorn Avenue, Toronto, Ontario, Canada M4V 3B2
Penguin Books (NZ) Ltd, 182–190 Wairau Road, Auckland 10, New Zealand

Penguin Books Ltd, Registered Offices: Harmondsworth, Middlesex, England

First published by Chatto & Windus 1987
Published in Penguin Books 1988
7 9 10 8 6

ACKNOWLEDGEMENTS
'The Changeling' 'On the Day that E. M. Forster Died'
and 'Precipice-Encurled' were first published in *Encounter*;
'Sugar' was first published in the *New Yorker*;
'The July Ghost' and 'Rose-Coloured Teacups'
were originally broadcast on the BBC's Radio 3,
and 'The July Ghost' has been printed in *Firebird I*
and *The Penguin Book of Ghost Stories*.

Printed in England by Clays Ltd, St Ives plc

For Michael Worton

CONTENTS

RACINE AND THE TABLECLOTH

When was it clear that Martha Crichton-Walker was the antagonist? Emily found this word for her much later, when she was a grown woman. How can a child, undersized and fearful, have enough of a self to recognize an antagonist? She might imagine the malice of a cruel stepmother or a jealous sister, but not the clash of principle, the essential denial of an antagonist. She was too young to have thought-out beliefs. It was Miss Crichton-Walker's task, after all, to form and guide the unformed personality of Emily Bray. Emily Bray's ideas might have been thought to have been imparted by Martha Crichton-Walker, and this was in part the case, which made the recognition of antagonism peculiarly difficult, certainly for Emily, possibly for both of them.

The first time Emily saw Miss Crichton-Walker in action was the first evening of her time at the school. The class was gathered together, in firelight and lamplight, round Miss Crichton-Walker's hearth, in her private sitting-room. Emily was the only new girl: she had arrived in mid-year, in exceptional circumstances (a family illness). The class were thirteen years old. There were twenty-eight of them, twenty-nine with Emily, a fact whose significance had not yet struck Emily. The fireside evening was Miss Crichton-Walker's way of noticing the death of a girl who had been in the class last term and had been struck by peritonitis after an operation on a burst appendix. This girl had been called Jan but had been known to the other girls as Hodgie. Did you hear about Hodgie, they all said to each other, rushing in with the news, mixing a kind of fear with a kind of glee, an undinted assurance of their own perpetuity. This was unfortunate for

Emily; she felt like a substitute for Hodgie, although she was not. Miss Crichton-Walker gave them all pale cocoa and sugar-topped buns, and told them to sit on the floor round her. She spoke gently about their friend Hodgie whom they must all remember as she had been, full of life, sharing everything, a happy girl. She knew they were shocked; if at any later time they were to wish to bring any anxieties or regrets to her, she would be glad to share them. Regrets was an odd word, Emily perhaps noticed, though at that stage she was already willing enough to share Martha Crichton-Walker's tacit assumption that the girls would be bound to have regrets. Thirteen-year-old girls are unkind and in groups they are cruel. There would have been regrets, however full of life and happy the lost Hodgie had been.

Miss Crichton-Walker told the girls a story. It made a peaceful scene, with the young faces turned up to the central storyteller, or down to the carpet. Emily Bray studied Miss Crichton-Walker's appearance, which was firmly benign and breastless. Rolled silver curls, almost like a barrister's wig, were aligned round a sweet face, very soft-skinned but nowhere slack, set mild. The eyes were wide and very blue, and the mouth had no droop, but was firm and even, straight-set. Lines led finely to it but did not carve any cavity or depression: they lay lightly, like a hairnet. Miss Crichton-Walker wore, on this occasion and almost always, a very fine woollen dress, nun's veiling with a pleated chest, long fitted sleeves, and a plain white Peter Pan collar. At her neck was a simple oval silver brooch. There was something essentially girlish – not skittish, or sullen, or liquid, but unmarked, about this face and body, which were also those of a neat, elderly woman.

The story was allegorical. It was about a caddis-grub which scuttled about on the floor of a pond, making itself a makeshift tube-house of bits of gravel, twigs and weed to cover its vulnerable and ugly little grub body. Its movements were awkward and painful, its world dank and dimly lit. One day it was seized with an urge to climb which it could not ignore. Painfully it drew its squashy length out of its abandoned house and made its way, bursting and anguished, up a tall bulrush. In the bright outer air it hardened, cased in, and then most painfully burst and split, issuing forth with fine iridescent wings and darting movements, a creature of light and air. Miss Crichton-Walker enjoyed this tale of contrasts. Emily Bray could not make out – she was never much to make out, it was her failing – what the other girls thought or felt. Always afterwards she imagined the dead Hodgie as grub-like and squashy. During the telling she imagined the others as little girls, although she herself was the smallest in size, puny and stick-like. They all sat in their dressing-gowns and pyjamas, washed and shapeless. Later in the dormitory they would chatter agitatedly, full of opinions and feelings, pointing fingers, jutting chins. Here they were secret and docile. Miss Crichton-Walker told them they had had a peaceful evening together and that had been good. Emily Bray saw that there were two outsiders in the room. There was herself, set aside from the emotion that was swimming around, and there was Miss Crichton-Walker who wanted them all to be sharing something.

Every Wednesday and every Sunday the school walked into the centre of the cathedral city to go to church. On Wednesday they had their own service, shared with their brother school, Holy Communion and Morning Prayer. On Sunday they made part – a large part – of the general congregation. There were rules about walking through the city; they did not go in a crocodile, but were strictly forbidden to walk more than two abreast through the narrow streets. Three laughing girls, horseplaying perhaps, had once swept over an old lady outside Boot's, had fractured frail bones and been cautioned by the Police. A result of this reasonable ruling was that it was important for each girl to have a partner, someone to walk with, a best friend. Girls of that age choose best friends naturally, or so Emily had observed, who had not had a best friend since her days in the junior school, before her unfortunate habits became pronounced. The church-walking added forms and rituals to the selection and rejection of best friends. Everyone knew if a couple split up, or a new couple was formed. Emily discovered quickly enough that there was a floating population of rejects, rag, tag, bobtail, who formed feebler ties, *ad hoc* partnerships, with half an eye on the chance of a rift between a more acceptable pairing. She assumed she would belong with these. She had no illusions about her chances of popularity in the class. The best she could hope for was decent anonymity. She also knew that decent anonymity was unlikely. When the exam results came, she would be found out. In the interim, she realized quickly enough the significance of the size of the class, twenty-nine girls. There would always be a final reject, one running round when all the musical chairs were occupied. That one would be Emily Bray.

You might suppose that grown-up, intelligent schoolmistresses would be capable of seeing the significance of twenty-nine, or that it might be possible for Emily to point it out, or recall it to them, if they did not. You also almost certainly know enough about conventional institutional rigours to be unsurprised that it was quite impossible for Emily to say anything coherent when, as happened regularly, she was caught up in the street and reprimanded for tagging along in a threesome. (Walking anywhere alone was an unthinkable and serious offence.) She dreaded Wednesdays and Sundays, working herself up on Tuesdays and Saturdays to beg, with mortified mock-casual misery, to be allowed to come along. After she began to get exam results, the situation, as she had foreseen, worsened. With appalling regularity, with unnatural ease and insulting catholicity, Emily Bray came first in almost everything except maths and domestic science. She came first in the theoretical paper of the domestic science, but her handiwork let her down. She was a simply intellectual creature. She was physically undeveloped, no good at sport, no one to chatter to about sex, or *schwärmerei*, delicious shoes or pony club confrontations. She had an image of herself in their minds as a kind of abacus in its limited frame, clicking mnemonics, solving problems, recording transactions. She waited to be disliked and they duly disliked her. There were clever girls, Flora Marsh for example, who were not so disliked: Flora was peaceably beautiful, big and slender and athletic and wholesome, genuinely modest, wanting to be mother of six and live in the country. Flora had a horse and a church partner, Catherine, she had known since she was five. Flora's handwriting was even and generous, flowing on in blue running curves and rhythmic spaces. Emily Bray wrote hunched over the page, jabbing at it with a weak-nibbed fountain pen. There was never a misspelled word, but the whole was blotted and a little smeared and grimy, the lines uneven, the characters without settled forms. In Emily's second year Miss Crichton-Walker addressed their class on its work and said in front of all of them that it was her habit always to read the best set of exam papers. In this case that was, as they all knew, Emily Bray's but she was afraid that she had had to return these unfinished since she was distressed by the aggressive handwriting. The papers were a disgrace in other ways too, nastily presented, and dirty. If Emily would be kind enough to make a fair copy she would be delighted to read them. She delivered this judgment, as was her habit, with a slight smile, not deprecating, not mitigating, but pleased and admiring. Admiring the accuracy of her own expressions, or pleased with the placing of the barb? It did not occur to young Emily to ask herself that question, though she noted and remembered the smile accurately enough to answer it, when she was ready, when her account was made up. But the child did not know what judgment the woman would make, or indeed that the woman would judge. The child believed she was shrugging off the judgment of herself. Of course the paper was dirty: schools thought dirt mattered; she believed it did not. She opposed herself like a shut sea-anemone, a wall of muscle, a tight sphincter. It is also true, changing the metaphor, that the judgment dropped in heavily and fast, like a stone into a pond, to rest unshifted on the bottom.

She noted the word, aggressive, as on that earlier occasion she had noted 'regrets'. She remembered writing those speedy, spattered pages – an essay on Hamlet's delays, a character-analysis of Emma Woodhouse. She had written for pleasure. She had written for an imaginary ideal Reader, perfectly aware of her own strengths and failings, her approximations to proper judgments, her flashes of understanding. If she had thought for ten minutes she would have known that no such Reader existed, there was only Miss Harvey and beyond Miss Harvey Miss Crichton-Walker. But she never yielded those ten minutes. If the real Reader did not exist it was necessary to invent Him, and Emily did so. The pronoun is an accurate rendering of Emily's vaguest intimation of his nature. In a female institution where justice, or judgment, was Miss Crichton-Walker, benign impartiality seemed to be male. Emily did not associate the Reader with the gods worshipped in the cathedral on Sundays. God the Judge and God the Friend and God the rushing wind of the Spirit were familiars of Miss Crichton-Walker invoked with an effort of ecstasy in evening prayers in the school, put together with music and branched stone and beautiful words and a sighing sentiment in the choir stalls. Emily could not reasonably see why the propensity to believe this myth should have any primary guarantee of touching at truth, any more than the propensity to believe Apollo, or Odin, or Gautama Buddha, or Mithras. She was not aware that she believed in the Reader, though as she got older she became more precise and firm about his attributes. He was dry and clear, he was all-knowing but not messily infinite. He kept his proportion and his place. He had no face and no imaginary arms to enfold or heart to beat: his nature was not love, but understanding. Invoked, as the black ink spattered in the smell of chalk dust and dirty fingers, he brought with him a foreign air, sunbaked on sand, sterile, heady, tolerably hot. It is not too much to say that in those seemingly endless years in that place Emily was enabled to continue because she was able to go on believing in the Reader.

She did not make a fair copy of her papers for Miss Crichton-

Walker. She believed that it was not really expected of her, that the point to be made had been made. Here she may have been doing Miss Crichton-Walker an injustice, though this is doubtful. Miss Crichton-Walker was expert in morals, not in *Hamlet* or *Emma*.

When she was fifteen Emily devised a way of dealing with the church walk. The city was mediaeval still in many parts, and, more particularly, was surrounded with long stretches of city wall, with honey-pale stone battlements, inside which two people could walk side by side, looking out over the cathedral close and the twisting lanes, away down to the surrounding plain. She discovered that if she ducked back behind the church, under an arched gateway, she could, if she went briskly, walk back along the ramparts almost all the way, out-flanking the mainstream of female pairs, descending only for the last few hundred yards, where it was possible to dodge through back streets to where the school stood, in its pleasant gardens, inside its own lesser barbed wall. No one who has not been an inmate can know exactly how powerful is the hunger for solitude which grows in the constant company, day and night, feeding, washing, learning, sleeping, almost even, with partition walls on tubular metal stems, excreting. It is said women make bad prisoners because they are not by nature communal creatures. Emily thought about these things in the snatched breathing spaces she had made on the high walls, but thought of the need for solitude as hers only, over against the crushing others, though they must all also, she later recognized, have had their inner lives, their reticences, their inexpressive needs. She thought things out on that wall, French grammar and Euclid, the existence of males, somewhere else, the purpose of her life. She grew bold and regular – there was a particular tree, a self-planted willow, whose catkins she returned to each week, tight dark reddish buds, bursting silvery grey, a week damp and glossy grey fur and then the full pussy willow, softly bristling, powdered with bright yellow in the blue. One day when she was standing looking at these vegetable lights Miss Crichton-Walker and another figure appeared to materialize in front of her, side by stiff side. They must have come up one of the flights of steps from the grass bank inside the wall, now bright with daffodils and crocus; Emily remembered them appearing head-first, as though rising from the ground, rather than walking towards her. Miss Crichton-Walker had a grey woollen coat with a curly lambskin collar in a darker pewter; on her head was a matching hat, a cylinder of curly fur. There were two rows of buttons on her chest; she wore grey kid gloves and sensible shoes, laced and rigorous. She stood there for a moment on the wall and saw Emily Bray by her willow tree. There was no question in Emily's mind that they had stared at each other, silently. Then Miss Crichton-Walker pointed over the parapet, indicating some cloud formation to her companion, of whose identity Emily formed no impression at all, and they passed on, in complete silence. She even wondered wildly, as she hurried away back towards the school, if she had not seen them at all.

She had, of course. Miss Crichton-Walker waited until evening prayers to announce, in front of the school, that she wanted to see Emily Bray, tomorrow after lunch, thus leaving Emily all night and half a day to wonder what would be said or done. It was a school without formal punishments. No one wrote lines, or sat through detentions, or penitently scrubbed washroom floors. And yet everyone, not only Emily Bray, was afraid of committing a fault before Miss Crichton-Walker. She could make you feel a real worm, the girls said, the lowest of the low, for having illegal runny honey instead of permitted hard honey, for running across the tennis lawns in heavy shoes, for smiling at boys. What she could do to those who cheated or stole or bullied was less clear and less urgent. On the whole they didn't. They were on the whole nice girls. They accepted Miss Crichton-Walker's judgment of them, and this was their heavy punishment.

Emily stood in front of Miss Crichton-Walker in her study. Between their faces was a silver rose bowl, full of spring flowers.

8

Miss Crichton-Walker was small and straight in a large upright arm chair. She asked Emily what she had been doing on the wall, and Emily said that she had no one to walk home from church with, so came that way. She thought of adding, most girls of my age, in reasonable day schools, can walk alone in a city in the middle of the morning, quite naturally, anybody might. Miss Crichton-Walker said that Emily was arrogant and unsociable, had made little or no effort to fit in with the community ever since she came, appeared to think that the world was made for her convenience. She set herself against everything, Miss Crichton-Walker said, she was positively depraved. Here was another word to add to those others, regrets, aggressive, depraved. Emily said afterwards to Flora Marsh, who asked what had happened, that Miss Crichton-Walker had told her that she was depraved. Surely not, said Flora, and, yes she did, said Emily, she did, that is what she *thinks*. You may have your own views about whether Miss Crichton-Walker could in sober fact have uttered the word depraved, in her soft, silvery voice, to an awkward girl who had tried to walk alone in mid-morning, to look at a pussy-willow, to think. It may be that Emily invented the word herself, saying it for bravado to Flora Marsh after the event, though I would then argue, in defence of Emily, that the word must have been in the air during that dialogue for her to pick up, the feeling was there, Miss Crichton-Walker sensed her solitude as something corrupt, contaminating, depraved. What was to be done? For the next four weeks, Miss Crichton-Walker said, she would walk back from church with Emily herself. It was clear that she found this prospect as disagreeable as Emily possibly could. She was punishing both of them.

What could they say to each other, the awkward pair, one shuffling downcast, one with a regular inhibited stride? Emily did not regard it as her place to initiate any conversation: she believed any approach would have been unacceptable, and may well have been right. You will think that Miss Crichton-Walker might have

9

taken the opportunity to draw Emily out, to find out why she was unhappy, or what she thought of her education. She did say some things that might have been thought to be part of such a conversation, though she said them reluctantly, in a repressed, husky voice, as though they were hard to bring out. She was content for much the larger part of their four weeks' perambulation to say nothing at all, pacing it out like prison exercise, a regular rhythmic pavement-tapping with which Emily was compelled to try to keep time. Occasionally spontaneous remarks broke from her, not in the strained, clutching voice of her confidential manner, but with a sharp, clear ring. These were remarks about Emily's personal appearance for which she felt – it is not too strong a word, though this time it is mine, or Emily's; Martha Crichton-Walker is innocent of uttering it – she felt disgust. "For the second week running you have a grey line round your neck, Emily, like the scum you deposit round the rim of the bath." "You have a poor skin, Emily. Ask Sister to give those blackheads some attention: you must have an abnormal concentration of grease in your nasal area, or else you are unusually skimpy in your attention to your personal hygiene. Have you tried medicated soap?" "Your hair is lank, Emily. I do not like to think of the probable state of your hatband." "May I see your hands? I have never understood how people can bring themselves to bite their nails. How unpleasant and profitless to chew away one's own flesh in this manner. I see you are imbued with ink as some people are dyed with nicotine: it is just as disagreeable. Perhaps the state of your hands goes some way to explain your very poor presentation of your work: you seem to *wallow* in ink to a quite unusual extent. Please purchase a pumice stone and a lemon and scour it away before we go out next week. Please borrow a knife from the kitchen and prise away the boot-polished mud from your shoe-heels – that is a lazy way of going on that does not deceive the eye, and increases the impression of slovenliness.'

None of these remarks was wholly unjust, though the number

of them, the ingenuity with which they were elaborated and dilated on, were perhaps excessive? Emily imagined the little nose sniffing at the armpits of her discarded vests, at the stains on her pants. She sweated with anxiety inside her serge overcoat, waiting outside Miss Crichton-Walker's study, and imagined Miss Crichton-Walker could smell her fear rising out of the wool, running down her lisle stockings. Miss Crichton-Walker seemed to be without natural exudations. A whiff of lavender, a hint of mothball.

She talked to Emily about her family. Emily's family do not come into this story, though you may perhaps be wondering about them, you might need at least to know whether the authority they represented would be likely to reinforce that of Miss Crichton-Walker, or to present some counter-balance, some other form of moral priority. Emily Bray was a scholarship girl, from a large Potteries family of five children. Emily's father was a foreman in charge of a kiln which fired a curious mixture of teacups thick with lilies of the valley, dinner plates edged severely with gold dagger-shapes, and virulently green pottery dogs with gaping mouths to hold toothbrushes or rubber bands. Emily's mother had, until her marriage, been an elementary school teacher, trained at Homerton in Cambridge, where she had developed the aspiration to send her sons and daughters to that university. Emily was the eldest of the five children; the next one, Martin, was a mongol. Emily's mother considered Martin a condign punishment of her aspirations to betterment. She loved him extravagantly and best. The three younger ones were left to their own resources, much of the time. Emily felt for them, and their cramped, busy, noisy little life, some of the distaste Miss Crichton-Walker felt for her, perhaps for all the girls. There are two things to note in this brief summing-up – a hereditary propensity to feel guilty, handed down to Emily from her briefly ambitious mother, and the existence of Martin.

Miss Crichton-Walker knew about Martin, of course. He had been part of the argument for Emily's scholarship, awarded on grounds of social need, in line with the principles of the school, rather than academic merit. Miss Crichton-Walker, in so far as she wanted to talk to Emily at all, wanted to talk about Martin. Tell me about your brothers and sisters, dear, she said, and Emily listed them, Martin, thirteen, Lorna, ten, Gareth, eight, Amanda, five. Did she miss them, said Miss Crichton-Walker, and Emily said no, not really, she saw them in the holidays, they were very noisy, if she was working. But you must love them, said Miss Crichton-Walker, in her choking voice, you must feel you are, hmm, not properly part of their lives? Emily did indeed feel excluded from the bustle of the kitchen, and more confusedly, more anxiously, from her mother's love, by Martin. But she sensed, rightly, that Miss Crichton-Walker wished her to feel cut off by the privilege of being at the school, guilty of not offering the help she might have done. She described teaching Amanda to read, in two weeks flat, and Miss Crichton-Walker said she noticed Emily did not mention Martin. Was that because she was embarrassed, or because she felt badly about him? She must never be embarrassed by Martin's misfortune, said Miss Crichton-Walker, who was embarrassed by Emily's inkstains and shoe-mud most sincerely, she must acknowledge her own. I do love him, said Emily, who did, who had nursed and sung to him, when he was smaller, who suffered from his crashing forays into her half-bedroom, from scribbled-on exercises, bath-drowned books. She remembered his heavy amiable twinkle. We all love him, she said. You must try to do so, said Miss Crichton-Walker.

Miss Crichton-Walker had her lighter moments. Some of these were part of the school's traditional pattern, in which she had her traditional place, such as the telling of the school ghost story at Hallowe'en, a firelit occasion for everyone, in the stark dining-room, by the light of two hundred candles inside the grinning orange skins of two hundred swedes. The girls sat for hours hollowing out these heads, at first nibbling the sweet vegetable, then revolted by it. For days afterwards the school smelled like a byre: during the story-telling the roasting smell of singed turnip overlay the persisting smell of the raw scrapings. For an hour before the storytelling they had their annual time of licence, running screaming through the dark garden, in sheets and knitted spiderwebs, jointed paper skeletons and floating batwings. The ghost story concerned an improbable encounter between a Roman centurion and a phantom cow in a venerable clump of trees in the centre of which stood an old and magnificent swing. Anyone meeting the white cow would vanish, the story ran, as in some other time the centurion had vanished, though imperfectly, leaving traces of his presence among the trees, the glimpsed sheen on a helmet, the flutter of his leather skirting. There was always a lot of suppressed giggling during Miss Crichton-Walker's rendering of this tale, which, to tell the truth, lacked narrative tension and a conclusive climax. The giggling was because of the proliferate embroidered legends which were in everyone's mind of Miss Crichton-Walker's secret, nocturnal, naked swinging in that clump of trees. She had once very determinedly, in Emily's presence, told a group of the girls that she enjoyed sitting naked in her room, on the hearth by the fire in the evening. It is very pleasant to feel the air on your skin, said Miss Crichton-Walker, holding her hands judicially before her chest, fingertips touching. It is natural and pleasant. Emily did not know what authority there was for the legend that she swung naked at night in the garden. She had perhaps once told such a group of girls that she would *like* to do so, that it would be good and pleasant to swoop unencumbered through the dark air, to touch the lowest branches of the thick trees with naked toes, to feel the cool rush along her body. There were in any case now several stories of her having been solidly seen doing just that, urging herself to and fro, milky-white in the dark. This image, with its moon face and rigid imperturbable curls was much more vivid in Emily's mind at Hallowe'en than any ghostly cow or centurion. The swing, in its wooden authority and weight, reminded Emily of a gibbet. The storytelling, more vaguely, reminded her of the first evening and the allegorizing of Hodgie's death.

Their first stirrings of appetite and anxiety, directed at the only vaguely differentiated mass of the brother school's congregation, aroused considerable efforts of repressive energy in Miss Crichton-Walker. It was said that under a previous, more liberal headmistress, the boys had been encouraged to walk the girls back from church. No one would even have dared to propose this to her. That there were girls who flouted this prohibition Emily knew, though only by remote hearsay. She could not tell one boy from another and was in love with Benedick, with Pierre, with Max Ravenscar, with Mr Knightley. There was an annual school dance, to which the boys were brought in silent, damp-palmed, hunched clumps in two or three buses. Miss Crichton-Walker could not prevent this dance: it was an ancient tradition: the boys' headmaster and the governors liked it to exist as a sign of educational liberality. But she spoke against it. For weeks before the arrival of the boys she spent her little Saturday evening homilies on warning the girls. It was not clear, from what she said, exactly what she was warning against. She was famous in the Lower Sixth for having managed explicitly to say that if any boy pressed too close, held any girl too tightly, that girl must say composedly 'Shall we sit this one out?' Girls rolled on their dormitory beds gasping out this *mot* in bursts of wild laughter and tones of accomplished parody. (The school was full of accomplished parodists of Miss Crichton-Walker.) They polished their coloured court shoes, scarlet and peacock, and fingered the stiff taffeta folds of their huge skirts, which they wore with demure and provocative silk shirts, and tightly-pulled wide belts. In later years Emily remembered as the centre of Miss Crichton-Walker's attack on sexual promptings, on the possibilities of arousal, a curiously elaborate disquisition on the unpleasantness and unnatural function of the female razor. She could not bring herself to mention the armpits. She spoke at length, with an access of clarity and precision, about the evil effects on the skin of frequent shaving of the legs, which left "as I know very well, an unsightly dark stubble, which then has to be treated more and more frequently, once you have shaved away the first natural soft down. Any gardener will tell you that grass grows coarser after it has once been cut. I ask all the girls who have razors in the school to send them home, please, and all girls to ask their parents not to send such things through the post." It was also during the weeks preceding the dance that she spoke against deodorants, saying that they were unnecessary for young girls and that the effects of prolonged chemical treatment of delicate skin were not yet known. A little talcum powder would be quite sufficient if they feared becoming heated.

I am not going to describe the dance, which was sad for almost all of them, must have been, as they stood in their resolutely unmingled ranks on either side of the grey school hall. Nothing of interest really happened to Emily on that occasion, as she must, in her secret mind, have known it would not. It faded rapidly enough in her memory, whereas Miss Crichton-Walker's peculiar anxiety about it, even down to her curious analogy between razors and lawn-mowers, remained stamped there, clear and pungent, an odd and significant trace of the days of her education. In due course this memory accrued to itself Emily's later reflections on the punning names of depilatories, all of which aroused in her mind a trace-image of Miss Crichton-Walker's swinging, white, hairless body in the moonlight. Veet. Immac. Nair. Emily at the time of the static dance was beginning to sample the pleasures of being a linguist. Nair sounded like a Miltonic coinage for Satanic scaliness. Veet was a thick English version of French rapidity and discreet efficiency. Immac, in the connexion of Miss Crichton-Walker, was particularly satisfying, carrying with it the Latin, maculata, stained or spotted, immaculata, unstained, unspotted, and the Immaculate Conception, which, Emily was taught at this time, referred to the stainless or spotless begetting of the Virgin herself, not to the subsequent self-contained, unpunctured, manless begetting of the Son. The girls in the dormitories were roused by Miss Crichton-Walker to swap anecdotes about Veet, which according to them had 'the – most – terrible – *smell*' and produced a stinking slop of hairy grease. No one sent her razor home. It was generally agreed that Miss Crichton-Walker had too little bodily hair to know what it was to worry about it.

Meanwhile, and at the same time, there was Racine. You may be amused that Miss Crichton-Walker should simultaneously ban ladies' razors and promote the study of *Phèdre*. It is amusing. It is amusing that the same girls should already have been exposed to the betrayed and betraying cries of Ophelia's madness. 'Then up he rose, and doffed his clothes, and dupped the chamber door. Let in the maid that out a maid, never departed more.' It is the word 'dupped' that is so upsetting in that little song, perhaps because it recalls another Shakespearean word that rhymes with it, Iago's black ram tupping the white ewe, Desdemona. Get thee to a nunnery, said Hamlet, and there was Emily, in a nunnery, never out of one, in a rustle of terrible words and delicate and gross suggestions, the stuff of her studies. But that is not what I wanted to say about Racine. Shakespeare came upon Emily gradually, she could accommodate him, he had always been there. Racine was sudden and new. That is not it, either, not what I wanted to say.

Think of it. Twenty girls or so – were there so many? – in the A level French class, and in front of each a similar, if not identical small, slim greenish book, more or less used, more or less stained. When they riffled through the pages, the text did not look attractive. It proceeded in strict, soldierly columns of rhymed couplets, a form disliked by both the poetry-lovers and the indifferent amongst them. Nothing seemed to be happening, it all seemed to be the same. The speeches were very long. There appeared to be no interchange, no battle of dialogue, no action. *Phèdre*. The French teacher told them that the play was based on the *Hippolytus* of Euripides, and that Racine had altered the plot by adding a character, a young girl, Aricie, whom Hippolytus should fall in love with. She neglected to describe the original play, which they did not know. They wrote down, Hippolytus, Euripides, Aricie. She told them that the play kept the unities of classical drama, and told them what these unities were, and they wrote them down. The Unity of Time = One Day. The Unity of Space = One Place. The Unity of Action = One Plot. She neglected to say what kind of effect these constrictions might have on an imagined world: she offered a half-hearted rationale she clearly despised a little herself, as though the Greeks and the French were children who made unnecessary rules for themselves, did not see wider horizons. The girls were embarrassed by having to read this passionate sing-song verse aloud in French. Emily shared their initial reluctance, their near-apathy. She was later to believe that only she became a secret addict of Racine's convoluted world, tortuously lucid, savage and controlled. As I said, the imagination of the other girls' thoughts was not Emily's strength. In Racine's world, all the inmates were gripped wholly by incompatible passions which swelled uncontrollably to fill their whole universe, brimming over and drowning its horizons. They were all creatures of excess, their secret blood burned and boiled and an unimaginably hot bright sun glared down in judgment. They were all horribly and beautifully interwoven, tearing each other apart in a perfectly choreographed dance, every move inevitable, lovely, destroying. In this world men and women had high and terrible fates which were themselves and yet greater than themselves. Phèdre's love for Hippolyte was wholly unnatural, dragging her world askew, wholly inevitable, a force like a flood, or a conflagration, or an eruption. This art described a world of monstrous disorder and excess and at the same time ordered it with iron control and constrictions, the closed world of the classical stage and the prescribed dialogue, the flexible, shining, inescapable steel mesh of that regular, regulated singing verse. It was a world in which the artist was in unusual collusion with the Reader, his art like a mapping trellis between the voyeur and the terrible writhing of the characters. It was an austere and adult art, Emily thought, who knew little about adults, only that they were unlike Miss Crichton-Walker, and had anxieties other than those of her tired and over-stretched mother. The Reader was adult. The Reader saw with the pitiless clarity of Racine – and also with Racine's impersonal sympathy – just how far human beings could go, what they were capable of.

After the April foolery, Miss Crichton-Walker said she would not have believed the girls were capable of it. No one, no one Emily knew at least, knew how the folly had started. It was 'passed on', in giggled injunctions, returning again embroidered to earlier tellers. It must have originated with some pair, or pairs, of boys and girls who had managed to make contact at the static dance, who had perhaps sat a few waltzes out together, as Miss Crichton-Walker had bidden. The instruction they all received was that on Sunday April 1st the boys were to sit on the girls' side of the church and vice versa. Not to mingle, that is. To change places *en bloc*, from the bride's side to the bridegroom's. No rationale was given for this jape, which was immediately perceived by all the girls and boys involved as exquisitely funny, a kind of epitome of disorder and misrule. The bolder spirits took care to arrive early, and arrange themselves decorously in their contrary pews. The others followed like meek sheep. To show that they were not mocking God, the whole congregation then worshipped with almost unnatural fervour and devotion, chanting the responses, not wriggling or shifting in their seats. The Vicar raised his eyebrows, smiled benignly, and conducted the service with no reference to the change.

Miss Crichton-Walker was shocked, or hurt, to the quick. It was as though, Emily thought very much later, some kind of ritual travesty had happened, the Dionysiac preparing of Pentheus, in his women's skirts, for the maenads to feast on. Though this analogy is misleading: Miss Crichton-Walker's anguish was a kind of puritanical modesty. What outraged her was that, as she saw it, she, and the institution of which she was the head, had been irrevocably shamed in front of the enemy. In the icy little speech she made to the school at the next breakfast she did not mention any insult to the church, Emily was almost sure. Nor did she dart barbs of precise, disgusted speech at the assembled girls: she was too upset for that. Uncharacteristically she wavered, beginning "Something has happened ... something has taken place ... you will all know what I am speaking of ..." gathering strength only when she came to her proposed expiation of the sin. "Because of what you have done," she said, "I shall stand here, without food, during all today's meals. I shall eat nothing. You can watch me while you eat, and think about what you have done.'

Did they? Emily's uncertainty about the thoughts of the others held for this extraordinary act of vicarious penance, too. Did they laugh about it? Were they shocked and anxious? Through all three meals of the day they ate in silence, forks clattering vigorously on plates, iron spoons scraping metal trays, amongst the smell of browned shepherd's pie and institutional custard, whilst that little figure stood, doll-like, absurd and compelling, her fine lips pursed, her judicial curls regular round her motion- less cheeks. Emily herself, as always, she came to understand, reacted with a fatal doubleness. She *thought* Miss Crichton- Walker was behaving in an undignified and disproportionate manner. She *felt*, gloomily and heavily, that she had indeed greatly damaged Miss Crichton-Walker, had done her a great and now inexpiable wrong, for which Miss Crichton-Walker was busily heaping coals of fire on her uncomprehending but guilty head. Miss Crichton-Walker was atoning for Emily's sin, which Emily had not, until then, known to be a sin. Emily was trapped.

When the A-level exams came, Emily developed a personality, not perhaps, you will think, a very agreeable one. She was approaching a time when her skills would be publicly measured and valued, or so she thought, as she became increasingly aware that they were positively deplored, not only by the other girls, but by Miss Crichton-Walker. The school was academically sound but made it a matter of principle not to put much emphasis on these matters, to encourage leadership, community spirit, charity, usefulness and other worthy undertakings. Girls went to university but were not excessively, not even much praised for this. Nevertheless, Emily knew it was there. At the end of the tunnel – which she visualized, since one must never allow a metaphor to lie dead and inert, as some kind of curving, tough, skinny tube in which she was confined and struggling, seeing the outside world dimly and distorted – at the end of the tunnel there was, there must be, light and a rational world full of aspiring Readers. She prepared for the A level with a desperate chastity of effort, as a nun might prepare for her vows. She learned to write neatly, overnight it seemed, so that no one recognized these new, confident, precisely black unblotted lines. She developed a pugnacious tilt to her chin. Someone in her form took her by the ears and banged her head repeatedly on the classroom wall, crying out "you don't even have to try, you smug little bitch . . ." but this was not true. She struggled secretly for perfection. She read four more of Racine's plays, feverishly sure that she would, when the time came, write something inadequate, ill-informed about his range, his beliefs, his wisdom. As I write, I can feel you judging her adversely, thinking, what a to-do, or even, smug little bitch. If I had set out to write a story about someone trying for perfection as a high diver, perhaps, or as a long distance runner, or even as a pianist, I should not so have lost your sympathy at this point. I could have been sure of exciting you with heavy muscles going up the concrete steps for the twentieth or thirtieth time, with the smooth sheet of aquamarine always waiting, the rush of white air, white air in water, the drum in the eardrums, the conversion of flesh and bone to a perfect parabola. You would have understood this in terms of some great effort of your own, at some time, as I now take pleasure in understanding the work of televised snooker players, thinking a series of curves and lines and then making these real, watching the balls dart and clatter and fall into beautiful shapes, as I also take pleasure in the skill of the cameramen, who can show my ignorant eye, picking out this detail and that, where the beautiful lines lie, where there are impossibilities in the way, where the danger is, and where success.

Maybe I am wrong in supposing that there is something inherently distasteful in the struggles of the solitary clever child. Or maybe the reason is not that cleverness – academic cleverness – is distasteful, but that writing about it is *déjà-vu*, wearisome. That's what they all become, solitary clever children, complaining writers, misunderstood. Not Emily. She did not become a writer, about her misunderstood cleverness or anything else.

Maybe you are not unsympathetic at all, and I have now made you so. You can do without a paranoid narrator. Back to Miss Crichton-Walker, always in wait.

On the evening before the first exam, Miss Crichton-Walker addressed to the whole school one of her little homilies. It was summer, and she wore a silvery grey dress, with her small silver brooch. In front of her was a plain silver bowl of flowers – pink roses, blue irises, something white and lacy and delicate surrounding them. The exams, she told the school, were due to begin tomorrow, and she hoped the junior girls would remember to keep quiet and not to shout under the hall windows whilst others were writing. There were girls in the school, she said, who appeared to attach a great deal of importance to exam results. Who seemed to think that there was some kind of exceptional merit in doing well. She hoped she had never allowed the school to suppose that her own values were wrapped up in this kind of achievement. Everything they did mattered, mattered very much, everything was of extreme importance in its own way. She herself, she said, had written books, and she had embroidered tablecloths. She would not say that there was not as much lasting value, as much pleasure for others, in a well-made tablecloth as in a well-written book.

While she talked, her eyes appeared to meet Emily's, steely and intimate. Any good speaker can do this, can appear to single out one or another of the listeners, can give the illusion that all are personally addressed. Miss Crichton-Walker was not a good speaker, normally: her voice was always choked with emotion, which she was not so much sharing as desperately offering to the stony, the uncaring of her imagination. She expected to be misunderstood, even in gaudier moments to be reviled, though persisting. Emily understood this without knowing how she knew it, or even that she knew it. But on this one occasion she knew with equal certainty that Miss Crichton-Walker's words were for her, that they were delivered with a sweet animus, an absolute antagonism into which Miss Crichton-Walker's whole cramped self was momentarily directed. At first she stared back angrily, her little chin grimly up, and thought that Miss Crichton-Walker was exceedingly vulgar, that what mattered was not exam results, God save the mark, but *Racine*. And then, in a spirit of almost academic justice, she tried to think of the virtue of tablecloths, and thought of her own Auntie Florence, in fact a great-aunt. And, after a moment or two, twisted her head, broke the locked gaze, looked down at the parquet.

In the Potteries, she had many great-aunts. Auntie Annie, Auntie Ada, Auntie Miriam, Auntie Gertrude, Auntie Florence. Auntie Florence was the eldest and had been the most beautiful. She had always looked after her mother, in pinched circumstances, and had married late, having no children of her own, though always, Emily's mother said, much in demand to look after other people's. Her mother had died when Florrie was fifty-four, demented and senile. Her husband had had a stroke, that year, and had lain helplessly in bed for the next ten, fed and tended by Auntie Florrie. She had had, in her youth, long golden hair, so long she could sit on it. She had always wanted to travel abroad, Auntie Florrie, whose education had ceased formally at fourteen, who read Dickens and Trollope, Dumas and Harriet Beecher

Stowe. When Uncle Ted died at last, Aunt Florrie had a little money and thought she might travel. But then Auntie Miriam sickened, went off her feet, trembled uncontrollably and Florrie was called in by her children, busy with their own children. She was the one who was available, like, Emily's mother said. She had always been as strong as a horse, toiling up and down them stairs, fetching and carrying for Gran, for Uncle Ted, and then for poor Miriam. She always looked so wholesome and ready for anything. But she was seventy-two when Miriam died and arthritis got her. She couldn't go very far. She went on with the embroidery she'd always done, beautiful work of all kinds, bouquets and arabesques and trellises of flowers in jewelled colours on white linen, or in white silk on white pillowcases, or in rainbow colours and patterns from every century, Renaissance, Classical, Victorian, Art Nouveau, on satin cushion covers. If you went to see her you took her a present of white satin to work on. She liked heavy bridal satin best. She liked the creamy whites and could never take to the new glaring whites in the nylon satins. When she was eighty-five the local paper had an article in it about her marvellous work, and a photograph of Auntie Florrie in her little sitting-room, sitting upright amongst all the white rectangles of her needlework, draped on all the furniture. Aunt Florrie still wore a woven crown of her own thinning hair. She had a good neighbour, Emily's mother said, who came in and did for her. She couldn't do much work, now, though. The arthritis had got her hands.

After Miss Crichton-Walker's little talk, Emily began to cry. For the first half-hour of the crying she herself thought that it was just a nervous reaction, a kind of irritation, because she was so strung-up for the next day's examination, and that it would soon stop. She cried at first rather noisily in a subterranean locker-room, swaying to and fro and gasping a little, squatting on a bench above a metal cage containing a knot of canvas hockey boots and greying gym shoes. When bed-time came, she thought she ought to stop crying now, she had had her time of release and respite. She must key herself up again. She crept sniffing out into the upper corridors, where Flora Marsh met her and remarked kindly that she looked to be in a bad way. At this Emily gave a great howl, like a wounded creature, and alarmed Flora by staggering from side to side of the corridor as though her sense of balance were gone. Flora could get no sense out of her: Emily was dumb: Flora said perhaps she should go to the nursery, which was what they called the sick bay, should see Sister. After all, they had A-level Latin the next day, she needed her strength. Emily allowed herself to be led through the already-darkened school corridors, moaning a little, thinking, inside her damp and sobbing head in a lucid tic-tac, that she was like an ox, no, like a heifer it would have to be, like Keats's white heifer in the Grecian urn . . . lowing at the skies . . . Dusty round white lamps hung cheerlessly from metal chains.

Sister was a small, wiry, sensible widow in a white coat and flat rubber-soled shoes. She made Emily a cup of Ovaltine, and put her into an uncomfortable but friendly cane armchair, where Emily went on crying. It became clear to all three of them that there was no prospect of Emily ceasing to cry. The salt tears flooded and filmed her eyes, brimmed over and ran in wet sheets down her face, flowing down her neck in cold streamlets, soaking her collar. The tic-tac in Emily's mind thought of the death of Seneca, the life simply running away, warm and wet, the giving-up. Sister sent Flora Marsh to fetch Emily's things, and Emily, moving her arms like a poor swimmer in thick water, put on her nightdress and climbed into a high hospital bed in the nursery, a hard, cast-iron headed bed, with white cotton blankets. The tears, now silent, darkened and gathered in the pillow. Emily put her knees up to her chin and turned her back on Sister, who pulled back some wet hair, out of her nightdress collar. What has upset her, Sister asked Flora Marsh. Flora didn't know, unless it was something the Headmistress had said. Emily heard them at a huge distance, minute in a waste of waters. Would she be fit to take her exams, Flora asked, and Sister replied, with a night's sleep.

Emily was double. The feeling part had given up, defeated, abandoned to the bliss of dissolution. The thinking part chattered away toughly, tapping out pentameters and alexandrines with and against the soothing flow of the tears. The next morning the feeling part, still watery, accepted tea and toast shakily from Sister; the thinking part looked out craftily from the cavern behind the glistening eyes and stood up, and dressed, and went wet-faced to the Latin exam. There Emily sat, and translated, and scanned, and constructed sentences and paragraphs busily, for a couple of hours. After, a kind of wild hiccup broke in her throat and the tears started again, as though a tap had been turned on, as though something, everything, must be washed away. Emily crept back to the nursery and lay on the iron bed, cold-cheeked and clammy, buffeted by a gale of tags from Horace, storm-cries from *Lear*, domestic inanities from Mrs Bennett, subjunctives and conditionals, sorting and sifting and arranging them, tic-tac, whilst the tears welled. In this way she wrote two German papers, and the English. She was always ready to write but could never remember what she had written, dissolved in tears, run away. She was like a runner at the end of a marathon, moving on will, not on blood and muscle, who might, if you put out a hand to touch him, fall and not rise again.

She received a visit. There was an empty day between the English and the final French, and Emily lay curled in the iron bed, weeping. Sister had drawn the blinds half-way down the windows, to close out the glare of the summer sun, and the cries of tennis players on the grass courts out in the light. In the room the air was thick and green like clouded glass, with pillars of shadow standing in it, shapes underwater. Miss Crichton-Walker advanced precisely towards the bedside, bringing her own shadow, and the creak of rubber footsteps. Her hair in the half-light glistened green on silver: her dress was mud-coloured, or seemed so, with a little, thickly-crocheted collar. She pulled out a tubular chair and sat down, facing Emily, her hands folded composed in her lap, her knees tightly together, her lips pursed. Crying had not thickened Emily's breathing but vacated its spaces: Miss Crichton-Walker smelled very thinly of moth-balls, which, in the context, Emily interpreted as the sharp mustiness of ether or chloroform, a little dizzy. She lay still. Miss Crichton-Walker said, "I am sorry to hear that you are unwell, Emily, if that is the correct term. I am sorry that I was not informed earlier, or I should have come to see you earlier. I should like you to tell me, if you can, why you are so distrssed?"

"I don't know," said Emily, untruthfully.

"You set high store by these examinations, I know,' said the mild voice, accusing. "Perhaps you overreached yourself in some way, overextended yourself, were overambitious. It is a pity, I always think, to force young girls to undergo these arbitrary stresses of judgment when it should surely be possible more accurately to judge the whole tenor of their life and work. Naturally I shall write to the Board of Examiners if you feel – if I feel – you may not quite have done yourself justice. That would be a great disappointment but not a disaster, not by any means a disaster. There is much to be learned in life from temporary setbacks of this kind."

"I have sat all my papers," said Emily's drugged, defensive voice. Miss Crichton-Walker went on.

"I always think that one real failure is necessary to the formation of any really resolved character. You cannot expect to see it that way just now, but I think you will find it so later, if you allow yourself to experience it fully.'

Emily knew she must fight, and did not know how. Half of her wanted to respond with a storm of loud crying, to drown this gentle concerned voice with rude noise. Half of her knew, without those words, that that way was disaster, was capitulation, was the acceptance of this last, premature judgment. She said, "If I don't talk, if I just go on, I think I may be all right, I think.'

"You do not seem to be all right, Emily."

Emily began to feel faint and dizzy as though the mothballs were indeed anaesthetic. She concentrated on the area below the judging face: the little knots and gaps in the crochet work, which lay sluggish and inexact, as crochet, even the best, always will, asymmetrical daisies bordered with little twisted cords. Little twisted cords of the soft thick cotton were tied at Miss Crichton-Walker's neck, in a constricting little bow that gathered and flounced the work and then hung down in two limp strands, each nearly knotted at its end. Where was Racine, where was the saving thread of reasoned discourse, where the Reader's dry air? The blinds bellied and swayed slightly. A tapestry of lines of verse like musical notation ran through Emily's imagination as though on an endless rolling scroll, the orderly repetitious screen of the alexandrine somehow visually mapped by the patterning of Aunt Florrie's exquisite drawn-thread work, little cornsheaves of threads interspersed by cut openings, tied by minute stitches, a lattice, a trellis.

> *C'était pendant l'horreur d'une profonde nuit.*
> *Ma mère Jézabel devant moi s'est montrée*
> *Comme au jour de sa mort pompeusement parée . . .*

Another bedside vision, highly inappropriate. The thinking Emily smiled in secret, hand under cheek.

"I think I just want to keep quiet, to concentrate . . ."

Miss Crichton-Walker gathered herself, inclining her silver-green coils slightly towards the recumbent girl.

"I am told that something I said may have upset you. If that is so, I am naturally very sorry. I do not need to tell you that what I said was well-meant, and, I hope, considered, said in the interest of the majority of the girls, I believe, and not intended to give offence to any. You are all equally my concern, with your varying interests and gifts. It may be that I felt the need of others more at that particular time than your need: perhaps I believed that you were better provided with self-esteem than most. I can assure you that there was no personal application intended. And that I said nothing I do not wholly believe."

"No. Of course not."

"I should like to know whether you did take exception to what I said."

"I don't want to –"

"I don't want to leave you without clearing up this uncomfortable matter. I would hate – I would be very distressed – to think I had caused even unintentional pain to any girl in my charge. Please tell me if you thought I spoke amiss."

"Oh no. No, I didn't. No."

How reluctant a judge, poor Emily, how ill-equipped, how hopeless, to the extent of downright lying, of betraying the principles of exactness. The denial felt like a recantation without there having been an affirmation to recant.

"So now we understand each other. I am very glad. I have brought you some flowers from my little garden: Sister is putting them in water. They should brighten your darkness a little. I hope you will soon feel able to return to the community. I shall keep myself informed of your well-being, naturally."

The French papers were written paragraph by slow paragraph. Emily's pen made dry, black, running little marks on the white paper: Emily's argument threaded itself, a fine line embellished by bright beads of quotations. She did not make it up; she knew it, and recognized it, and laid it out in its ordered pattern. Between paragraphs Emily saw, in the dark corners of the school hall, under dusty shields of honour, little hallucinatory scenes or tableaux, enacting in doorways and window embrasures a charade of the aimlessness of endeavour. She wrote a careful analysis of the clarity of the exposition of Phèdre's devious and confused passion and looked up to see creatures gesticulating on the fringed edge of her consciousness like the blown ghosts trying to pass over the Styx. She saw Miss Crichton-Walker, silvery-muddy, as she had been in the underwater blind-light of the nursery, gravely indicating that failure had its purpose for her. She saw Aunt Florrie, grey and faded and resigned amongst the light thrown off the white linen cloths and immaculate bridal satins of her work, another judge, upright in her chair. She saw Martin, of whom she thought infrequently, on an occasion when he had gleefully tossed and rumpled all the papers spread on her little table, mild, solid, uncomprehending flesh among falling sheets of white. She saw even the long racks of ghost-glazed, unbaked pots, their pattern hidden beneath the blurred film of watery clay, waiting to go into the furnace of her father's kiln and be cooked into pleasantly clean and shining transparency. Why go on, a soft voice said in her inner ear, what is all this fuss about? What do you know, it asked justly enough, of incestuous maternal passion or the anger of the gods? These are not our concerns: we must make tablecloths and endure. Emily knew about guilt, Miss Crichton-Walker had seen to that, but she did not know about desire, bridled or unbridled, the hooked claws of flame in the blood. She wrote a neat and eloquent paragraph about Phèdre's always-present guilt, arching from the first scene to the end, which led her to feel terror at facing Minos her father, judge of the Underworld, which led her ultimately to feel that the clarity of her vision dirtied the light air, the purity of daylight. From time to time, writing this, Emily touched nervously the puffed sacs under her swollen eyes: she was struggling through liquid, she could not help irrelevantly seeing Phèdre's soiled clarity of gaze in terms of her own overwept, sore vision, for which the light was too much.

In another place, the Reader walked in dry, golden air, in his separate desert, waiting to weigh her knowledge and her ignorance, to judge her order and her fallings-off. When Emily had finished her writing she made her bow to him, in her mind, and acknowledged that he was a mythical being, that it was not possible to live in his light.

Who won, you will ask, Emily or Miss Crichton-Walker, since the Reader is mythical and detached, and can neither win nor lose? Emily might be thought to have won, since she had held to her purpose successfully: what she had written was not gibberish but exactly what was required by the scrupulous, checked and counter-checked examiners, so that her marks, when they came, were the highest the school had ever seen. Miss Crichton-Walker might be thought to have won, since Emily was diagnosed as having broken down, was sent home under strict injunctions not to open a book, and was provided by her mother with a piece of petit-point to do through the long summer, a Victorian pattern of blown roses and blue columbine, stretched across a gripping wooden hoop, in which she made dutiful cross after cross blunt-needled, tiny and woollen, pink, buff, crimson, sky-blue, royal blue, Prussian blue, creating on the underside a matted and uncouth weft of lumpy ends and trailing threads, since finishing off neatly was her weakest point. Emily might be thought to have won in the longer run, since she went to university indeed, from where she married young and hastily, having specialized safely in French language. If Emily herself thought that she had somehow lost, she thought this, as is the nature of things, in a fluctuating and intermittent way, feeling also a steady warmth towards her mild husband, a tax inspector, and her two clever daughters, and beyond that a certain limited satisfaction in the translation work she did part-time for various international legal bodies.

One day, however, she was called to see the deputy head of her eldest daughter's school, a shining steel and glass series of cubes and prisms, very different from her own dark, creeper-covered place of education. The deputy head was birdlike, insubstantial and thin in faded denim; his thin grey hair was wispy on his collar; his face was full of mild concern as he explained his anxieties about Emily's daughter. You must try to understand, he told Emily, that just because you are middle-class and university-educated, you need not expect your daughter to share your priorities. I have told Sarah myself that if she wants to be a gardener we shall do everything we can to help her, that her life is her own, that everything all the girls do here is of great importance to us, it all matters equally, all we want is for them to find themselves. Emily said in a small, dull voice that what Sarah wanted was to be able to do advanced French and advanced maths and that she could not really believe that the school had found this impossible to timetable and arrange. The deputy head's expression became extensively gentler and at the same time judicially set. You must allow, he told Emily, that parents are not always the best judge of their child's aptitudes. You may very well – with the best of intentions, naturally – be confusing Sarah's best interests with your own unfulfilled ambitions. Sarah may not be an academic child. Emily dared not ask him, as she should have done, as furious Sarah, frustrated and rebellious, was expecting her to do, if he *knew* Sarah, on what he was founding this judgment. Sarah's French, she said, is very good indeed; it is my subject, I know. She has a natural gift. He smiled his thin disbelief, his professional dismissal, and said that was her view, but not necessarily the school's. We are here to educate the whole human being, he told Emily, to educate her for life, for forming personal relations, running a home, finding her place in society, understanding her responsibilities. We are very much aware of Sarah's needs and problems – one of which, if I may speak frankly, is your expectations. Perhaps you should try to trust us? In any case, it is absolutely impossible to arrange the timetable so that Sarah may do both maths and French.

That old mild voice sounded through this new one: Emily walked away through the glassy-chill corridors thinking that if it had not been for that earlier authority she would have defied this one, wanting to stone the huge, silent panes of glass and let the dry light through, despising her own childishness.

At home, Sarah drew a neat double line under a geometric proof, laid out for the absent scanning of an unfalteringly accurate mind, to whose presence she required access. What Sarah made of herself, what Sarah saw, is Sarah's story. You can believe, I hope, you can afford to believe, that she made her way into its light.

ROSE-COLOURED TEACUPS

There were three women in the room, two sitting in low, oval-backed armchairs, and one on the end of a bed, her pale head lit by a summer window, her face slightly shadowed. They were young women, full of energy; this could be seen in the quick, alert turns of the heads, the movements of hand to mouth, carrying a cigarette in a long holder, a rose-coloured teacup. They wore knee-length shifts, one olive, one russet (sometimes it was a kind of dull crimson), one, belonging to the pale head, a clotted cream or blanket-wool colour. They all had smooth but not shining pale stockings and barred, buttoned shoes, with pointed toes and very small heels. One dark woman, in a chair, had long hair, knotted in the nape of her neck. The other two were shingled. The pale-headed woman, when she turned her head to look out of the window, could be seen to have the most beautiful slanting ledge of shorn silver and gold from the turn of her skull to the fine neck. She had a fine-edged upper lip, still and calm; a composed look, but expectant. The third woman was harder to see; the haircut was decisive and mannish; Veronica had to resist seeing it as she had always known it, pepper and salt.

She could see the chairs very clearly, one with a pale green linen cover, fitted, and one with a creased chintz, covered with large, floppy roses. She could see the little fire, with its dusty coal scuttle and brass fire-irons. Sometimes she saw it burning brightly, but mostly it was dark, because it was summer outside, and through the window, between the rosy chintz curtains, there was the unchanging college garden with its rosebeds and packed herbaceous border, its sunken pool and smell of mown grass. There were leaves coiling into the picture round the outside of the window-frame – a climbing rose, a creeper, what was it? She could see a desk, not very clearly. It was no good straining to see; it was necessary to wait quietly. There was a dark corner containing a piece of furniture she had never managed to see at all – a wardrobe? She could always see the low table, set for tea. There was a little kettle, on a trivet, and a capacious sprigged teapot, a walnut cake, on a plate, slices of malt loaf, six pink lustre teacups, rosily iridescent, with petal-shaped saucers. The lustre glaze streaked the strong pink with cobwebs of blue-grey and white-gold. And little butter knives with blunt ends and ivory handles there would be, there were, and a little cut glass dish of butter. And one of jam, yes, with a special flat jam spoon. The women talked to each other. They were waiting for someone. She could not hear their conversation or their occasional laughter. She could see the tablecloth, white linen with a drawn thread-work border, and thick embroidered flowers spilling in swags round its edges, done in that embroidery silk that is dyed in deepening and paler shades of the same colour. She mostly saw the flowers as roses, though many of them, looked at more closely, were hybrid or imaginary creations. She was overdoing the pink.

Her daughter Jane called from upstairs, peremptory and wailing. Jane was unusually at home because of some unexpected hiatus in her very busy social life, which flowed and overflowed from house to house, from friend's kitchen to friend's kitchen, loud with rock, pungent with illegal smoke, vigorous-voiced. Jane had decided to sew something. The sewing-machine was in the spare bedroom. She appeared to be slicing up a pillowcase and reconstructing it into the curiously formed bandeaux and rag-ribbons that went with certain versions of her hair. The sewing-machine had given up, Jane said, it was a stupid thing. She sat at the sewing-table and gave the machine a decisive slap, looking up with her extravagant face surrounded by a rayed sooty star of erect and lacquered hair, a jagged work of art. She had her father's big black eyes, outlined in kohl, and Veronica's father's wide and shapely mouth, painted a glossy magenta. She was big and compact, round and slender, very much alive, a woman and a cross child. It wouldn't *pick up*, the needle, Jane said, rattling the wheel round and round, clattering antique pistons and hinges. It was the tension. The tension had gone to pot. She pulled furiously at the pieces of rag and thread whirred out of the underparts of the machine where the shuttle bustled and nattered. The top thread was snapped. Veronica's mother had had the machine as a wedding present in 1930; it had been second-hand then. Veronica had had it since 1960, when Jane's elder sister had been born. She had made baby clothes on it and nightdresses. Only simple things. She was no seamstress. Her mother had been only moderately efficient with the thing, though she had used it to make do in the war, turning collars, cutting down trousers, making coats into skirts, and curtains into dungarees. Her mother's mother had been a dressmaker in the 1890s. And had also done hand-embroidery, cushions and handtowels, handkerchiefs and 'runners' for dresser-tops.

Jane tugged at her multiple earrings, coils of gold wire and little glass beads. I had a go at the tension, she said. I can't get it to go back. Jane was forthright and attacking with many things Veronica had her generation's classic inadequacy about: machines, group living, authority. Jane inhabited a mechanical world. She walked the pavements with a pendant black box, she lived amongst a festoon of electricity, hi-fi, hairdryer, tape-deck, curling-tongs, crimper. She had undone the tension-gauge on the elderly Swan Vickers and spattered various metal discs over the sewing-table. She had become irritated with the irregular coil of fine wire, with its needle-eye hook at the end, on which the thread bobs jerkily and peacefully when the machine is in running order. She had tugged and jerked at it, teasing it out of its coil so that it now protruded, a wavering, threatening, disconnected spike, pointing out nowhere.

Veronica felt rage. She said, 'But that is a coiled *spring*, Jane —'

and heard in her mind's ear a preliminary ghost of her own voice about to embark on a howling plaint, how *could* you, have you no feelings, my mother kept that machine all her life, I always looked after it, it was cared for ...

And abruptly remembered her own mother's voice in the 1950s, unrestrained, wailing, interminable, how *could* you, how *could* you, and saw briefly the pair of them, her mother with her miserable disappointed face, the mouth set in a down-droop, and her own undergraduate self, sugar-petticoated, smooth-skinned, eye-lined and passionate, staring at the shards of pink lustre teacups in a road-delivered teachest. The teacups had been given by her mother's old college friend, to take back a new generation to the college. She had not liked the teacups. She did not like pink, and the floral shape of the saucers was most unfashionable. She and her friends drank Nescafé from stone mugs or plain cylinders in primary colours. She had left folded in her drawer the tablecloth embroidered for her by her grandmother, whose style of embroidery was now exemplified by the cloth, so stiff and clean and brilliant, in the visionary teaparty she had taken to imagining since her mother died. It was a curious form of mourning, but compulsive, and partly comforting. It seemed to be all she was capable of. The force of her mother's rage against the house and housewifery that trapped her and, by extension, against her clever daughters, who had all partly evaded that trap, precluded wholehearted mourning. The silence of her absence was like coming in out of a storm. Or like the silence of that still little room, in its bright expectancy, one or any afternoon in the late 1920s.

She could not reproduce that fury against Jane. She repeated, "It's a spring, you can't uncoil it" and Jane said half-heartedly that she didn't see why not, and they sat down together to try to make sense of the scattered parts of the tension-regulator.

Veronica remembered packing the pink cups. Something had been terribly wrong. She remembered moving around her college room in a daze of defeat and anguish barely summoning up the strength to heap the despised crockery, all anyhow, into the crate, thinking that there should have been newspaper to wrap things in and that she didn't have any. And that the effort of finding any was beyond her. But although she could remember the fine frenzy in which the fate of the teacups had seemed immaterial, the cause was gone. Had she lost a lover? Missed a part in a university play? Said something and regretted it? Feared pregnancy? Or had it been merely vaguer fears of meaninglessness and inertia which had assailed her then, when she was lively, and had been replaced now by the stiffer and more precise fears of death and never getting things done? The girl in her memory of that passively miserable day's packing seemed discontinuous with herself — looked in on, as much as the imaginary teaparty. She could remember vividly taking a furtive look through a door in the part of the college where her mother's room had been, and seeing two low chairs and a bed under a window. The chairs in her constructed vision were draped anachronistically in the loose covers they had worn in her brief, half-reluctant glimpse of them. Her mother had wanted her to be at the college and had felt excluded, then, by her daughter's presence there, from her own memories of the place. The past had been made into the past, discontinuous from the present. It had been a fantasy that Veronica would sit in the same chairs, in the same sunlight and drink from the same cups. No one steps into the same river twice. Jane's elder sister, Veronica's elder daughter, had also gone to the college, and Veronica, forewarned, had watched her assert her place in it, her here and now.

The telephone rang. Jane said that would be Barnaby and her cross lassitude fell away. At the door on the way out, she turned and said to Veronica, "I'm sorry about the machine. I'm sure it'll mend. And anyway it's geriatric." She could be heard singing on the stairs, on the way to the telephone, to take up her life again. She sang beautifully in a large clear voice, inherited from her father, who could sing, and not from Veronica and her mother who scraped tunelessly. She was singing in the Brahms Requiem in the school choir. She rolled out joyfully, "Lord make me to know mine end, and the measure of my days, what it is; that I may know, that I may know how frail I am."

The three women sat in the little room, imagined not remembered. Veronica detected in her mother's cream-coloured dress just a touch of awkwardness, her grandmother's ineptness at a trade for which she was not wholly suited, a shoulder out of true, a cuff awry, as so many buttons and cuffs and waistbands had been during the making-do in the time of austerity. This awkwardness in her mother was lovable and vulnerable. The other shingled woman raised the teapot and poured amber tea into rosy teacups. Two of these cups and one saucer, what was salvaged, stood now on Veronica's dresser, useless and, Veronica thought, exquisitely pretty. Her mother raised her pale head expectantly, lifting that fine lip, fixing her whole attention on the door, through which they came – Veronica could see so much – the young men in blazers and wide flannels, college scarves and smoothed hair, smiling decorously. Veronica saw him smile with the wide and shapely smile that had just reappeared, deprecating and casual, on Jane's different, darker face. She saw the little, blonde, pretty face in the window lit with pure pleasure, pure hope, almost content. She could never see any further: from there, it always began again, chairs, tablecloth, sunny window, rosy teacups, a safe place.

THE JULY GHOST

"I think I must move out of where I'm living," he said. "I have this problem with my landlady."

He picked a long, bright hair off the back of her dress, so deftly that the act seemed simply considerate. He had been skilful at balancing glass, plate and cutlery, too. He had a look of dignified misery, like a dejected hawk. She was interested.

"What sort of problem? Amatory, financial, or domestic?"

"None of those, really. Well, not financial."

He turned the hair on his finger, examining it intently, not meeting her eye.

"Not financial. Can you tell me? I might know somewhere you could stay. I know a lot of people."

"You would." He smiled shyly. "It's not an easy problem to describe. There's just the two of us. I occupy the attics. Mostly."

He came to a stop. He was obviously reserved and secretive. But he was telling her something. This is usually attractive.

"Mostly?" Encouraging him.

"Oh, it's not like *that*. Well, not . . . Shall we sit down?"

They moved across the party, which was a big party, on a hot day. He stopped and found a bottle and filled her glass. He had not needed to ask what she was drinking. They sat side by side on a sofa: he admired the brilliant poppies bold on her emerald dress, and her pretty sandals. She had come to London for the summer to work in the British Museum. She could really have managed with microfilm in Tucson for what little manuscript research was needed, but there was a dragging love affair to end. There is an age at which, however desperately happy one is in stolen moments, days, or weekends with one's married professor, one either prises him loose or cuts and runs. She had had a stab at both, and now considered she had successfully cut and run. So it was nice to be immediately appreciated. Problems are capable of solution. She said as much to him, turning her soft face to his ravaged one, swinging the long bright hair. It had begun a year ago, he told her in a rush, at another party actually; he had met this woman, the landlady in question, and had made, not immediately, a kind of *faux pas*, he now saw, and she had been very decent, all things considered, and so . . .

He had said, "I think I must move out of where I'm living." He had been quite wild, had nearly not come to the party, but could not go on drinking alone. The woman had considered him coolly and asked, "Why?" One could not, he said, go on in a place where one had once been blissfully happy, and was now miserable, however convenient the place. Convenient, that was, for work, and friends, and things that seemed, as he mentioned them, ashy and insubstantial compared to the memory and the hope of opening the door and finding Anne outside it, laughing and breathless, waiting to be told what he had read, or thought, or eaten, or felt that day. Someone I loved left, he told the woman. Reticent on that occasion too, he bit back the flurry of sentences about the total unexpectedness of it, the arriving back and finding only an envelope on a clean table, and spaces in the bookshelves, the record stack, the kitchen cupboard. It must have been planned for weeks, she must have been thinking it out while he rolled on her, while she poured wine for him, while . . . No, no. Vituperation is undignified and in this case what he felt was lower and worse than rage: just pure, child-like loss. "One ought not to mind places," he said to the woman. "But one does," she had said. "I know."

She had suggested to him that he could come and be her lodger, then; she had, she said, a lot of spare space going to waste, and her husband wasn't there much. "We've not had a lot to say to each other, lately." He could be quite self-contained, there was a kitchen and a bathroom in the attics; she wouldn't bother him.

There was a large garden. It was possibly this that decided him: it was very hot, central London, the time of year when a man feels he would give anything to live in a room opening on to grass and trees, not a high flat in a dusty street. And if Anne came back, the door would be locked and mortice-locked. He could stop thinking about Anne coming back. That was a decisive move: Anne thought he wasn't decisive. He would live without Anne.

For some weeks after he moved in he had seen very little of the woman. They met on the stairs, and once she came up, on a hot Sunday, to tell him he must feel free to use the garden. He had offered to do some weeding and mowing and she had accepted. That was the weekend her husband came back, driving furiously up to the front door, running in, and calling in the empty hall, "Imogen, Imogen!" To which she had replied, uncharacteristically, by screaming hysterically. There was nothing in her husband, Noel's, appearance to warrant this reaction; their lodger, peering over the banister at the sound, had seen their upturned faces in the stairwell and watched hers settle into its usual prim and placid expression as he did so. Seeing Noel, a balding, fluffy-templed, stooping thirty-five or so, shabby corduroy suit, cotton polo neck, he realized he was now able to guess her age, as he had not been. She was a very neat woman, faded blonde, her hair in a knot on the back of her head, her legs long and slender, her eyes downcast. Mild was not quite the right word for her, though. She explained then that she had screamed because Noel had come home unexpectedly and startled her: she was sorry. It seemed a reasonable explanation. The extraordinary vehemence of the screaming was probably an echo in the stairwell. Noel seemed wholly downcast by it, all the same.

He had kept out of the way, that weekend, taking the stairs two at a time and lightly, feeling a little aggrieved, looking out of his kitchen window into the lovely, overgrown garden, that they were lurking indoors, wasting all the summer sun. At Sunday lunch-time he had heard the husband, Noel, shouting on the stairs.

"I can't go on, if you go on like that. I've done my best, I've tried to get through. Nothing will shift you, will it, you won't *try*, will you, you just go on and on. Well, I have my life to live, you can't throw a life away . . . can you?"

He had crept out again on to the dark upper landing and seen her standing, half-way down the stairs, quite still, watching Noel wave his arms and roar, or almost roar, with a look of impassive patience, as though this nuisance must pass off. Noel swallowed and gasped; he turned his face up to her and said plaintively,

"You do see I can't stand it? I'll be in touch, shall I? You must want . . . you must need . . . you must . . ."

She didn't speak.

"If you need anything, you know where to get me."

"Yes."

"Oh, well . . ." said Noel, and went to the door. She watched him, from the stairs, until it was shut, and then came up again, step by step, as though it was an effort, a little, and went on coming, past her bedroom, to his landing, to come in and ask him, entirely naturally, please to use the garden if he wanted to, and please not to mind marital rows. She was sure he understood . . . things were difficult . . . Noel wouldn't be back for some time. He was a journalist: his work took him away a lot. Just as well. She committed herself to that "just as well". She was a very economical speaker.

So he took to sitting in the garden. It was a lovely place: a huge, hidden, walled south London garden, with old fruit trees at the end, a wildly waving disorderly buddleia, curving beds full of old roses, and a lawn of overgrown, dense rye-grass. Over the wall at the foot was the Common, with a footpath running behind all the gardens. She came out to the shed and helped him to assemble and oil the lawnmower, standing on the little path under the apple branches while he cut an experimental serpentine across her hay.

Over the wall came the high sound of children's voices, and the thunk and thud of a football. He asked her how to raise the blades: he was not mechanically minded.

"The children get quite noisy," she said. "And dogs. I hope they don't bother you. There aren't many safe places for children, round here.'

He replied truthfully that he never heard sounds that didn't concern him, when he was concentrating. When he'd got the lawn into shape, he was going to sit on it and do a lot of reading, try to get his mind in trim again, to write a paper on Hardy's poems, on their curiously archaic vocabulary.

"It isn't very far to the road on the other side, really," she said. "It just seems to be. The Common is an illusion of space, really. Just a spur of brambles and gorse-bushes and bits of football pitch between two fast four-laned main roads. I hate London commons.'

"There's a lovely smell, though, from the gorse and the wet grass. It's a pleasant illusion."

"No illusions are pleasant," she said, decisively, and went in. He wondered what she did with her time: apart from little shopping expeditions she seemed to be always in the house. He was sure that when he'd met her she'd been introduced as having some profession: vaguely literary, vaguely academic, like everyone he knew. Perhaps she wrote poetry in her north-facing living-room. He had no idea what it would be like. Women generally wrote emotional poetry, much nicer than men, as Kingsley Amis has stated, but she seemed, despite her placid stillness, too spare and too fierce – grim? – for that. He remembered the screaming. Perhaps she wrote Plath-like chants of violence. He didn't think that quite fitted the bill, either. Perhaps she was a freelance radio journalist. He didn't bother to ask anyone who might be a common acquaintance. During the whole year, he explained to the American at the party, he hadn't actually *discussed* her with anyone. Of course he wouldn't, she agreed vaguely and warmly. She knew he wouldn't. He didn't see why he shouldn't, in fact, but went on, for the time, with his narrative.

They had got to know each other a little better over the next few weeks, at least on the level of borrowing tea, or even sharing pots of it. The weather had got hotter. He had found an old-fashioned deck-chair, with faded striped canvas, in the shed, and had brushed it over and brought it out on to his mown lawn, where he sat writing a little, reading a little, getting up and pulling up a tuft of couch grass. He had been wrong about the children not bothering him: there was a succession of incursions by all sizes of children looking for all sizes of balls, which bounced to his feet, or crashed in the shrubs, or vanished in the herbaceous border, black and white footballs, beach-balls with concentric circles of primary colours, acid yellow tennis balls. The children came over the wall: black faces, brown faces, floppy long hair, shaven heads, respectable dotted sun-hats and camouflaged cotton army hats from Milletts. They came over easily, as though they were used to it, sandals, training shoes, a few bare toes, grubby sunburned legs, cotton skirts, jeans, football shorts. Sometimes, perched on the top, they saw him and gestured at the balls; one or two asked permission. Sometimes he threw a ball back, but was apt to knock down a few knobby little unripe apples or pears. There was a gate in the wall, under the fringing trees, which he once tried to open, spending time on rusty bolts only to discover that the lock was new and secure, and the key not in it.

The boy sitting in the tree did not seem to be looking for a ball. He was in a fork of the tree nearest the gate, swinging his legs, doing something to a knot in a frayed end of rope that was attached to the branch he sat on. He wore blue jeans and training shoes, and a brilliant tee shirt, striped in the colours of the spectrum, arranged in the right order, which the man on the grass found visually pleasing. He had rather long blond hair, falling over his eyes, so that his face was obscured.

"Hey, you. Do you think you ought to be up there? It might not be safe."

The boy looked up, grinned, and vanished monkey-like over the wall. He had a nice, frank grin, friendly, not cheeky.

He was there again, the next day, leaning back in the crook of the tree, arms crossed. He had on the same shirt and jeans. The man watched him, expecting him to move again, but he sat, immobile, smiling down pleasantly, and then staring up at the sky. The man read a little, looked up, saw him still there, and said,

"Have you lost anything?"

The child did not reply: after a moment he climbed down a little, swung along the branch hand over hand, dropped to the ground, raised an arm in salute, and was up over the usual route over the wall.

Two days later he was lying on his stomach on the edge of the lawn, out of the shade, this time in a white tee shirt with a pattern of blue ships and water-lines on it, his bare feet and legs stretched in the sun. He was chewing a grass stem, and studying the earth, as though watching for insects. The man said, "Hi, there," and the boy looked up, met his look with intensely blue eyes under long lashes, smiled with the same complete warmth and open-ness, and returned his look to the earth.

He felt reluctant to inform on the boy, who seemed so harmless and considerate: but when he met him walking out of the kitchen door, spoke to him, and got no answer but the gentle smile before the boy ran off towards the wall, he wondered if he should speak to his landlady. So he asked her, did she mind the children coming in the garden. She said no, children must look for balls, that was part of being children. He persisted – they sat there, too, and he had met one coming out of the house. He hadn't seemed to be doing any harm, the boy, but you couldn't tell. He thought she should know.

He was probably a friend of her son's, she said. She looked at him kindly and explained. Her son had run off the Common with some other children, two years ago, in the summer, in July, and had been killed on the road. More or less instantly, she had added drily, as though calculating that just *enough* information would preclude the need for further questions. He said he was sorry, very sorry, feeling to blame, which was ridiculous, and a little injured, because he had not known about her son, and might inadvertently have made a fool of himself with some casual reference whose ignorance would be embarrassing.

What was the boy like, she said. The one in the house? "I don't – talk to his friends. I find it painful. It could be Timmy, or Martin. They might have lost something, or want . . ."

He described the boy. Blond, about ten at a guess, he was not very good at children's ages, very blue eyes, slightly built, with a rainbow-striped tee shirt and blue jeans, mostly though not always – oh, and those football practice shoes, black and green. And the other tee shirt, with the ships and wavy lines. And an extraordinarily nice smile. A really *warm* smile. A nice-looking boy.

He was used to her being silent. But this silence went on and on and on. She was just staring into the garden. After a time, she said, in her precise conversational tone,

"The only thing I want, the only thing I want at all in this world, is to see that boy."

She stared at the garden and he stared with her, until the grass began to dance with empty light, and the edges of the shrubbery wavered. For a brief moment he shared the strain of not seeing the boy. Then she gave a little sigh, sat down, neatly as always, and passed out at his feet.

After this she became, for her, voluble. He didn't move her after she fainted, but sat patiently by her, until she stirred and sat up; then he fetched her some water, and would have gone away, but she talked.

"I'm too rational to see ghosts, I'm not someone who would see anything there was to see, I don't believe in an after-life, I don't see how anyone can, I always found a kind of satisfaction for myself in the idea that one just came to an end, to a sliced-off stop. But that was myself; I didn't think *he* – not *he* – I thought ghosts were – what people *wanted* to see, or were afraid to see . . . and after he died, the best hope I had, it sounds silly, was that I would go mad enough so that instead of waiting every day for him to come home from school and rattle the letter-box I might actually have the illusion of seeing or hearing him come in. Because I can't stop my body and mind waiting, every day, every day, I can't let go. And his bedroom, sometimes at night I go in, I think I might just for a moment forget he *wasn't* in there sleeping, I think I would pay almost anything – anything at all – for a moment of seeing him like I used to. In his pyjamas, with his – his – his hair . . . ruffled, and, his . . . you said, his . . . that *smile*.

"When it happened, they got Noel, and Noel came in and shouted my name, like he did the other day, that's why I screamed, because it – seemed the same – and then they said, he is dead, and I thought coolly, *is* dead, that will go on and on and on till the end of time, it's a continuous present tense, one thinks the most ridiculous things, there I was thinking about grammar, the verb to be, when it ends to be dead . . . And then I came out into the garden, and I half saw, in my mind's eye, a kind of ghost of his face, just the eyes and hair, coming towards me – like every day waiting for him to come home, the way you think of your son, with such pleasure, when he's – not there – and I – I thought – no, I won't *see* him, because he is dead, and I won't dream about him because he is dead, I'll be rational and practical and continue to live because one must, and there was Noel . . .

"I got it wrong, you see, I was so *sensible*, and then I was so shocked because I couldn't get to want anything – I couldn't *talk* to Noel – I – I – made Noel take away, destroy, all the photos, I – didn't dream, you can will not to dream, I didn't . . . visit a grave, flowers, there isn't any point. I was so sensible. Only my body wouldn't stop waiting and all it wants is to – to see that boy. *That* boy. That boy you – saw."

He did not say that he might have seen another boy, maybe even a boy who had been given the tee shirts and jeans afterwards. He did not say, though the idea crossed his mind, that maybe what he had seen was some kind of impression from her terrible desire to see a boy where nothing was. The boy had had nothing terrible, no aura of pain about him: he had been, his memory insisted, such a pleasant, courteous, self-contained boy, with his own purposes. And in fact the woman herself almost immediately raised the possibility that what he had seen was what she desired to see, a kind of mix-up of radio waves, like when you overheard police messages on the radio, or got BBC 1 on a switch that said ITV. She was thinking fast, and went on almost immediately to say that perhaps his sense of loss, his loss of Anne, which was what had led her to feel she could bear his presence in her house, was what had brought them – dare she say – near enough, for their wavelengths to mingle, perhaps, had made him susceptible . . . You mean, he had said, we are a kind of emotional vacuum, between us, that must be filled. Something like that, she had said, and had added, "But I don't believe in ghosts."

Anne, he thought, could not be a ghost, because she was elsewhere, with someone else, doing for someone else those little things she had done so gaily for him, tasty little suppers, bits of research, a sudden vase of unusual flowers, a new bold shirt, unlike his own cautious taste, but suiting him, suiting him. In a sense, Anne was worse lost because voluntarily absent, an absence that could not be loved because love was at an end, for Anne.

"I don't suppose you will, now," the woman was saying. "I think talking would probably stop any – mixing of messages, if that's what it is, don't you? But – if – *if* he comes again" – and here for the first time her eyes were full of tears – "if – you must promise, you will *tell* me, you must promise."

He had promised, easily enough, because he was fairly sure she was right, the boy would not be seen again. But the next day he was on the lawn, nearer than ever, sitting on the grass beside the deck-chair, his arms clasping his bent, warm brown knees, the thick, pale hair glittering in the sun. He was wearing a football shirt, this time, Chelsea's colours. Sitting down in the deck-chair, the man could have put out a hand and touched him, but did not: it was not, it seemed, a possible gesture to make. But the boy looked up and smiled, with a pleasant complicity, as though they now understood each other very well. The man tried speech: he said, "It's nice to see you again," and the boy nodded acknowledgement of this remark, without speaking himself. This was the beginning of communication between them, or what the man supposed to be communication. He did not think of fetching the woman. He became aware that he was in some strange way *enjoying the boy's company*. His pleasant stillness – and he sat there all morning, occasionally lying back on the grass, occasionally staring thoughtfully at the house – was calming and comfortable. The man did quite a lot of work – wrote about three reasonable pages on Hardy's original air-blue gown – and looked up now and then to make sure the boy was still there and happy.

He went to report to the woman – as he had after all promised to do – that evening. She had obviously been waiting and hoping – her unnatural calm had given way to agitated pacing, and her eyes were dark and deeper in. At this point in the story he found in himself a necessity to bowdlerize for the sympathetic American, as he had indeed already begun to do. He had mentioned only a child who had "seemed like" the woman's lost son, and he now ceased to mention the child at all, as an actor in the story, with the result that what the American woman heard was a tale of how he, the man, had become increasingly involved in the woman's solitary grief, how their two losses had become a kind of *folie à deux* from which he could not extricate himself. What follows is not what he told the American girl, though it may be clear at which points the bowdlerized version coincided with what he really believed to have happened. There was a sense he could not at first analyse that it was improper to talk about the boy – not because he might not be believed; that did not come into it; but because something dreadful might happen.

"He sat on the lawn all morning. In a football shirt."

"Chelsea?"

"Chelsea."

"What did he do? Does he look happy? Did he speak?" Her desire to know was terrible.

"He doesn't speak. He didn't move much. He seemed – very calm. He stayed a long time."

"This is terrible. This is ludicrous. There *is no boy*."

"No. But I saw him."

"Why you?"

"I don't know.' A pause. "I do *like* him."

"He is – was – a most likeable boy."

Some days later he saw the boy running along the landing in the evening, wearing what might have been pyjamas, in peacock towelling, or might have been a track suit. Pyjamas, the woman stated confidently, when he told her: his new pyjamas. With white ribbed cuffs, weren't they? and a white polo neck? He corroborated this, watching her cry – she cried more easily now – finding her anxiety and disturbance very hard to bear. But it never occurred to him that it was possible to break his promise to tell her when he saw the boy. That was another curious imperative from some undefined authority.

They discussed clothes. If there were ghosts, how could they appear in clothes long burned, or rotted, or worn away by other people? You could imagine, they agreed, that something of a person might linger – as the Tibetans and others believe the soul lingers near the body before setting out on its long journey. But clothes? And in this case so many clothes? I must be seeing your memories, he told her, and she nodded fiercely, compressing her lips, agreeing that this was likely, adding, "I am too rational to go mad, so I seem to be putting it on you."

He tried a joke. "That isn't very kind to me, to imply that madness comes more easily to me."

"No, sensitivity. I am insensible. I was always a bit like that, and this made it worse. I am the *last* person to see any ghost that was trying to haunt me."

"We agreed it was your memories I saw."

"Yes. We agreed. That's rational. As rational as we can be, considering."

All the same, the brilliance of the boy's blue regard, his gravely smiling salutation in the garden next morning, did not seem like anyone's tortured memories of earlier happiness. The man spoke to him directly then:

"Is there anything I can *do* for you? Anything you want? Can I help you?"

The boy seemed to puzzle about this for a while, inclining his head as though hearing was difficult. Then he nodded, quickly and perhaps urgently, turned, and ran into the house, looking back to make sure he was followed. The man entered the living-room through the french windows, behind the running boy, who stopped for a moment in the centre of the room, with the man blinking behind him at the sudden transition from sunlight to comparative dark. The woman was sitting in an armchair, looking at nothing there. She often sat like that. She looked up, across the boy, at the man; and the boy, his face for the first time anxious, met the man's eyes again, asking, before he went out into the house.

"What is it? What is it? Have you seen him again? Why are you . . .?"

"He came in here. He went – out through the door."

"I didn't see him."

"No."

"Did he – oh, this is so *silly* – did he see me?"

He could not remember. He told the only truth he knew.

"He brought me in here."

"Oh, what can I do, what am I going to *do*? If I killed myself – I have thought of that – but the idea that I should be with him is an illusion I . . . this silly situation is the nearest I shall ever get. To him. He was *in here with me?*"

"Yes."

And she was crying again. Out in the garden he could see the boy, swinging agile on the apple branch.

He was not quite sure, looking back, when he had thought he had realized what the boy had wanted him to do. This was also, at the party, his worst piece of what he called bowdlerization, though in some sense it was clearly the opposite of bowdlerization. He told the American girl that he had come to the conclusion that it was the woman herself who had wanted it, though there was in fact, throughout, no sign of her wanting anything except to see the boy, as she said. The boy, bolder and more frequent, had appeared several nights running on the landing, wandering in and out of bathrooms and bedrooms, restlessly, a little agitated, questing almost, until it had "come to" the man that what he required was to be re-engendered, for him, the man, to give to his mother another child, into which he could peacefully vanish. The idea was so clear that it was like another imperative, though he did not have the courage to ask the child to confirm it. Possibly this was out of delicacy – the child was too young to be talked to about sex. Possibly there were other reasons. Possibly he was mistaken: the situation was making him hysterical, he felt action of some kind was required and must be possible. He could not spend the rest of the summer, the rest of his life, describing non-existent tee shirts and blond smiles.

He could think of no sensible way of embarking on his venture, so in the end simply walked into her bedroom one night. She was lying there, reading; when she saw him her instinctive gesture was to hide, not her bare arms and throat, but her book. She seemed, in fact, quite unsurprised to see his pyjamaed figure, and, after she had recovered her coolness, brought out the book definitely and laid it on the bedspread.

"My new taste in illegitimate literature. I keep them in a box under the bed."

Ena Twigg, Medium. The Infinite Hive. The Spirit World. Is There Life After Death?

"Pathetic," she proffered.

He sat down delicately on the bed.

"Please, don't grieve so. Please, let yourself be comforted. Please . . ."

He put an arm round her. She shuddered. He pulled her closer. He asked why she had had only the one son, and she seemed to understand the purport of his question, for she tried, angular and chilly, to lean on him a little, she became apparently compliant. "No real reason," she assured him, no material reason. Just her husband's profession and lack of inclination: that covered it.

"Perhaps," he suggested, "if she would be comforted a little, perhaps she could hope, perhaps . . ."

For comfort then, she said, dolefully, and lay back, pushing Ena Twigg off the bed with one fierce gesture, then lying placidly. He got in beside her, put his arms round her, kissed her cold cheek, thought of Anne, of what was never to be again. Come on, he said to the woman, you must live, you must try to live, let us hold each other for comfort.

She hissed at him "Don't *talk*" between clenched teeth, so he stroked her lightly, over her nightdress, breasts and buttocks and long stiff legs, composed like an effigy on an Elizabethan tomb. She allowed this, trembling slightly, and then trembling violently: he took this to be a sign of some mixture of pleasure and pain, of the return of life to stone. He put a hand between her legs and she moved them heavily apart; he heaved himself over her and pushed, unsuccessfully. She was contorted and locked tight: frigid, he thought grimly, was not the word. *Rigor mortis*, his mind said to him, before she began to scream.

He was ridiculously cross about this. He jumped away and said quite rudely, "Shut up," and then ungraciously, "I'm sorry." She stopped screaming as suddenly as she had begun and made one of her painstaking economical explanations.

"Sex and death don't go. I can't afford to let go of my grip on myself. I hoped. What you hoped. It was a bad idea. I apologize."

"Oh, never mind," he said and rushed out again on to the landing, feeling foolish and almost in tears for warm, lovely Anne.

The child was on the landing, waiting. When the man saw him, he looked questioning, and then turned his face against the wall and leant there, rigid, his shoulders hunched, his hair hiding his expression. There was a similarity between woman and child. The man felt, for the first time, almost uncharitable towards the boy, and then felt something else.

"Look, I'm sorry. I tried. I did try. Please turn round."

Uncompromising, rigid, clenched back view.

"Oh well," said the man, and went into his bedroom.

So now, he said to the American woman at the party, I feel a fool, I feel embarrassed, I feel we are hurting, not helping each other, I feel it isn't a refuge. Of course you feel that, she said, of course you're right – it was temporarily necessary, it helped both of you, but you've got to live your life. Yes, he said, I've done my best, I've tried to get through, I have my life to live. Look, she said, I want to help, I really do, I have these wonderful friends I'm renting this flat from, why don't you come, just for a few days, just for a break, why don't you? They're real sympathetic people, you'd like them, I like them, you could get your emotions kind of straightened out. She'd probably be glad to see the back of you, she must feel as bad as you do, she's got to relate to her situation in her own way in the end. We all have.

He said he would think about it. He knew he had elected to tell the sympathetic American because he had sensed she would be – would offer – a way out. He had to get out. He took her home from the party and went back to his house and landlady without seeing her into her flat. They both knew that this reticence was promising – that he hadn't come in then, because he meant to come later. Her warmth and readiness were like sunshine, she was open. He did not know what to say to the woman.

In fact, she made it easy for him: she asked, briskly, if he now found it perhaps uncomfortable to stay, and he replied that he had felt he should move on, he was of so little use ... Very well, she had agreed, and had added crisply that it had to be better for everyone if "all this" came to an end. He remembered the firmness with which she had told him that no illusions were pleasant. She was strong: too strong for her own good. It would take years to wear away that stony, closed, simply surviving insensibility. It was not his job. He would go. All the same, he felt bad.

He got out his suitcases and put some things in them. He went down to the garden, nervously, and put away the deck-chair. The garden was empty. There were no voices over the wall. The silence was thick and deadening. He wondered, knowing he would not see the boy again, if anyone else would do so, or if, now he was gone, no one would describe a tee shirt, a sandal, a smile, seen, remembered, or desired. He went slowly up to his room again.

The boy was sitting on his suitcase, arms crossed, face frowning and serious. He held the man's look for a long moment, and then the man went and sat on his bed. The boy continued to sit. The man found himself speaking.

"You do see I have to go? I've tried to get through. I can't get through. I'm no use to you, am I?"

The boy remained immobile, his head on one side, considering. The man stood up and walked towards him.

"Please. Let me go. What are we, in this house? A man and a woman and a child, and none of us can get through. You can't want that?"

He went as close as he dared. He had, he thought, the intention of putting his hand on or through the child. But could not bring himself to feel there was no boy. So he stood, and repeated,

"I can't get through. Do you want me to stay?"

Upon which, as he stood helplessly there, the boy turned on him again the brilliant, open, confiding, beautiful desired smile.

THE NEXT ROOM

The two young men in the front of the hearse had rolled up their shirtsleeves, very neatly, and opened the windows. They were basking a little, parked on the tarmac. You couldn't blame them. It was so hot out there, incandescent you might say, if that were not an unfortunate choice of word. Joanna Hope, stepping out of the dark chapel into the bright sun, blinked tearlessly and looked at them with approval. They were sleekly and pleasantly alive. They had brought her mother to that place safely and would not be wanted to take her anywhere else. Behind her Mrs Stillingfleet plucked at her sleeve and said they must wait for the smoke. Mrs Stillingfleet's eyes were wet and screwed-up, though not flowing. Behind Mrs Stillingfleet Nurse Dawes and the minister were both solemn and dry-eyed. They constituted the whole party.

"The smoke," echoed Joanna, not at first understanding, and then, catching up, affirmatively, "of course, the smoke." The garden of remembrance stretched away enticingly in the bright light, still under arching boughs, bright with roses, crimson, gold and white. She had chosen Pink Perpetue to commemorate her mother, who had been very fond of pink, who had lain only ten minutes ago inside her satin casing clothed in a soft pink silk nightdress Joanna had once bought for her in Hong Kong, which she had always declared too good to wear. Joanna looked up at the sky above the chimney; a 1920s brick chimney, slightly cottagey. The sky was a hot dark blue and the air danced a little, reminding Joanna, inappositely, of the simmering heat on the North African desert where she had sat, by the hour, in a jeep, counting the intermittent traffic, six camels, two mules, three lorries, two land-rovers, sixteen tramping, burdened women. She remembered Mike's wrist next to hers, holding the clipboard, gold hairs and sweat round the canvas strap of his watch. The smoke, creamy and dense, began to stain the still dancing blue. Joanna fancied she saw fine filaments of papery black in it. Her body shook with an emotion to which, firmly and with shame, she put a name. It was elation. It had been sweeping across her, intermittently and more and more strongly, ever since Nurse Dawes had woken her in the small hours to break the sad news. Her mother was free carbon molecules and potash. It was the end. She had dutifully given her mother a large part of her life, for which she had been castigated and thanked. Now it was over. It was the end. "She's in a better place now, I know it," said Mrs Stillingfleet, looking round at the silent rosy alleys. "She's at peace." Joanna nodded, not wanting to contradict. For herself, she was absolutely sure that there was no *better* place, that the end was the end. She thought Mrs Stillingfleet, who had borne her mother's mocks and scorn and disparagement with almost saintly patience, might have been glad to think so too. She had told Mrs Stillingfleet that Molly Hope had left her £500, which was not true; Joanna had suggested it and Molly had replied tartly that she hardly did enough to earn the very generous wages she received, let alone any posthumous bonus. Without Mrs Stilling-fleet, and latterly Nurse Dawes, Joanna herself could not have gone on. She was also beholden to the Economic Development Survey, who had kept her on, during all the years of Molly's immobility, without insisting that she did any foreign tours or fieldwork. She had mastered the computer, and processed other people's statistics. She co-ordinated. Now at last the world was all before her, as she had intended, when choosing her profession. Except that now, she was fifty-nine.

The house, now her house, was still full of her mother's presence. Little sounds, scratchings and rattles, were automatically trans-lated by Joanna as her mother putting down teacups on the Russian metal tray, or rearranging the tooth mugs in the bath-room. She went into her own bedroom, the bedroom of her early days at the Survey, of her father's precipitate and still unexplained retirement from the Ministry of Defence. Her own eyes met her steadily from the mirror. A handsome, tall, thin woman in white-spotted navy-blue pleated silk, her well-cut hair heavily flecked with silver. The room was north-facing, and outside was the road. Her parents' bedroom, and her mother's later downstairs room, once the breakfast room, faced south onto the garden for which the house had been bought. I shall sell this house, she thought, safely inside this admittedly chilly room. I shall start again. Not precipitately: I need to think things out. The room had no character, and dark green silk hangings. Stairs creaked under no foot. Joanna went out and toured all the empty rooms. They were instinct with her mother's presence and absence in about equal proportions. The presence was worst inside the wardrobe – some of the small pastel crimplene dresses still held Molly's increasingly angular shape. In a dark depth she saw her father's burberry and his gardening jacket. He had been dead twelve years. A tweed hat of his, pale-blue herringbone, gathered dust on a shelf. She herself, over the years, had given away most things, driving down to the Salvation Army with dark suits folded into black plastic binliners. Dark suits were particularly useful to the Salvation Army. They rendered the unemployed respectable for interviews for jobs. They gave them a chance. Joanna had never understood the indifference with which Molly had accepted Donald's persisting presence, in the shape of his things, after he was gone. She had never even moved his empty twin bed out from beside her own: she lay there at night, under her fringed, clip-on reading lamp, receiving her Benger's Food from Joanna, sometimes carping, sometimes gracious, and beyond her in the shadows was the square outline of his mattress, naked under a shotsilk counterpane, and an identical reading-lamp, dangling its egg-shaped switch, extinguished.

Both these beds were now empty: so was Molly's more recent downstairs bed, in the most pleasant room, with its bay overlooking the lawn, and hung with wisteria and summer jasmine. Her dressing-gown was still across the foot of this bed: her alarm clock still ticked beside it. Joanna, moved by grief and a ferocious need to clear all this away, dropped both of them into the woven cane linen-basket, pale green, braid-trimmed. She heard the clock cluck in protest, and felt an absence of outrage, in which she felt herself expand, as though she could skip in this room, or shout, or whirl around, and no one would hear to condemn. She added the hairbrush. There was something terrible and pathetic in the last shining white hairs in its thick, real bristles. She listened to the empty silence. Outside on the lawn, a thrush churred. She stood in the bay and looked at the bird, strutting busily, staring arrogantly about it. The lawn was white with daisies and pink with fallen petals from the rose pergola. The garden was at its loveliest, in the summer sun. Her father's ashes had been scattered at the feet of these climbing roses; she and Molly had done it together, in silence and disaccord. Molly objected to the pergola which she called "your father's folly". She was right that it was too large and obtrusive for the space it occupied. But he had loved it, had loved Albertine, and Madame Alfred Carrière and Mme Grégoire Staechelin. Joanna liked to think that he now, perhaps, was indissolubly part of these vegetable beauties, climbing and tumbling and breathing over the wooden arch. She had not known him very well and had not understood him at all: he was mediated for her by Molly's disappointment, disapproval, wrath and disgust. Now in Molly's empty room she looked out at his pergola and thought of him in peace.

She made herself a sort of supper on a tray, intending to sit down with a good book, not to watch the television – Molly's last years, and perforce her own, had been increasingly dominated by long serial dramas Molly had initially condemned as vulgar, and had later, contradictory and unapologetic, become obsessed by. *Dallas*, *Dynasty*, Wimbledon. The World Cup, *Eastenders*, Embassy Snooker, *The Edge of Darkness*. Not now dear, it's time for my serial. Always "my", as though the television companies planned with Molly's interests foremost in their mind. The opaque, grey, lightless screen was the sharpest reminder yet of Molly's absolute absence: reflected in it Joanna saw her parents' drawing-room furniture, bulging slightly, and the colour of a photograph from her childhood. I shall sell the house, she said to herself, tapping her egg. As soon as possible, but not without some sort of sensible thought about how I want to live now. Nothing precipitate and silly. The screen reflected Molly's knitting bag, a tapestry sack on wooden handles. It had pathos. Joanna rose in the middle of her egg to close it into a bureau drawer before sitting down again. What do I do with one and a half sides of a manically complicated fair-isle pullover?

She became aware of two quite different aspects of her sense of her mother who was not here. The first was an expectation of her imminent arrival, querulous or ready with a piece of witty self-deprecation, to take up her seat in her chair and ask for this and that to be fetched or taken away. This almost comfortable expectation was uncanny only because Molly would never come again; it was usual, and would not be switched off to order, or for reason's sake. The second was not expectation, but reminiscence and later came to constitute itself in Joanna's thought as "the jigsaw". She had had such a jigsaw during the long and tedious years at boarding school – a set of images, strip-cartoon pictures, patches of colour, she seemed to snip out with mental scissors and fit together awkwardly and with overlaps or gaps, labelling this for reference "my mother", an entity which had little or nothing to do with the living, slippered creature who would not again patter between Cliff Thorburn and the toaster, or take up the knitting-needles and count stitches. "My mother" in Joanna's schooldays had, like most people's mothers, worn embarrassing and strident hats. She was frozen forever in Joanna's playroom doorway like an avenging angel crying out against powder paint on the carpet fifty-four years ago. A comforting corner of the jigsaw held a kitchen mother with a wooden spoon, dripping cochineal into birthday icing: she was good at cakes, and enjoyed Joanna's pleasure. Joanna turned the finished jigsaw in her mind like a kaleidoscope; there were things now, that constituted sharp corners and jagged edges, that she had never brought out to look at in those long flickering evenings in case Molly overlooked or overheard her thoughts. Many of these pieces were to do with her vanished father, who had begun to vanish long before he had in fact choked gently to death, who had begun to vanish at precisely the moment when he had become perpetually present, when his premature retirement, or whatever it had been, had confined him to Molly's territory and its margins, the far reaches of the garden, the bonfire, the compost heap, the battle with ground elder from next door. Molly had been a great requirer: she had expected much from life, and had not had it, and had made her disappointment vociferous. Joanna was not, and now never would be, quite sure *what* she had wanted – it was not particularly to do anything, but to be something, the wife of an influential and successful man. (Joanna's own life, a career devoted to useful work for underdeveloped societies, had been conceived in direct opposition to this want.) Joanna sometimes suspected that her mother had married her father simply because he represented the nearest thing she knew to this vicarious influence and success. He had been clever, shy, and formal, a step up the social scale for the daughter of a sub-postmistress. He might have become an Under-Secretary or even better. He never talked about his work, and then, suddenly, there was trouble – "the silly mess your father got into" – Joanna would never know what – and it was at an end.

He had become ill, almost immediately, within a year at most. A wasting disease had attacked him. Joanna had heard him say once, in the conservatory, "I wasted time, and now doth time waste me," but he had been saying it into the trumpets of his lilies, not to her. He said nothing to Molly, who said a great deal to him, and Joanna had always bitterly felt that he saw Joanna herself as an extension of his wife. He had had fine, cobwebby grey hair, that when he worked he sleeked, briefly, with water. As he wasted away he became all grey; his face grew thinner, and ashen, and developed long fine downwards pleats and incisions, and then a crazy criss-cross of cracks as he diminished steadily. His eyes had always been a pale, smoky grey. He wandered among the smoke of his bonfires in a grey V-necked pullover, carrying increasingly small forkfuls of twigs and dried weeds, ghost-grey. Joanna had been very startled that the ashes which she sifted onto the roots of Madame Alfred Carrière, at the last, had been creamy-white.

The stages of his slow decline were marked on the whole by jigsaw pieces depicting, not him, but Molly's dealings with him. Molly declaring, after the fateful interview with the specialist, "There's nothing really wrong with him: he just needs to pull himself together, you'll see." Molly's distaste for his bodily presence and all his activities. He had tried, in the early days, to have a glass of beer in the early evenings. Molly had taken exception to this. The smell, she said, disgusted her. Beer was a sickening smell. (The fact that Joanna also disliked its smell had rendered her icily neutral in this dispute.) Molly had pounced on his beer glass the moment it was emptied, when the air still lingered in the fringe of froth at its brim, and had washed and washed it, her mouth set. Later, she had commented to Joanna on every small eructation. Your father's tummy grumbles all the time. He makes awful belching noises. It's the beer. It's disgusting. Towards the end, when the discreet belches were an inevitable function of his failing body, she had not even waited for his absence to comment. He appeared not to hear. He gave up the beer. The plant dispute had been harder and longer. The plants were his great love, and he was good with them. The conservatory was ranged with brave and brilliant exotics. If he could have had his way, every windowsill would have been fringed with leafage, every table scented with its own perfume. He brought things in from the conservatory, tentatively, in ones and twos, and Molly, decisively, swiftly, returned these intruders to where, she seemed to believe, they belonged, often balancing them dangerously on the edge of shelves, or breaking off delicate new growth in the process. "Earth is poisonous," she would say. "You know that.

Things have their proper places." The windowsills were airless inside the double glazing. Joanna's jigsaw Mother brandished a pot in her hand, her face blazing. But she was an ambiguous figure. After his death, though with no hint, before it, of this extraordinary turnabout, she had tended the plants herself, clumsily and diligently, keeping alive what she could, practising propagation by layering and leaf-cuttings. Donald's pride had been a collection of Christmas cactuses, which flower in the dark days, brief and brilliant at the end of their fleshy segments. He had bred a new variety of this plant, and had asked Molly whether it should be called "Molly Hope" or "Mrs Donald Hope". Molly had replied that this was a matter of indifference to her. The plant, called in the event "Joanna Hope", a deep salmon-pink bloom when it came, now occupied, in various exemplars, many windowsills and whatnots about the place. Even in Molly's own room.

Joanna's jigsaw-mother was densest at the points of medical crisis. It was during Joanna's last African tour that her father had become finally bed-ridden. Molly had been wonderful about this for just long enough, a prop and a stay admired and trusted by her GPs and neighbours, coping brilliantly, turning to. On Joanna's return, her own spectacular collapse had set in. The blood pressure – "I just *sensed* it was unnatural, dear, but I was really shocked when Dr Highet told me just *how* high it was, and when I was doing so much for your unfortunate father, which really can't have done it any good, now can it?" The palpitations, the blue lips, the partially paralysed shoulder muscles, the unstable legs, culminating in a collapse into unconsciousness at Joanna's feet when the daughter had been preparing to announce that she was setting off on a road-feasibility study in Burma. We shall not be with you long, now, Molly had declared on that occasion, twenty years ago, putting out a tremulous hand from under a crocheted bed-jacket. It's a lot to ask, but it won't be for long, and then you will be free as the wind. The illnesses were real: Joanna had asked. They gave serenity and dignity to Molly Hope. Pain was an occupation. They won't want to employ me any longer, Joanna had said, the terms of my contract don't allow it. But they had been so generous. So accommodating. This was civilized society: a series of accommodations to need and helplessness. After Donald's death, Molly had recovered a little, enough to take holidays with her daughter in the Trossachs and once in Paris. On that occasion Molly had had her handbag snatched by a crowd of vehement dancing gipsy children, who had flapped at her face with sheets of newspaper and irregular slabs of cardboard, keeping up a shrill mesmeric cry. Joanna saw her now as she had been then, bewildered, turning her little face from side to side, all tremulous, weeping slow tears of impotent rage. At home, a woolly chrysalis between sheets, she was threatening. Out there she had been pathetic, little and lost, and Joanna's own feelings unbearable. Oh I am *sorry*, Joanna had cried, as though it was all her fault, and her mother had recovered her look of disapproval and her vitality.

Joanna noticed that she had toothache. Psychosomatic, she told herself briskly, thinking of Molly's endlessly discriminated neuralgias and fibrositis. She was a little rattled by the image of her mother in the dusty Paris street, mocked by the wild children. She felt cruel. She turned on the television, a final concession to the silence. A Red Indian chief was talking, fully feathered, black and white, his ancient face lined and thoughtfully set. "My people", he said, "can hear the voices of the creatures; we love the earth, which you white men tear up with your railroads and level for your agriculture. We can hear the spirit-voices of our ancestors, close to us, not gone away, in the grass and trees and stones we know and love. You send your ancestors away in closed boxes to your faraway Heaven. We leave our people in the spirit hunting-grounds, open to the air we know. We do not go very far away. You may not notice, as you hunt amongst our trees with your cracking guns, but behind you press a whole company of our people, invisible but present, inhabiting our land." He was, the credits informed Joanna, a real chief, filmed in 1934, a lasting, mouthing, echoing, mobile ghost-face of a defeated alien, long crumbled. Ghosts too of trembling trees and chuckling icy water flickered in Joanna's drawing-room; a white hunter penetrated silence, crunching twigs, and behind him crowded a greater silence. Joanna did not like this, though foreign faces and unravaged lands were her desire and hope. In black Africa, spirits came to drink blood and strangle children; in South America they were propitiated, at cross-roads, in building-sites, with bunches of bloody feathers and ears of corn. In a home counties drawing room, what buzzed was the electric circuit, what tapped at the casement the long tendrils of the creeper, looking for a place to adhere to. Where had her mother gone, particles and smoke? The twinge in her jaw became a gimlet-boring, intermittent enough to be shocking every time it began again.

The toothache was no better at the Survey the next day. Joanna's colleagues confused its effects with those of grief, and tried to persuade her that she should have stayed at home and looked after herself, that they could easily have managed without her, which was what she feared. "I'm not upset, I have toothache," she told Mike, at the end of the morning. Mike spent much less time in England than on tour; it might have been seen as Joanna's luck that he was here, at the time of Molly's death, for three months. Mike, her only lover, and now for many years her limited but real and only friend, might be relied on to see that she meant exactly what she said. "Then you must go to the dentist," he said. "Though you can't expect not to be upset at all, Joanna." Joanna wanted to speak to him in a rush, about her limited but important future, about the possibility of other work, of seeing other parts of the world, but was inhibited by the presence of his latest assistant, Bridget Connolly, dark and pretty and just back from a course in Japan. She said, for Bridget's benefit, "Of course I miss Mother. It hasn't yet at all sunk in that she isn't there. I hear her rummaging in the cupboards and moving things in the conservatory, you know, things like that. But I did what I could, I consider, and now it's all over, there is some relief, I must admit. That part of my life is finished, now. I shall sell the house. When I've thought what to do next."

Bridget spoke. She spoke with disproportionate urgency, as though saying something she needed to say, that was not quite called for now, but could be inserted in their talk. "In Tokyo," she said, "I had breakfast every day with the family's grandfather, who was dead. He was present at every meal – his picture, anyway, in the middle of the table – we all bowed to it, and he had his own little servings of meals. They all went off to work at some unearthly hour so by the time I ate there was only me and him – and the maid brought tea for both of us, and asked him respectfully if he'd enjoyed it. He was a terribly fierce-looking old man. It was his house. They consulted him about everything."

There was a little silence. Then Bridget and Joanna spoke simultaneously. Bridget said, "I'm sorry: it was all rather a culture-shock: I was quite frightened, actually: I just wanted to say . . ."

Joanna said, "I'm quite sure death is the end. I'm sure one just goes nowhere, as one came from nowhere. I'm sure."

Mike said, "I think I'll ring my dentist and make you an emergency appointment, Joanna. I shall charge it to the Survey. I've done it before. In the interests of efficiency, I shall say. You look a bit washed-out." He touched both their arms. The young woman looked up at him, quick, electric, wanting contact and reassurance. Joanna looked down at her desk, remembering. She was embarrassed – yes, that was the exact word – to feel Mike moving into a place that had always been cramped by the exigencies of her parents. She supposed she had loved him, though she had never for a moment doubted that he preferred his wife to her – both in and out of bed – and this certainty had made her morally comfortable, not guilty about his wife, not desirous of supplanting her. Now she thought, watching him telephone, that although she had ancestors, she would not be one, she was the end of some genetic string. Was she unnatural not to have wanted him – or someone – more? What she wanted, was the time back. The empty desert and her own young eyes, watching for signs of life, out of a young face in a young body. Her tooth shrilled. Mike put down the phone. "Mr Kestelman will see you right away," he said. "He's got another emergency patient there. He'll manage to help you both as quickly as possible. I'll order you a cab, Joanna."

The dentist's waiting-room was white and streamlined, somewhere between the modernist and the clinical. Its walls were white and its tables spotless and unscratched white melamine: its lighting came from huge opaque white bowls, suspended or supported on chrome. It was like a time capsule in a science fiction film, colourless, and therefore about equally soothing and alarming. No flowers, not a speck of dust. It was already inhabited by a restless woman when Joanna arrived. The other emergency case. Joanna sat on a white tweed sofa, slung on chrome with leather bands, and put her feet together on an off-white Berber rug. The other woman, sitting opposite, leafed through and again through a heap of glossy magazines. She had pure white hair arranged in curls round her face and in a longer fall to her shoulders: this white had a spun-silk, glossy quality, full of vitality. Her skin was, by contrast, darkish, moist though, not desiccated. She was difficult to put an age to. She wore a puce angora sweater, with a low scoop neckline, embroidered with iridescent bugles and beads: the perceivable edge of her breasts seemed rounded and lively, with a few freckles. She was made up, lavishly but not grotesquely, a fuchsia lipstick to match the angora, huge hoops of violet shadow between black lashes and silver eyebrows. She wore gipsyish hooped earrings, silver, not gold. Joanna put a hand to her own jaw and gave the other an opening.

"Does it hurt? Does it hurt badly?"

"Pretty bad."

"I'm a coward about pain. Or I used to be, I should say, before things changed. Mr Kestelman thinks I've got an abscess. I only came here as a last resort. I'm ashamed, really. I tried healing by other means, but it didn't work."

"Other means?"

"What you might call faith healing. Spiritual healing. I have the gift. It is a marvellous gift, I don't know if you know anything about it, I developed it only fairly recently. I've achieved extraordinary things, marvellous cures, *mysterious* things, but for some reason I can't soothe away this pain. Physician, heal thyself, and all that. My theory is, the pain distracts me from the necessary concentration. My husband said I should give conventional medicine a go, it also exists in the world for a reason, and has helped many, don't you agree, so here I am.'

"How did you discover you had the gift?" asked Joanna, politely and with some curiosity.

"It's a fairly frequent consequence of an NDE. I didn't know that at the time, naturally. But it turns out, many of those who experience NDEs have these gifts."

"NDE?"

"Near Death Experience. I was clinically dead, and brought back. Really." She laughed, and Joanna laughed, and both put their hands to their painful faces. "I had a heart attack, two years ago now – you wouldn't think it to look at me, would you? – and I was clinically dead, stopped breathing, everything, and then they brought me back. And when I was dead, I had this wonderful experience. It changed my life. Changed absolutely."

"Tell me," said Joanna, who would have been told anyway, who had encountered her own Ancient Mariner, in this antechamber. The other swung into a well-polished narration, impeded by twinges of dental agony.

"I didn't mention it for ages, I thought I wouldn't be believed. But I knew all along it was true, truer than most things, if you see what I mean, *more* true. There I was, swimming as it were, up and up, away from myself – I could see myself lying there, it was in an underpass at Pimlico tube station actually – I could see this body lying there like a banana-skin someone had dropped – and there was I, moving away quite fast *up* a kind of tunnel – or funnel-thing – and at the other end was a sort of opening and an indescribable light, ever so bright. And more than anything I wanted to go through that door. It was bliss. Bliss. I can't describe it. When I got near, there were Figures, who Opened, and I came out into a kind of green place – a *clean* green place, all washed clean, it made me see how polluted our poor earth is – you've never dreamed such green – and there across a field was a little bungalow, ever such a lovely bungalow, with a garden *brimming* with every kind of peony, and I thought: Mum would have *loved* that, she always said her idea of heaven was a labour-saving bungalow and a garden full of peonies – and when I came to the door, there they all were, inside, Mum and Dad, and Uncle Charlie I never liked much, and my auntie Beryl, and a quietish lady who I knew was my grandmother, though I'd never set eyes on her, she died before I was born, I proved it later from photographs. They were all sort of young and healthy-looking. The *scent* of those peonies. Mum was baking cakes, and I stood in the doorway and said, "Oh Mum, can I come in, oh can I come in, how good it all looks." And Mum said, "No, you can't come now. This cake is for your uncle Jack. Not you. It's not your time. You must go back. You are needed back there." And a shining kind of person, dark-skinned like a Red Indian maybe, came up the path, and said – he didn't exactly speak but I *heard* him tell me, no, Bonnie, you've got to go back, it isn't your time, there are things for you to do, and people who need you. And then I was back in my body in intensive care in St George's and I heard them cry out, she's breathing. Ever since then, I've *known*. I've *known* death was good and not frightening. But all the rest – the healing and the clairvoyance and all that – I discovered when I joined the Academy."

"The Academy?"

"The Academy of the Return. We're a research group and a

therapeutic community. You see, it turns out that my experience wasn't unusual really, not in terms of the other experiences of NDE. The experience seems to be the same – in all cultures and religions – the tunnel and the light and the figures, and seeing your parents again –"

"I've just lost my mother," said Joanna, involuntarily.

"Well, there you are. We were brought together, because of your need to know what I have to impart. Our two toothaches were brought about with a purpose, and that's why I couldn't cure mine, of course it is, our meeting was *meant*."

"But," said Joanna, her face furiously stabbing. How can you say, I don't want heaven, I want . . .

A white-clothed figure beckoned from the inner room. "Mr Kestelman will see you now, Mrs Roote."

Mrs Roote rose, a little tremulously, looked to Joanna for reassurance, and crossed the threshold.

Joanna remembered Molly, in her last few months, complaining of noises. Joanna did not wish to remember the exact nature of these complaints, but they rose in her mind, with a difference. It was Molly's habit to wake herself with an automatic radio-teamaker, so that the voices of the world's news and the chatter and gossip of the BBC's presenters mingled with the vanishing veils of her uneasy sleep and the half-apprehended creatures of dream and nightmare. Or so Joanna now imagined, having tried out the device herself once and found her mind slipping in and out of what she vaguely felt were Molly's apprehensions and not her own. Anyway, she had thought Molly's last visions, if they could be dignified with that name, were functions of that domestic machinery. Molly, it was fair to admit, had insisted that they were not. She had asked for sympathy which Joanna had failed to offer. "I don't know often", she had said, trying to characterize these experiences, "if I'm waking or sleeping, I don't know where I am, either, but I do hear your grandparents, dear, quarrelling dreadfully in the next room, ever so close, and it's as though I can't quite be heard or seen yet, but I might be at any minute, they might turn on me and draw me into it at any minute, and I always tried so hard not to be drawn in . . ."

And once, "Oh, Joanna, they are waiting for me—I almost said, lying in wait, but that would be an awful thing to say, about one's own parents, wouldn't it? I don't want you to miss me, dear, when I'm gone, I want you to have a good time and know I was grateful for all you did, even if I'm a cantankerous old bitch a lot of the time. I've had my time, and that's it, and if it wasn't much of a time, it's no good crying over spilt milk, is it?"

And the next day, "I can hear more and more of what they're saying, in the next room. Just as it always was, nothing changed. Ma feels neglected and Pa feels nagged and put-upon, *just* the same . . ."

"Old memories are re-activated in your brain, mother. It's usual. People remember things in their seventies they haven't thought of for thirty years."

"I know. But I can't sleep for their wrangling. And I can't wake up enough to stop hearing it."

Bonnie Roote came out of the surgery, clutching a wad of tissues to her face, like a huge peony, the edges of its petals stained with bright pink lipstick and scarlet threads of blood. The attendant told Joannna Mr Kestelman would be ready in a moment. Bonnie Roote sat on the sofa, the side of her lively face swollen and awkward.

"Was it bad?" said Joanna.

Bonnie shook her head, indicating no. She mopped at her mouth. She opened her handbag, and held out a card to Joanna. She said, carefully, slurring, "We were destined to meet, dear, that's the meaning of it. Here is the address — come when you need us, if you need us."

The card said, "The Academy of the Return. Thanatology and the study of the Afterlife. Therapeutic groups: spiritual and physical health alike our concern. We may have the answers to the questions you have always been asking. Try us."

Mr Kestelman, taciturn and scientific in his sterile workplace, removed one of Joanna's teeth, which, he explained, had had a mosaic of tiny cracks and had finally crumbled altogether. Joanna must not, on any account, he said, disturb the blood-clot, which would eventually form the new gum in the gap. Joanna tasted blood, iron and gravy combined, and felt the temporary absence of a huge segment of her head. She nodded with heavy gravity to his instructions, which included going home immediately and lying down, trying to have a sleep, to get over the shock. Munificent in small things, he filled her handbag with paper tissues and little strips of encapsulated painkillers in foil. "You'll feel queasy when it comes back to life, at first," he told her. "But don't worry. It doesn't last." He told her not to explore with her tongue and she withdrew its tip guiltily from what felt like a huge soft cabbage of congealing flabby matter, replacing the lost grinder, the shining citadel of the toothpaste advertisements of her childhood. Under lost childish teeth, fringed and rootless, had been the purposeful saw-ridge of the mature, the real thing. She remembered the taste and the intricacy. It was a shock that there would, this time, be no replacement.

The house was unwelcoming, rebarbative and reproachful. She hurried through it, ignoring it, to her bedroom, and drew the curtains for the prescribed lying-down. Then she got up again and opened them. Closed curtains in daylight meant death. The good weather persisted: let the sun shine in. It didn't shine in, much: Joanna's room was not on the sunny side of the house. She got into the bed, in her petticoat, and closed her eyes; her inner vision immediately projected, on a screen, a terrible horse head, a stripped skull long in the tooth, its empty sockets and gaunt jaws running with pale carnation-coloured blood, the colour of the inside of her eyelid no doubt, crawling on the ivory bones, long,

long in the tooth. Joanna said to herself, precisely, that loss of a tooth aroused all sorts of primitive fears and opened her eyes waterily focussing on the pelmet, the dressing-table, the silk lampshade. When she closed her eyes again all she could see was the carnation colour, turbulent in tossing waves. She sighed, and slept.

There were voices in the next room. Aggrieved voices, running on in little dashes like a thwarted beck clucking against pebble-beds and rooted impediments. They had the ease of long custom and the abrasiveness of new rage. Joanna could not put words together, only the tone, which pricked the skin of her shoulders, primeval hackles shaved away by centuries of civilization. She could hear other sounds: the clink of teacups and once, surely, the angry smack of iron on ironing board. Sleep and throbbing washes of toothache insulated her for a while but she had in the end to acknowledge that she was awake and that the yammer persisted; it could not be extinguished, as she had extinguished the horsehead, by appeal to daylight. She got up and walked to and fro in her bedroom, and the voices in the next room sharpened and faded as she approached and retreated. She could see this non-existent room very clearly, a dusty place, with a table, two chairs, a gas cooker and a high, inaccessible closed window. The room next to hers was in fact an airing-cupboard; she went to open its door, where its innocent shelves held her innocent nightdresses, tidily folded. The voices spoke beyond their flimsy wall. "I shall put the house on the market," Joanna told the airing-cupboard, to see if her live voice would banish these dusty ones. They rustled furiously. Phrases came through. "*No* consideration . . . *No* imagination . . ." And then, "Out of sight, out of mind, I see." And then, silence. She could not see why silence should ever have supervened. Or for how long it might last.

She put the house on the market. The estate agent, Mr Maw, called, and Joanna showed him over it, room by room, and lastly the garden, early one morning before she left for the Survey. In the garden, swifts swooped and a blackbird sang, and the pergola roses breathed soft and sweet. In the house Mr Maw was effusive. A delightful property, he said, entering its vital statistics on a kind of abstract map on yellow paper, as Mr Kestelman had earlier entered Joanna's ravaged or vanished teeth on some archetypal mouth-plan. He paced the rooms, measuring them with his bright black shoes, toe to heel. In parts of the house, even while he was there, the voices hissed and jangled. It was as though these brick walls were interwoven with some other tough, flexible, indestructible structure, containing other rooms, other vistas, other jammed doors. Like a dress and its lining, with the slimmest space between. He should have no trouble selling this lovely residence, Mr Maw told Joanna, in such good repair and so tastefully done up. Anyone could see it had been lived in very happily: it was *homely*, it had good vibrations, you came to recognize them in his business. It must be a real wrench for Miss Hope, leaving this pleasant spot. Could he recognize *bad* vibrations, Joanna asked him? Oh yes, he assured her. Like the smell of unattended drains, on very rare occasions. He had had a client once who had had to resort to an exorcist. The property had been brimful of rage and hatred. You could feel it like a temperature change, like a damp chill, coming over the threshold. Now here, you can feel love and consideration, like the polish on good furniture. Joanna said, I mean to travel. I never meant to settle down in this way. This was my mother's house, my mother's idea of. She could not say, of what. Nor did Mr Maw want to know. He said he was sure she would find a nice holiday abroad very restorative, and then he could perhaps help her to find a labour-saving little maisonette.

Mike found her crying amongst the filing-cabinets in the Survey Record Room. She did not say that she had been looking up their official report on the North African desert road, which had concluded in fact that it need never be built, that there was not enough demand. She had been thinking of the close bright stars, the bargaining in the bazaar, the heat in the jeep. Mike made her a plastic beaker of nasty but welcome coffee and put his arm round her shoulder. "Poor old Jo," he said, and she did not take offence, for that was what he had said then, when the mosquitoes bit her and her feet blistered. "Poor old Jo. What's up exactly?"

"I put the house on the market."

"Isn't that a bit precipitate?"

"I don't want it. And I keep hearing my parents quarrelling in the next room."

She did not expect him to believe her, but there was relief in the statement.

"You did them proud. They're gone now. You can get a place of your own."

And if I had had, once, a place of my own . . . we should not now be sitting companionably here. She persisted.

"I keep feeling they're not gone. I hear them."

"You need a change."

"I know. I was going to ask. I wondered. I've lived all these years hoping – believing I could travel again, do another tour, get away – I suppose it's hopeless."

"On the whole," said Mike gently, "the foreign tours are saved for the tough young men, the single ones at that. You know how it is. But I did have an idea. If it appeals. It isn't glamorous. It's a change, though. Would you want to go to Durham? We've got a project on, on the feasibility of new small industries in mining villages. You know, the Survey always did a little local work, as well as the international. Nowadays, that's on the increase. You'd be talking to skilled men, interviewing local planners, What do you think?"

The African moon faded and the horizon contracted like a brace. All the same.

"It's a challenge."

"Right. Exercise the old fieldwork techniques even if not exactly breaking new ground? Get you away from the voices in the next room."

"They won't like that."

"Now you're being silly. I'll fix you up with a lunch with Protheroe, who's liaising with the finance companies, and we'll get you off next week."

The night before she left for Durham, Joanna spent a considerable time in the conservatory. The plants were silent, living their own lives. Mrs Stillingfleet would come in and attend to them until the house was sold. Mr Maw had had one or two tempting nibbles, he said, but nothing definite yet. It was early days, he said. He could get in touch if Miss Hope was needed. Durham wasn't the end of the earth. The conservatory had a harsh pool of light in its centre, and a peripheral population of ghostly plants, reflected amongst harsh slivers of glitter off dark glass squares. The sky was very close; a black layer on black walls and roof, apparently solid above the solid glass. Tendrils hung softly from invisible struts, feathery fronds of jasmine, corkscrew curls of passion flowers, a contained little jungle, neatly trained and tied. The potted plants were banked on trays of sandy gravel on benches, smelling paradoxically of cold, moonlit steam. Joanna moved amongst them, breaking off a dead leaf here, removing a spent bloom there. Several of these had blushed unseen; she had not visited them since Molly's death. Now she looked at the cactuses and their pups, Molly's favourites. "I must see to my pups," she had said, the week after Donald's scattering, though she had mocked him when he boasted of their health and multiplicity. Pups, indeed, Molly had then said. Anyone would think they were sentient creatures, the way you go on. Looking at the major cactus, now, swollen and furry, sprouting cobwebs of silvery hairs, and surrounded by little, fat, arachnoid replicas of itself, Joanna more or less felt its discomfort in her own blood. It was unbalanced, sprawling heavily over the rim of its container. Carefully she broke off and repotted some of the younger tumuli, digging with Molly's little brass shovel in Molly's little tub of gritty, arid potting compost. Not a creak, not a whisper. The

Christmas cactus, Joanna Hope, was not a true cactus. It needed watering and feeding freely, it needed a good loam, like any other flowering plant. It did not of course flower in summer, but it did put on new growth. Joanna picked one up. It had strange, gawkily bent arms, made of segments at slight angles to each other. The lower segments were dark green and ridged. The higher ones were paler green. The newest, perhaps the size of Joanna's little finger-nail, were glossy with health and were flushed with a roseate glow that hinted at the pure salmon-flesh pink the improbable bloom would be, in midwinter. This pink colour, and the hooked, serrated end of the segment, gave it a resemblance to the claw of some marine creature; this was enhanced by the little fringe of hairy feelers that sprouted where the new segment joined the old, and so, repeated and invariable, down all the joints of the awkward stem or arm. These feelers were of course roots. If you broke off one of these segments, delicately, roots and all, and planted it firmly in a new pot of new earth, it would expand into another plant, darken and lose its translucent pinkness, sprout more segments. Some of these plants must be parts of other plants her father himself had teased into shape, fed and watered. They represented a sort of eternity, predictable, cyclical, unchanging in form and colour. The roseate segments with their very new crenellated edges reminded her of her baby teeth: but after the baby teeth had come the rooted teeth, and after the rooted teeth this fleshed and shrinking hole. Joanna picked up a small, unassuming "Joanna Hope" stuck, by Molly no doubt, into a pale blue plastic plant pot, and took it up to bed with her. It was quiet, and alive. It might be possible to take it out of this house, up to Durham.

In the next room, the voices had acquired a certain ruggedness and clarity. Why not irises, said one, an iris bed, a raised iris bed, is a splendid feature. Not for most of the year, said the other, querulous granite, just a mass of ugly old leaves, taking up space, you want something serviceable and adaptable. You never give any credit to the larger things of the imagination, said the first voice, never. It's worth the old leaves for its time of glory. You never could see that, you never could see glory. You could have one or two at the back, said the ungiving voice, by the cistern there, one or two. What use are one or two, said the sad voice, and was answered, you never understand the proper *scale* of things, a bed of that size is just silly, just presumptuous, in the space you've got. One or two by the cistern. The roots need sun, said the other, you fool, the roots need sun, they must be baked in sun, soaked in light, you never understood that, never, you never admitted how much light they needed, you moved that bronze bearded one I had under the laurels where it rotted . . .

There must, Joanna thought, be endless quarrelling singing voices attached to this piece of earth: why do I hear only these? Are the happy silent? Bonnie Roote's relatives were in suburban bliss. The Academy of the Return might explain this anger, but I will not go there. I will go north and leave the field to them, the garden and the next room both, and they can call on Mr Maw to arbitrate, who will not hear them, who experiences them, if he senses them at all, as, what was it, full of love and consideration. Be quiet, she said to them, aloud or not, she hardly knew, and she heard them hear her protest and ignore it. Impossible to come to any civilized arrangement with you, one said to the other, impossible, impossible.

County Durham was full of ancient things that had once been powerful new beginnings. The cathedral, slipping slightly into the river down its craggy steep, houses the bones of St Cuthbert and the black slab under which rests the Venerable Bede, who changed the shape of the English sense of the English and their history. The mining villages are scattered in pockets amongst purple and grey moorland, not strung in a black chain as they are further south in Yorkshire. Ancient mills have become industrial archaeological sites, as Roman camps became before them, where the wind whistles in over heather and soughing bracken. New steel mills stand, silent, empty and cold; colliery wheels above their conical slag heaps are rusty and forever still. Joanna for some reason noticed the dead, though her work was with the living and despondent. Legionaries from Scythia and Mesopotamia and the sunlit Provincia Romana lay under that heather. Undernourished girls and boys haunted the mills and the old workings, perhaps still lacerated by the straps with which they had hauled loads of ore. Joanna listened for them and could not hear them. She herself was housed in the splendid Mitre Hotel in Durham, where the assize judges had slept when not housed in the Castle, where they still slept, feeding well, laughing sonorously, going out to admonish sinners, release the innocent, and command the confinement of the guilty in the fortress-like gaol where other dead lay in quicklime and where the sheriff's hair had gone white with horror at a hanging. The hotel was, it claimed in its parchment-like, tasteful brochure, quite possibly haunted by a wrongfully hanged highwayman and a distraught Jacobite widow who had ridden vainly to save her beloved from his terrible march to the Tower. Their presence, the brochure said, announced itself respectively by a feeling of great coldness and panic, or by a kind of sighing noise and unbearable apprehension. Joanna liked the hotel, which had ancient uneven floors and romantically low and heavy doorways, newly embellished with heavy firedoors. She dined in the dining-room amongst warm smells of good cooking, brandy *flambé*, crisp hot pastry, garlic-simmered sauces, a long and splendid way away from poached eggs on toast and Benger's food. Her terror of the presences in the next room in her own house, she thought, over apple pie and crumbly Wensleydale and fresh cream, was not a gut terror such as that evoked by highwayman and mourning lady. Her ghosts only grumbled, they did not threaten, nor did they bear with them any searing experience of unbearable pain. No, the truth was, they were simply *theoretically* frightening. She did not wish to believe the revenant of the Academy of the Return. She did not wish to spend eternity, or even an indefinable future life or lives, in the company of Donald and Molly, the iron and the kettle. She had formed the hypothesis, for want of a better one, that her parents did indeed persist in death, much as they had been in life. She might conceivably be schizophrenic and hallucinating, of course, but she believed she was not, and was by no means going to waste her valuable and abbreviated future on discussion of raised iris beds with an expensive psychiatrist. She had formed the further hypothesis, or hope, that these spirits, or presences, were attached to the earth where they had lived and died, as the Red Indian so providentially revealed to her had suggested. They were there, and she was here. Mr Maw would sell them, and their husks of housing, with the bricks and mortar they had been previously confined by. This view was encouraged by the *local* nature of their disputes, in so far as she had heard them. There was another hypothesis, a worse one, which she refused to entertain. She slept soundly the first night in her brown and gold hotel room, enjoying everything, a dark blood-red bathroom *en suite*, a marvellous tray full of instant teas, coffees, little sugar biscuits, a television, a radio, everything anonymous, user-friendly, you might say, or simply indifferent to its users, who were not inhabitants, who were rootless passengers on the earth, as Joanna had always wished to be. She slept one night in silence. Two. Three. She went into Durham and met the team of economists and market researchers and computer experts who were testing out various job-creation plans. She met also the local unemployed, the skilled men, whose predicament funded her own precarious livelihood. She sat in Job Centres across scarred formica tables on hard leatherette chairs and discussed retraining. She had some hopes. Joanna had always been a believer in human ingenuity. Also in progress. It is hard to become a development economist if you do not believe in those things. She had supposed human ingenuity would find ways round food shortages and over-population, round scarcity of fossil fuels and the joblessness initially caused by the second industrial revolution, round third world hunger and starvation wages battling with first world standards of living and normal requirements for a decent day's work. Beyond that she had more vaguely believed in men becoming wiser, cleverer, healthier, more adaptable and accommodating, outgrowing war and anger as childish things. It was hard to maintain these beliefs in the face of the kind of cultural and personal vertigo experienced by whole communities of men with complex crafts which would never be needed again, never again be a guarantee of wit, or pride or marvel. The ones who distressed her were those a little younger than herself, who had invested a life in this form of activity, whose bodies and brain-cells were excited functions of cutting *this* tool, gauging *this* kind of coal-face, wiring *this* kind of digger. One she talked to, a large man who had been foreman of a specialized tube-making team in the steel mills, turned on her with a kind of personal accusation. "Me father worked in t'mill, and his father before him, and I wanted nowt for me son, nowt but that he should do an honest day's wek in t'mill, the same as I did. We have us pride, you know, we have us sense of community, we know who and what we are, and now they come along and say no, you're not economic, you're not competitive, we don't want to know. But we have *the skills* . . ."

"You could acquire other skills."

"Oh yes. To do what. What skills? Young men might learn to operate them computers, but us as are set in our ways, we're dead men, and you know it, you've written us off, a whole generation, you can't wait for us to be tidied away. Come on, admit it."

"I'm not here for that reason."

"No. O'course you aren't. But you're not here to help men like me, are you? Th'young, maybe. Th'bright ones. I'd give up investigating us and let us die wi decency as fast as we can, Miss. Honest I would."

Later, in her hotel room again, Joanna felt despondent after this conversation with a self-styled dead man. The mass of men, she thought, are disappointed and angry. Why should the dead be any different, why should we suppose that it isn't our absolute nature to want more than we can have and yet to cling like limpets to what we know and have made of ourselves? Why not bungalows with peonies, why not a department of the afterlife full of fine steel tubing? Why should not the worst and most tenacious aspects of our characters persist longest? Why should I suppose that I have any right to hope either to change the world or to be quietly annihilated: those hopes are just part of what I am, which goes on and on within certain clearly defined and very narrow limits. As if in answer to her thoughts on disappointment and anger the voices started up, muttering behind the bathroom door, indistinguishable but furious, furious, purely enraged. Joanna's second hypothesis had been that it is indeed our ancestors who form our eternity, the time before and the time after our short time on earth, like the Japanese grandfather who presided at breakfast, like Bonnie Roote's happy family gathering. For an individual man or woman was an object not unlike the Christmas cactus, "Joanna Hope", bearing its eternal genes which dictate its form and future forever and forever. The voices were attached, not to the vacated garden, but to her own blood and presence. She could go to the Academy of the Return and enquire what quality in her it was that enabled her to hear them, or she could close her mind to them, confront and ignore them. She went to the bathroom door. She imagined the alternatives behind it: shower curtain, non-slip rubber bathmat, glistening red porcelain, or the dusty garret the voices inhabited. There was a susurration: shifting plastic, dripping tap, monotonous plaint.

"Please be quiet," she said. "I can hear you. I can't help you, and I don't want to hear you. You must make things better yourselves . . . Please, I beg of you, leave me alone. Now."

Silence. More silence. Courage, Joanna thought, turning back towards the delightful anonymous bed, with its strip of discreet lighting, with its warm gold sheets.

As she raised her knee to get into it, the voice said, "Of course, if you'd treated her a bit better, she wouldn't be so spiteful, she'd show more understanding, more consideration, she was often lacking in feeling but I put some of it down to your mismanagement ..."

"She'll learn, in the fullness of time."

In the fullness of time, the fine barrier would indeed be opened, Joanna concluded, and she would in her turn pass, none too quietly, into that next room.

THE DRIED WITCH

She was dry. It was the dry season, but this was her own dryness. Her inside-mouth felt like cloth dried into creased folds in the sun; her tongue scrubbed the silky-dry palate with its sand-ripples of flesh. The wet film was gone from her eyes; the rims and the lash-roots pricked. Between the legs was dry too. She washed out her mouth with a scoop of water but this wetness vanished like water spilled on a stone in the sun. She moved round her house, sweeping dust from the clay floor that sweated more dust. She scrubbed spots of grease from the little cooking-stove and wiped traces of white scum from the necks of large jars of salted vegetables. She picked at loose ends on woven sacks of millet and baskets of lentils. She refolded the quilts on her upper floor, and brushed the stone steps in the shuttered shadow. She took up her bright brass pot and set out for the tank.

The village had two streets, crossing. The houses were yellow stone, cemented, with wooden windows, painted pigeon-blue, and golden-brown doors. Half the houses backed onto the high crawling mountains; some had cave-cellars. Others faced the narrow plain in the valley and the mountain-ridge beyond, laced ice-blue on simmering air, river-blue shot with copper. The tank was fed by a small spring that came out of the mountain and went back into it, a little lower, making an angry, sucking sound. Women cleaned their pots, or beat their long skirts, on the stone edge of the trough.

A-Oa needed to see her eyes. She looked into the unruffled tank, deep and dark, greenish at its lower edges and on its floor. Her face looked back at her, an oval shadow on the glitter, and then, as she came nearer, provided with features, an empty fall of black hair, a black mouth, the dark holes of the eyes. The water turned everything into dark purple and greenish-brown shadows: unsmiling and uniformly olive her dark mask peered back at her, wrinkling its eyes, which, it was true, were very dark.

She took up a scouring stone and a handful of white sand and rubbed the vessel, which did not need it. She looked at herself in its convex surfaces, and finally in its curved bottom, spun with fine scratches, glinting white lights, brief coloured lights. Her pot-face, unlike her water-face, was round and beaming, a sunny shape in hot metal. Her hair scattered light, her features melted and shifted shape with the contour of the bowl. Here there were colours if they could be read, in the brassy refractions, brass-brown cheek-hollows, brass-russet closed lips, burning. Her eyes, under their arched brows, appeared to be ruddy.

The house of a jinx is spotlessly clean and her eyes are red. There was an age when a woman might become a jinx, and she had perhaps arrived there. There were few men in the village. Many of the young ones had been taken by the army, which had taken A-Oa's husband, to fight many months' march away, on the frontier. Others had joined the bandits in their mountain-fortress. Those who were left no longer looked at A-Oa in the street in the way she had once feared and needed. Her breasts were small and soft and dry inside her shirt; the cloth was slack over slackness. A woman could not see herself in a man's eye, that was simply what the old poems said, but she could read the firmness of her body in his attention, the spring of her step. When she combed her hair she caught up now long silver hairs, not many, among the dark ones. These hairs were thicker and livelier in texture than the dark ones, brighter. Were her eyes red?

There was life in the village street, even in the dry afternoon heat. Cha-An's two daughters and Bo-Me's frog-agile son squatted and chattered in the dust. When they saw A-Oa they scattered, calling shrilly, the old woman, the old woman, not meeting her eye. A-Oa tightened dry lips: an old woman was what she was, or was about to be, but it was also a sweet way, a roundabout way, of saying something else, the other thing. She was not friendly to children. Before her husband went she had buried four, eggshell-skulls under fine hairless skin, stick arms strapped to blown bellies, dead trailing feet with their beautiful useless bones, parcels wrapped in banana leaves tucked gently into pits scooped in the dust and hard clay. One, a boy, had seen two summers, had had a few piping words, her name, a complaint of pain, a contented chuckle when he recognized the fat hen. His head had been huge, a wise head, a fool's head, on a body that never swelled or wriggled. It was always known that he too would not last. He was the third: after the fourth, the army had taken his father.

Kun was outside his shop. He was always to be seen, smiling his own smile, which was not happy, which crumpled his fat face into a shape as though it might be gently about to weep for its own hopelessness and helplessness. Kun had a cellar in the mountain, in which were stored pickled pork and pickled vegetables, linen and cotton thread, oil and quilting, baskets and jars: Kun was a necessary man, a man aware of others' needs, a good, sharp dealer, respected for it. Kun knew everything that happened in the village before anyone else: he knew when births and deaths would be, and was ready with gifts and offerings, he knew that Bo-Me's eldest son had run away to the bandits when she was still searching the fields for him, he knew when Ma-Tun's young wife was alone with a visiting cousin and was able to tell Ma-Tun what had been spoken between them, not much, but enough; he knew, A-Oa was convinced, what had happened to her own young brother-in-law, Da-Shi, who had gone away one night, leaving no message, a year or so after his brother, A-Oa's husband, had been taken by the army. Kun divulged such knowledge reluctantly and with many cautions. He advised against haste when there were crimes to be judged, or failings to be punished. Like A-Oa he had now no close family in the village: his mother, with whom he had lived, had died at a great age, lovingly tended by her son, mourned with howls and streams of tears. Kun had never been wanted by the army or coerced by the bandits. He was a fat man, with soft triangular breasts like a woman, resting on his smooth pale belly like overlapping mountain ledges. He wore the usual cotton loincloth, and over it a long cotton robe or coat in dark blue, embroidered at the neck and cuffs in red and yellow. He had soft pointed slippers, over which his fat ankles hung, and could come up behind you silently, if he chose, or if he chose, make an important flapping sound, that announced him for some distance. A-Oa felt that they were in some ways the same, she and Kun, singletons on the edge of the circle, not woven in by kin or obligation. But Kun had known how to make himself necessary and a little feared. A jinx was feared. A jinx could dry up a child, or cause crops to fail, or pigs to be barren. A jinx could cause a tree to burst into flames. A-Oa had never seen this happen, but it was known to be so, to be within the power of those who cast their minds, who made charms. The person who could most certainly have told her whether she had red eyes, whether a change had been effected in her, was Kun. But she did not want to hear it from him. She knew that Kun did not like her, that he wished her ill. She did not know why. It was even possible that Kun wished everybody ill, indiscriminately. She had no one with whom to discuss this.

The next day she went up the valley to the Temple. She packed a little meal to offer to the carved Wise Ones: a small dish of chick peas, an oboe-fruit, ridged brownish green, pointed at both ends, which when pierced with a knife produced a flow of clear, thin red juice. Women desiring children offered these fruits at certain times of the year, carving them open, lavishly displaying their dimpled and pimpled concavity, the rows of fat white seeds on their thread-stalks in the moon-shaped cradle. She took too a few pods of the white beans that grew in her garden-strip, almost all of which were now gathered and heaped in the sun to dry. The beans were pale and waxy, flecked with crimson; their papery pods were whitish, splashed with purple-red.

The valley mounted steeply amid rustling yellow bamboos, harbouring insects with scraping monotonous songs and the occasional rush of sooty wings. The Temple was at the head of the valley and higher still, up four hundred steps, carved in the rock, in whose natural and carved niches sat perhaps four hundred carved sages and petty gods, staring with blind intelligence. It was built on a plateau, within a high wall, painted blood colour, on which charms were written in soot black characters against evil ones, sorcerers and demons. Round the foot of this wall crouched and wandered a collection of the rootless and the lost, the homeless and the holy, black-veiled women huddled like clustering bats, naked holy men, still as stone, or rhythmically prostrating themselves and rising. There was a smell of sour cooking, the smell of burning pats of dung, a weaker smell of hot flour on griddles, a tinge of spice. In the past they had crowded to put out their hands to A-Oa, displaying huge sores, or running wasted fingers in the channels of their children's bowed ribs. Today they wailed a little but did not hurry, as though she appeared to offer no hope. There was a well out here, deep under a conical canopy. A-Oa stopped and hauled up bucket and dipper to assuage the dryness. She sipped, turned the cold water in her dry mouth, feeling it run over, not soak into, the shiny-dry flesh, catch, as it went down, on the sore dryness of her throat.

The courtyards were busy and chattering: worshippers moved between greater and lesser temples, brown-robed monks carried baskets of grain and vegetables, families squatted in the dust and argued. In the greater Temple were the huge figures of the Wise Ones, three and awful, taller and wider than the eye could ever see at once, so that it was as much as you could do to focus on a heavy knee, or monstrous, mountainous hand, or far away the three faces, up in the dark of the roofspace, staring quietly out over the heads of the worshipping ants, wonderfully, characteristically blank, bearing a family resemblance in their perfect stillness. The brass lamps were all at the level of the altars, which were themselves below the level of the vast feet, which were dusty but not travel-stained. This gave the illusion that the Wise Ones towered away for ever, out of sight, out of apprehension, out of form. A-Oa bought an incense stick from a monk, lit it, and stood it with the others on one of the smaller altars; she bowed repeatedly, and set out her dishes of beans and fruit before kneeling to pray, her black and silver hair in the dust. It seemed to her that she did not know how to pray or what to ask for. In the past she had asked for sons: or to be forgiven for whatever had caused the sons she had to sicken and fail. To one side of her, standing beside the altar, was a small squat brass boy, a fat and polished child, not dusty like everything else in the huge, smoky and rattling place, but gleaming where countless soft dark hands had touched and caressed him. He wore a small scarlet cloth on a string, just large enough to cover whatever he had between his legs. It was known that his touch brought luck, brought boy-children. On every previous visit A-Oa had touched him. When she was young and humorous she had tickled him like a lover, laughing back quietly at her husband; after the loss of the first child she had touched the warm metal with fearful fingertips. Once she had come with Da-Shin and had touched the boy furtively, laying her fingers over his metal ones, asking friendship, complicity. He had a smile that took up his whole face, curling both mouth and eyebrow corners. She tried to tell the Wise Ones that she was afraid, that she was not herself, that there were changes she couldn't describe. All she was conscious of was the presence of the grinning boy, the sheen of countless handlings, gratified or denied, the dangling red cloth that was never lifted. She thought: when I am dead, this will be over, meaning by "this" the boy and all his works. The Wise Ones vouchsafed no relief, perhaps because she expected so little, was closed to their silent lines of life as her tongue and palate were to water.

Outside again, she embarked on the real business she had come on. There was an old woman from whom she had once had a charm to keep yellow worms from the bitter melon roots, and from whom Da-Shin had had something else, he later confessed. An old woman who knew about certain things. She had lived then in a minimal shelter of canes and flat leaves, with a wooden dish in front of her for offerings and various skin bags and linen bags propped against her squatting haunches, containing her secrets. In those days which now seemed far off, like a fairy tale, the days of Da-Shin and the running blood, A-Oa had looked at this woman with a mixture of repugnance, fear, and something approaching pity. A-Oa was a good housewife: she loved the things she had, her solid stone walls, her perfectly bright cooking pot, the blade of the hoe with which she cleared her ridges of plants so that nothing noxious should poke its head above the soil, or spread leaves or tendrils out of place. The old woman, in her flimsy hutment and her dry black cloths seemed unnecessary, waste, fragile as the fine black disintegrating films left when paper or cloth had been burned. She walked round the outer wall of the Temple, expecting mostly not to find her. But there she was, shelter, begging bowl, skin and linen bags, resting lightly on the earth almost exactly where she had been in the days of Da-Shin.

A-Oa squatted in front of her and put a handful of seeds into the bowl. Be well, Mother, she said, and, the years have spared you in well-being. The old woman rustled and shifted a little, creaking. Her face was fine dark skin stretched over bare bone, working its way out, mapped with finest lines, delicate as veiling, with no flesh or fat to thicken. Her eyes were gone into her head, black and reddened, the stubby row of lashes white ghosts on mahogany. I remember you, she said to A-Oa in a thin voice. You wanted the possible and the impossible. You wanted a secret thing and also the death of the yellow worms. I hope the worms do not trouble you. A-Oa said that the worms had vanished as though they had never been. The old woman sucked her lips and said, "And now you want other knowledge."

"I want a charm against dryness, mother," said A-Oa. "I am

dry through my whole body, like a smoked fish."

The old woman fumbled in her clothes and produced a limp lemon and a triangular blade. The skeletal dark hands sliced into the fruit flesh on the wooden bowl: the old mouth twisted and fumbled and spat on the segments. She turned and turned the segments in the bowl, and then handed one to A-Oa.

"Bite," she said. "This will tell if the juice of your body has dried up, like a failed spring, or been sucked out by a witch, to have power over you. Bite and tell me exactly what happens."

A-Oa bit, inhaling the warm rind: under her tongue saliva welled, not much, but some, not as she remembered from her youth, the gush of human water at the very sight of the sharp yellow shining globules. Even the thought of a lemon on a dry day could once bring such a rush of liquid. Now the thing itself alleviated, no more.

"There is water, but not much."

"As I thought. If there was true water, the charmed lemon would have it running out over your chin. You have lost your true water. Your blood also is dried up?"

"For many months."

"Bring your face nearer. My sight is poor."

A-Oa leaned forward, so that her head was under the shelter, her brow under the canopy of the black hood. She could smell the other's breath as it curled from her nostrils, an incorrupt smell, dusty, spicy, airy. She could see the lines cut in brow and lip, the purple-black sunk curves of the eye-sockets. She cast her eyes down and did not meet those others, whose whites were yellow, whose huge iris was coal-black, whose rims were reddened.

"You have red eyes," said the old woman. "A jinx has ways of replacing juices: there are magics you could learn, if you are willing, if that is what you want."

"I have always lived quietly and properly. I have had four sons, whose life was sucked out of them before it was theirs. I have kept my garden well and my house is clean. My husband is gone and I have no one to live for; also no one who would be unhappy if tomorrow I fell and died, or began to rave as She-At did some years ago, until the village cast her out and stoned her. I have no respect in the village. I have no sons to care for me when I am old and weak. Every year will be a little worse. To know your knowledge, Mother, that would be some help against what took my sons, against my state."

"Knowledge must be paid for," said the old one. She put out no hand, and may have been talking about life, not money. A-Oa, however, brought out three coins from her waistband and laid them beside the pool of lemon juice in the wooden trough, from where, in the deft flicker of a long hand and the twitch of a fold, they vanished into the old woman's clothing.

"These things are necessary," said the old woman. "You must set up an altar and put on it some things I shall tell you, that you must find, and some things I shall give you. You must wait until all moisture has parted from the things that have moisture, and the dried things are plumped out. Then you will have power over wet and dry, to heal or, if need be, to harm. You will be respected and feared. Unless you come against some more powerful magic."

Various people watched her come back through the village, in silence, in the simmering heat. Kun stood in the shadow of his house, with a crescent of glistening sweat on the curve of his belly. His eyes moved with her passage; his lips were pursed in his peevish frown. The children scattered. Everyone in the village knows almost everything about everyone else. She had the pieces of root and fibre, the dusty dried beans, black and crimson, tucked away in her long skirts. In her own house the kitchen was dark and earth-warm, cooler than the street outside. The fat hen ran in importantly to greet her, chucking quietly, shaking dusty wattles. Its bright golden eye peered at her out of the tipped side of its face; its red flabby comb nodded. She put on water for tea, and lit the candle in front of the little altar behind the stove, the house-spirit's own altar: the other altar must stand invisible from the window, behind the vegetable jar, the other side of the stove. In the roof, in the mouths of sacks and jars were various other charms, tied bunches of quills and twigs, fur and seed pods, to propitiate nameless little demons or wandering spirits.

She made tea, and broke up a sweet rice-cake, sitting on the ground with her back to the window, staring at her knives, her chopper, her strainer on the low table. The hen bustled round her, making a great business about the odd rice-crumb, rattling companionably in its throat. It was a good layer, the hen; it took care of its own visits to Bo-Me's noisy cockerel. It was only infrequently broody – it tended to abandon its eggs in various places A-Oa knew about and rush back to the kitchen to supervise the chopping of the supper vegetables, to pick up strayed grains. A-Oa considered it: one of the old woman's requirements was an egg about to hatch but unhatched, an egg with a chick curled inside it which must be left to rot and go beyond rotting to dryness. That was not so easy; she might be reduced to thieving other women's unhatched clutches, she who had always kept herself to herself, correct and virtuous. It was a thin time for chicks, the height of the dry season. Also required was a lash-snake, a wiry poisonous, fast-moving pallid worm that struck from under stones in field pathways and was best avoided. For that reason A-Oa knew where some of these were, or had been. Da-Shin had known how to trap them with a forked stick and a noose. He had showed her how, though she had never done it. They had sat shoulder to shoulder at the edge of the pumpkin-field, setting up the contraption and the bait, scarcely breathing. She remembered the quick twist of his wrists in the sun, the line of his spine above his squatting haunches, the smell of his male sweat drying quickly, the heat stirring between them. She would try to catch a lash-snake: it was safer than paying boys. The other things were not so bad to acquire: certain organs of a large desert rat still relatively easy to catch even in this sparse time, one which she could either catch or naturally buy from the boys for her supper. Certain combinations of seeds. She sipped her tea and considered ways and means, not as though she any longer had a choice, not, in a way, as though she herself were there any more with her passions and her irrelevant needs and hopes. She had a task, a place in the world again. She would have to steal the egg. She could wait months and months for the fat hen to decide capriciously to sit again. It might never do so. Even when it did sit, it was not notably successful in rearing chicks. It produced eggs in plenty, which was A-Oa's reason, or excuse, for not snapping its neck and putting it into the pot.

When the charms were assembled, neatly laid out in their little dishes, A-Oa had a bad time, a sultry, transitional time of terrible smells, corruption and deliquescence whilst the egg rotted, exploded and fell away, whilst the desert rat's entrails pullulated and squirmed, whilst the stiff hoop of the lash-snake went puffy and pimply and then fell into desiccation. It was imperative, the old woman had said, that no one should touch, move, or disturb the relations of these components of the charm whilst the drying went on, and that no one but A-Oa should set eyes on them. That was easy enough: no one came into her house, no one was curious, except perhaps Kun, and Kun was a man, and, as such, prohibited from ever going into a woman's part of the house. Male children until they were two years old could be with their mother in the kitchens. After that they were kept out, beyond the sliding door, or woven hanging carpet, or rush curtain, depending on the wealth of the house. So no one came into A-Oa's kitchen during the days of rotting and drying, which were long and troublesome, in which she slept badly and had terrible dreams, of demons circling in the air, of Da-Shin lying smashed on the rocky foothills of the mountains, his belly blown in the sun, of fire crackling in the trees in the village meeting-place on the plain, where they came at certain seasons of the moon to dance, and drink, and sing and stumble, and lie where they fell, in the warm dark, a man freely feeling for his neighbour's wife, an untouched girl for her sister's husband, for at these times they were filled with spirits, not themselves, not the children of their house, nor the property of their men, nor prohibited from touching their men's male relations, father or brother, under pain of death. The kitchen became full of the smell, it hung in the fine smoke and permeated the oil of A-Oa's hair, it inhibited the hen, who stayed in the rest of the house, squawking crossly. And then after its time, it went, and there was quiet dryness. The egg was chalky shards of shell, burst by escaping gases, fallen away from fine bones and undeveloped quills and the curved beaked skull. The snake was papery dry scales over the fine humps of vertebrae in their curled chain, fragile eye-sockets, and needle fangs from which the palate and mouth had shrunk. The rat parts were a brown stain, no more. Whereas the wrinkled dried beans, crimson and black, had plumped out, were glossy and round, and the strange dried vegetable-flesh the woman had given her, spongy mushroom heads or hairy root-tangles were fat and soft and springy, resuscitated. The ghost of the smell hung over all, as for days the smell of burning may, in a kitchen where there has been an accident with the fat, a sheet of sudden flame and black fine cinders.

It became widely accepted that A-Oa was a jinx when she cured the running sores on Bo-Me's son's legs. It was also of course accepted that A-Oa had caused these sores, had started to suck out the child's life through the sores, through the daily thickening yellow pus on which flies gathered. Bo-Me spoke very casually to A-Oa one day at the edge of the tank, addressing her respectfully for the first time as "Mother". "My Cha-Tin is sickening, Mother," said Bo-Me. "There are wet wells on his legs and he is shrivelling away. I have asked everyone for advice and no one has been able to help me. Do you happen to know of any remedy I might try?" Bo-Me knew, and A-Oa knew, that to a close friend, a mother or a sister, Bo-Me would have said that some witch or jinx was attacking the child with her thoughts, or with spells. But she answered in kind, that she had various remedies her mother had taught her, it might be that one of them would prove helpful. Bo-Me should bring the child to her house at dusk. When he came, walking painfully, his sharp little face fearful, A-Oa made Bo-Me wait outside the kitchen whilst she took the boy in and touched his stick-legs with various bunches of fronds and put a mixture of mashed bitter herbs and spiderweb, about which all the women knew, on the bubbling places. She reached down into one of her tall jars and pulled a pickled lime from its darkness. "Eat this," she said. "It will bring the water back to where it should be, under your tongue." The boy stared at her with dark, serious eyes. "Thank you, old one," he said. "It is nothing," said A-Oa, and took him back to his mother. "He will get well now," she told Bo-Me, and he did.

Then there was Di-Nan's diarrhoea, which she cured with a seed-pellet and the instruction to walk four times round the periphery of the village from left to right and four times in the other direction. There was a pig of Ta-Shin's, that wouldn't eat, that lay on its side making self-pitying moans, which, grown confident now, she cured simply by predicting that it would stand again, if it was starved for two days, on the second day, and should be fed three hours after it stood. She had respect: grandmothers brought her small gifts of preserved fat or cooked rice: she was greeted deferentially in the streets. "Go well, Mother." Something had happened, but it was neither what she had hoped for nor what she, more obscurely, waited for, with a fear like a hot stone inside her. Then the boy came, Bo-Me's second son, not the tiny Cha-Tin but the beautiful, gleaming Cha-Hun, his long black hair plaited down his spine and moving like a bright snake as he shook his head. He was a young man, not a boy, A-Oa saw, as he sauntered past her door, the muscles of his buttocks standing out, and his stomach hard and small and taut. When he had gone past, casually, casually, he came back, even more casually, and leaned on her doorpost, glancing quickly into the dark inside of her house.

"How is it with you, Mother?"

"Well enough. And the little brother?"

"Skipping like a young goat. A marvel of your working. May I come in, Mother, out of the sun and the dusty street?"

"I am too old to forbid you," said A-Oa drily, meaning that there would have been a time when it would have been sinful and punishable for him to enter a house alone with a woman who was no kin of his, but that now it was not, for she was no woman, she was something else.

He came in, like bright dark oil poured into a cup and sat on the ground, sniffling the smells of her house, taking in the bunches in the roof, the bedlinen, the cleanliness, the journeying hen. In the dark some of his confidence deserted him. He looked up at A-Oa as a child might look, expecting a sweet, or comfort, or knowledge of his predicament to come automatically to her, as knowledge of the gas in a baby's stomach comes to its mother, when its face puckers, and she helps it. A-Oa, no mother, stepped back a pace or two, and looked impassively down on Cha-Hun, waiting. The bright light in the doorway was temporarily blocked by bulk: the dark hump of Kun's fat shoulders was there, and then his frowning face, peering for a long moment before his slippers flapped away. Cha-Hun was rattled and began one of those interminable polite conversations the villagers delighted in, discussing the health of every man and woman, from the headman down to the newest baby, and then moving on to cows and bean fields, pumpkins and honey bees, all discussed and named safely and in order. A-Oa answered politely – there were ritual prescribed responses which she gave absently – and watched him. After a little time, Kun passed again, in the opposite direction, on the other side of the street. They saw him stare in at the doorway as he passed. Cha-Hun rose to leave. In the doorway, he said, following nothing that had gone before, "And charms, Mother? Do you make charms, not to take away sickness, *other* charms?"

"It could be so," said A-Oa, from the inside. "How can I say, not knowing what you might require?"

"Oh, it is not for me," said Cha-Hun, turning on his heel, too lightly. "May I come again and pass the time of day?"

"Any day," said A-Oa.

When he had gone, she talked over the talk they had had, he and she, with her hen, until she found the flaw in it. There was a member of his own immediate family he had not mentioned, when enumerating them all in order. A member he should have dwelt on with particular respect. "I think *that* is it," said A-Oa to the hen. They sat side by side on the floor, and A-Oa pulled thread from goats' hair. The hen settled comfortably, fluffing up its breast feathers in the dust. "Does he want a love-charm, or a poison, or perhaps one first and then the other?" said A-Oa to the hen which stared with one round, silly eye. "Shall we help him, or leave him to cry and be safe?"

The one he had left unnamed was his elder brother's young wife, An-At. His elder brother, like A-Oa's husband, but hardly so willing, it seemed likely, had been taken by the army, at the beginning of the dry season a year ago, when An-At, child and woman, had barely stepped over his mother's threshold. Bo-Me's family was large and vigorous and noisy: the girl had come from a neighbouring village and had cost two goats, several sacks of grain and an unusual metal cooking pot a travelling soldier in Bo-Me's family had once brought back from beyond the mountains. (Soldiers did come back, with hacked ankles, with burned-out eyes, with rotted fingers, those neither dead nor useful nor wholly incapable of the struggle to return.) The girl was thin and fastidious, picking at her food and saying little, occasionally smiling a momentary, secretive, contemptuous smile. Bo-Me did not like her. She worked, the village said, but foolishly made it seem as though she didn't, appeared to move lazily, to sit around languidly when her tasks had been rapidly done. She spent time combing and coiling and loosing her beautiful hair: when her husband had been at home, she had put flowers in it, and some beaded pins and ties which she had brought with her and now no longer wore.

In large households, everyone slept together. It was not permissible for a man to enter the women's quarters, or to be alone in a house with an unmarried woman to whom he was not related. It was permissible for him to share a bed with his brother's wife, his sister, but not of course to touch her. He must sleep as though long knives lay between them. So she had slept with Da-Shin, in the early years a boy, and then not. Night after night, never looking at each other, hearing each other breathe. The penalty for putting a hand across those invisible knives, a hand flung in sleep, a hand darkly unrelated to the still-sleeping face on the pillow, was death. Death for the woman, that was. Expulsion from the family for the man, if the family chose to enforce it. They often did not: men were rare in the village and such temptations were understood to be the fault of women – it was their nature. A-Oa believed it was their nature, as she had been taught. She also knew what Cha-Hun wanted from her, which was something not so natural.

During the next day or two she observed, without surprise and without alarm – only with an increase in the heat and bulk of the dry hot stone inside her – that Kun was following Cha-Hun. He stood in his doorway and watched the young men go out to work: that was usual: he stood behind them, at a quiet distance, when they sat in the street in the shadow and argued: that was also usual. But when Cha-Hun came out alone, perhaps to the water-tank, perhaps to relieve himself in the fields, perhaps simply to stroll past A-Oa's front door and think of returning to make the request he hadn't made, the heavy figure came behind him, lightly, lightly, rolling along with his fat calves above his folded ankles, his face bland and empty. So he had once followed Da-Shin, who had been neither the first nor the last. The women said of him that he was like a woman, and shuddered a little: they knew what they meant by this but there were no stories to tell about Kun as there had been about other soft men who followed boys, or soft boys who followed soldiers. Kun had been married some time in the dark past. His wife had been put to death for trying to bewitch him, to gain control over his thoughts with little cakes made of honey and other things, unmentionable. He had had no child and had never remarried. A-Oa did not know what the men said about Kun's padding surveillances. She had foolishly never spoken to Da-Shin about it. Things between her and Da-Shin had been all unspoken, a bulk of silence, substantial and shadowy as Kun himself. On the night when Kun talked to Da-Shin she had wished that she had said something, asked something, used words. But words were unnecessary and dangerous. She would say to Cha-Hun, from her new authority, when he came back, "Watch Kun."

He came back of course. He sat inside her doorway, his face pulled long with passion, his eyes glittering, and Kun passed by, inclining his head, tucking in his chins, compressing his lips in that way he had, to hold back breath, speech, anything. "Can you make a love-charm, Mother?" Cha-Hun blurted out, clasping his squatting knees with desperate fingers, meeting her eye and then dropping his gaze. A-Oa in her dry distance thought he was a love-charm in himself and said, to mock him, "I do not see how you should need such a thing, Cha-Hun."

"It is not for me."

"If I am to make such a thing, I must have truth."

He frowned, and committed himself. "The girl — is not mine. She does not see me."

"You can surely make her see you."

"*She cannot*. She must."

"If she should be forbidden," said A-Oa, out of sadness, "nothing can come of this but death and misery. This you know."

"Nothing can come of it but — something — I *must have* — a joy — I would pay for with my life, with my life, gladly." It will not be your life, A-Oa thought of saying, and was prevented, partly by a memory of Da-Shin, vanished overnight, to where, to what fate? And by her own mean awareness of the force of his youth, maybe the girl's youth, that blazed and would not be denied. So she would help it along, would she? Help them to burn? If that was what they wanted.

She told him the things he must bring, things not easily obtained, hairs, slivers of nail, the girl's blood, seeds from the sacks in her kitchen and honey from her combs, flour she had ground, and seed of his own which she would mix, when the moon was right, with things she herself would bring and which he would cook, in a way she would show him, in his own way. Cha-Hun glowered at the earth and said it would not be easy. His pale tongue moistened his gold-shadowed lips, with distaste, with anxiety, with desire? A-Oa sat dry beside him and said sharply that he could not expect such a thing to be easy, it was difficult and dangerous, as what he wanted was difficult and dangerous. If in the honeycomb was embedded a hatching bee, drowned in its own running amber, this was particularly propitious, though not absolutely necessary. She must have these in the third week of the waxing moon, if it could be managed. Otherwise Cha-Hun must wait, another month.

A shadow crossed their talk, heaved raggedly across Cha-Hun's silk shoulders and A-Oa's watching face, turned up sideways towards him, like the hen. Kun stood in the doorway, his hand on her door-frame, his fat body between her and the square of sun.

"Can I help you, Kun?" she said, naming him directly, which in certain ways was unlucky, or threatening, depending on whether either of them, he or she, had any power of ill-will.

"I trust Cha-Tin is well," he said by way of answer, gloomily.

"As a young goat, says Cha-Hun," replied A-Oa.

"Let us all hope he continues so," said Kun, with heavy politeness, and heaved himself lightly away again. The hot stone inside A-Oa shifted in its dark furnace. She opened her mouth to say to Cha-Hun, watch Kun, and could not speak for dryness, could not summon moisture even to croak. In any case to speak was surely unnecessary. Cha-Hun was no fool. He must know. Moreover, no one could avoid Kun, if they were not fated to be able to. Kun made it his business to know things. Cha-Hun was peculiarly his business. She had seen Kun's eyes, calculating pig's eyes, measure herself, her dry self.

He came back, Cha-Hun, with his little leaf-wrapped packets and clay pots, within the allotted time, and at night, knocking at her door softly under the misshapen moon that lurched above the mountain. His hands were ostentatiously empty: inside he drew the things from here and there, knotted inside his loincloth, and laid them out before her, explaining curtly and with distaste what each was, though not how he had obtained it, as other anxious clients might have done, demonstrating their resourcefulness or good faith. She took the things from him in the metal-light and carried them back into her kitchen, back to the secret altar. When Cha-Hun came back, as instructed, the next day, she had mixed them with secrets of her own, liquids and solids of her own, some of the old woman's mushroom-flesh crumbled to powder, a speck of snakeskin, a scrap of rat stain. Under her eyes Cha-Hun himself shaped them all in a wooden bowl, his long fingers sticky with honey and rusty with blood, doing woman's work, awkwardly making the cake that he must then, she told him, cook in the heat of his own body until the new moon. She showed him, as was necessary, where to put the cake to cook, and as her fingers indicated drily, here, he hung his head and watched his prick curve and helplessly rise with its own life towards her, hot-red and wet and shining. That is a good sign, she told the hot and trembling boy, that shows the magic is good, that the cake is right, that the charm will work. After the cooking, you must give it to her to eat, or if you think she will not, hide it in her food. It is better if she takes it all at once, willingly, but you are the judge of that. And he stood there, shamed and eager, his thin, strong rod swaying blindly upright like a charmed snake's hood, after her hand. And she felt her own scraping, squeaking dryness and said Go now, before anyone comes. Meaning Kun, but she dared not name him.

That night she dreamed of the boy, or perhaps not of that boy but of Da-Shin, as he had once been, naked and risen like that boy. She often thought of Da-Shin as though he had been there last week, or yesterday, as though the shock of his departure was fresh, although it must, she saw now, have been years, many years, since he went. This boy, who she thought of as Da-Shin's contemporary, was in fact nearer in age to her own buried sons, those tiny, fragile, male bodies. In her dreams she reached out to embrace him, reached up from amongst her quilts to clutch him as he bent over her, intent and golden, and her hands and her mind slipped through him, grey and vanishing. It was not that she desired the boy: she desired only to be able to desire him, and was dry. So she played with his spirit, teased and teasing, impotent.

The new moon came and went. Cha-Hun did not come to say whether his cake had been accepted or not, openly or by trickery. In the street he avoided A-Oa's eye and Kun padded after him. He did not need to tell A-Oa whether he had been successful: it shone from him, from his gleaming plait to his cocky strut, from his involuntary singing to his swinging arms. The girl too had lost her lethargy. She was restless and lively: she swept what had already been swept: she ran to and from the tank, smiling. What A-Oa could deduce Kun too could deduce, probably, though not certainly, her own part in it, which she was privately sure was wholly unnecessary. Then the smiling of An-At was replaced by a deepening frown, and the light running by a hunched plodding. A-Oa waited. A train of events had been set in motion. When the screaming began, she assumed that the voice was An-At's. It began early one morning, before dawn, one huge howl and then a choking wail, then another huge howl, a voice to swallow the moon. Doors opened, bare feet padded on the street. A crowd gathered in the grey, behind Kun, who was there first, quietly ready. Bo-Me burst out of her house tearing herself away from the frightened restraining hands of An-At and Cha-Hun, lashing her hair from side to side like an enraged beast, rolling in the dust, howling. She is possessed, said one. The house is cursed, said another. Her son is killed by witchcraft, said An-At. Cha-Tin is dead where he was sleeping. A witch has come at night and sucked out his soul, said Kun. Perhaps. My house is cursed, shrieked Bo-Me, from the dust. My child is killed and my hearth is dishonoured. A-Oa stood at her own door and wondered if they would behead An-At. It was her brain that wondered this, occupying itself vainly. The fat hen came running out beside her, dusty-feathered. She knew very well where the blame would be laid, where the evil would be detected. She had always known. She wanted to go to Bo-Me and say, it is terrible, the death of a son, and knew she could not and must not. The death of her own sons, her grief, Da-Shin, her dryness had brought about this evil, this death in its turn. Her pain was responsible. Let us look into this, Kun said, as she had always known he would say. Let us think clearly where the witchcraft is in this village, where this evil begins. And the gathering turned round, away from Bo-Me's sobbing, and looked at A-Oa with its common intention, its single thought.

"Does anyone know of any spell made against Bo-Me's family?" said Kun, then, looking not at A-Oa but at Cha-Hun, who also, stammering, seeing a chance, or a possible chance, in this moment of danger, began to confess. He confessed that he had been visited by spirits in his sleep, that he had seen an old woman perched on his pillow, that she had tied his will with strings, had spat in his mouth and subdued him to her evil desires. That he had gone to her, driven by this spell, and had been given a witchcake, which he had hidden in An-At's porridge. That An-At, under the influence had . . . The whole household was cursed by this dry old woman's terrible jealousy, of Bo-Me's sons, of An-At's youth and beauty; she had brought them down. Bo-Me sobbed in the dust.

"Answer," said Kun, to A-Oa.

"I have no spittle," said A-Oa, whispering.

The crowd began agitatedly to reminisce. She had looked at

one, and that night he had had stomach pains. Another, coming to the water-tank after her, had seen a swimming snake vanish in its shadows. It was true that Cha-Hun had seemed possessed for some moons. They had remarked on it. An-At, who had stood with her arms crossed under her breasts during Cha-Hun's recital, now gave A-Oa one look, one quick look of complicity, hostility, perhaps guilt, and abased herself deliberately beside her mother-in-law, crying out that she had sinned but not by her own doing, that she was guilty but the victim of witchcraft, that the village was under a spell . . .

Kun said, "This woman tempted her own brother-in-law to wickedness. He was so shamed that he could live no longer under the same roof, but ran away and threw himself from the high ridge into the gully. His bones were there white and unburied. No man can get down there. He has been eaten by birds and worms, under the sky. I saw this in a vision, and climbed up there, and saw that it must be true. Now she is old, and can do no more harm with her beauty, she has turned to making spells, as we all know, to invading our thoughts and our pillows. None of us are safe. We are all tainted by this woman. How shall we clean ourselves?"

They chattered, for a timeless time, discussing the ill-fortunes that the village had experienced, yellow worms and wilted kale, mould in a millet-crock, the sudden drying up of one man's goat's milk, the barrenness of a new and expensive wife. An-At, daring, fighting for her life, put her arms round Bo-Me and was not shrugged away. Her proud little face was bony with fear and attention. What shall we do, they asked each other uncertainly, whilst more complaints bubbled up and frothed like the gases in fermented beans stored in a badly-scoured jar. A-Oa stood impassively in her doorway, with the hen fussing at her feet. She did not think of speaking in her own defence: this had always been coming, and speech would be a puff of air to the conflagration. Kun said nothing, but she knew it depended on Kun. He was watching the boy, Cha-Hun, who knelt beside his mother, afraid of touching her in case he accidentally came into contact with the tenacious and desperate An-At. There was a kind of desperate pout to his lips, and a deep frown driving down to his eyes. Finally he turned to Kun, and said, sullen and smouldering, "What should we do then? What do you advise?" Kun made a quieting little gesture with his puffy smooth hands in the air above Cha-Hun, and moved a step or two towards him. He touched his shoulder and looked from Cha-Hun to An-At and Bo-Me and onwards to A-Oa. His answer was a question. "How have we done in the past, to clean the village?" And it was Cha-Hun who answered, "We sun the jinx. We put the jinx to dry in the sun." "In the sun," said Bo-Me's voice, liquid with tears and wailing. She shook her swollen face from side to side and An-At moved with her, making their movements one. Kun said no more. It was taken up by the common voice. "We must sun the jinx. The sun will dry out the evil."

A-Oa had seen this done to others, in her time. They took her outside the village, pummelling her a little, but not much, made uneasy by her dogged silence. They tied her with linen bands and hemp cords to a dead stump of a tree in the middle of the dust and mud, in the space outside the village where they danced on sacred days. They tied her sitting down, in the hot sun, looking across at the row of thorn trees and the distant mountain slopes and rim, dancing with unreal blue and white. Three days, the time was. If she was still alive after three days, they could fetch her in and the evil would be judged to have been searched out by the sun and shrivelled away. The heat this year was the worst in living memory, and had gone on unduly long. The rains might come. It was possible that A-Oa might have braced, or stilled her spirit and flesh to endure, to wait quietly, quietly, to live on, for the rain, for the end of the boiling and bubbling which she had seen on other flesh and knew she must expect. Dried old women had been brought in again, blistered and baked like badly-cured leather, given sips of honey-water. One had had no mind, fried brains, the children called her, and one had babbled like a child of times long forgotten and children long dead. She found no such tenacity in herself, considering her plight, in the first few lucid hours. Nor did she find fear, even animal fear, a need to scrabble at her bands and moan for pity. The truth was, she had known when she had seen the glistening life of Cha-Hun's prick, its blind, swaying *need*, that she had no answering need, not for anything, she was finished. She wondered if they would behead An-At. She would not know what they did. She thought briefly of her hen, and its little pleasures, its conceited expectant trotting. Perhaps they had wrung its neck already. Her mouth twisted with pain for the hen.

Before the sun was at its height she did look about her, at the black, sooty-barked thorn trees, so baked that their leaves were gone and no one knew whether they would come again in the spring or stand like wet skeletons when the rain came. The mountains were cold and slightly glassy, on the high snow, smoky and slaty lower down. The sky was not yet heavy: it was blue, angry blue and dry. It moved with dryness as water moves finely in deep rivers, a surface always the same but with a shimmer of shifting depth. The sun came up behind her, stood over her, and went down behind the thorns in front of her. At first sweat came, more moisture than she'd thought she had, standing fleetingly on the hair on her upper lip, vapouring away. Parts of her body hurt in turn. Her eyelids: a last desperate prickle amongst the lashes and then the fine skin began to lift away into blisters as she saw her own veins boil bloody on her retina. Her tongue, huge, a weightless boulder, cracking against her teeth. Heat ran down her spine and killed and fetched up the colourless scales and cushions of skin above the vertebrae, where it was thin, where it flaked back to expose raw wet flesh that dried, fast. A sound came in her ears, a hissing and squeaking, the contents of her skull writhing and shrinking like intestines in a frying pan.

Pain is one thing when it is local, a smashing or bursting of healthy flesh, an arm cracked by a falling boulder, a narrow passage ruptured by the huge head of a child. Pain everywhere, eating drily inwards, diminishing the body, turning it into part of the air, of the surrounding sky, as the snake, the egg, the rat stain had shrunk and departed on her altar, is something else. She was it, and she watched it, with her whole attention, and when cold night came she shivered at its cessation, reluctant to return to her sore self. All her body desired water, in the night. She thought of wet cloth, pressed on her brow when the doomed sons were struggling into the world: she thought of lingering dregs in the rice bowl when the wet breakfast rice had been supped up. She thought of water on leaves when the rains had begun, running, collecting, hanging, falling. She thought of her hen, sipping puddles in the rainy season, turning its beak up to swallow. She was tormented by very small quantities of water, in drops rather than in cups. The thought of the tank would have been insupportable, annihilation by too much. In the night her bones hurt, the marrow creaking in them, her knees and ankles hideous knobs. She slept, some of the time, or fell into the pain, hurrying the end.

On the second day, in the morning, before the heat of the day, she saw them vaguely, watching her from between the thorn trees. Their shapes were outlined in excruciating flame, they burned on the air as they moved, with such fluent ease, gesturing with an arm, planting a foot, as though this was natural and possible. She could see only through slits, could not tell who they were or what they were. As the sun rose, a kind of merciful oven-black rose inside her, a black not of shade but of heated iron into which nevertheless she dipped for respite, for loss of herself, as one might dive into a pool. Long sores snapped open in her arms and legs, peeled back blackly and darkened. She saw dark, dark, and round it like beads in dark hair, blue flashes of the uniform but splintering sky.

The second night was the worst time, cool enough to restore locality to splits and fissures, to make her want to move the immovable hummock of her tongue, to want to raise a bound wrist and brush at her terrible many-pustuled eyes. She thought of herself: so this is where I was coming: and everything that had once belonged to herself seemed small and husked, dust to sweep, a stain to be wiped from the grid of the cooking-stove where something had spilled, and been baked blackly on, and had tenaciously adhered. Why begin, thought A-Oa, if we come here so quickly?

On the third day, she was two. Her mind stood outside herself, looking down on the shrivelling flesh, with its blues and umbers, on the cracked face, the snarling mouth, the bared, dry-bone teeth. Her mind moved in its own shape, stepping rapidly, so it had feet of a kind, looking out of angled vision, so it had eyes of a kind, at the poor thing tied to the tree trunk, at the thorns in their dusty blackness, at the blue bowl of the hot sky through which power and heat rippled uninterrupted and through her shape too, bathing in the heat, scooping up the heat with mental hands as one might scoop spring-water in the bathing-pool in the river, after the rains, when the river wasn't dry. After a time, she thought, she would step away from the thing altogether, and the dry snort and rattle would go out of its throat. Meanwhile she stepped this way and that testing the dryness, displacing heat and light as though she was what they were, but more dense. A flicker of life came and went in the thorn trees. She could not see clearly who was there: the moving bodies were sluggish blots on her quick, hot vision, humped and awkward. There was a thing she could do, she thought, to make them skip and jump: she turned her bright, airy head towards them and gathered a long stream of heat and dryness, which coiled round the thorn trees like a flung rope, like a garment, and here and there the thorns in their turn flickered into a new life, little points of silver and gold and dusky red rose on the twiggy fingers and danced along the dry black arms, and the heat and dryness could be seen for what they were, a translucent but visible veil of moving air, and then the whole tree was one huge head of flaring hairs, rising and crying. So it was true, she thought, I can set trees alight, and she danced a little, to the cracking and rushing sound of the conflagration. Small figures scuttled away like woodlice out of cut straw and she watched them with satisfaction as a child might watch ants run from a smashed nest. The eddies of heat from the burning swirled out across the muddy ground and took her with them, away from the strapped and cracking thing, away.

LOSS OF FACE

They travelled, every day, three sides of a rectangle. Down eighteen floors of one rectangular tower, under the wide motorway, with its moving belts of fast cars, up nineteen floors of a fatter, less glittering tower on the other inaccessible shore of the throughway. It was possible to get lost, like rats in an orientation maze, and perform several journeys in the polished grey subways, but these zigzags were straightened out as though a line had been jerked taut, and up they came, to the nineteenth floor.

In front of them, as they stood briefly beside the melancholy roar of the motors, reared a brown tower whose purpose seemed to be the raising and display of a rectangular number, made up of hot little red lights like so many brakelights up above the city. The first day the number was 379. On the second, 378. By the third, they had established, tentatively, the hypothesis that it diminished by one, each day. One of them had hazarded the guess that the number might be the stock exchange closing price, perhaps in Tokyo, perhaps in Singapore. They could not tell how many regular descending steps the figure would have to take to be statistically unlikely to be a closing price. They were lecturers in English literature. They could have asked, on the nineteenth floor, where the conference was, but their brief conversational breaks were hectic with serious oriental questions about Kristeva's views on Desire and Harold Bloom's map of misreading. Celia Quest, who was speaking on John Milton and George Eliot, was also puzzled by the liquid red numbers above the lifts that translated them from ground to air. In the smaller, lecture tower, there was no fourth floor. In the larger, where she slept under oyster satin and ate a New World version of a Continental breakfast, there was no thirteenth. Her room was 1840, which

Professor Baxter said was easy to remember, since that was the year of publication of Browning's *Sordello*. When he said *Sordello* Celia's inner eye was visited by an irrelevant but very clear image of the curious mediaeval tall turrets of San Gimignano in Tuscan sunlight, threatening, slit-eyed, ramshackle fortresses in another world in another time. And beyond these Brueghel's vertiginous, cracking Tower of Babel. Out of the heavily mesh-curtained window of 1840 could be seen only the deep ravine between massive, graceless erections, in daylight all muddy, liverish brown and khakis, indistinct in the thick petrol-iridescent air. At night it was a black gulf where lights ran in bright streamers. Out of the window across the road, on the nineteenth floor, could be seen the veined and rounded chalky knobs of intractable mountains, whose black on white clefts descended into a line of trees before the towerscape intervened. This sunny chalk, and an occasional pungent smell, partly garlic, partly something unidentifiably fishy, rising from odd gratings in the pavement, were the only indications that they had come half-way round the world, crossing above deserts and mountain-ranges, typhoon-whipped yellow waves and spicy cities, outside which they had sat confined in their metal-cigar prison, circum-spectly confined for fear of turbaned terrorists.

Celia gave two lectures. The first was on Milton's figures of virtue. Milton was very sure what virtue was. Celia described the certainties of the incorruptible Christ in *Paradise Regained*, rejecting food for his hunger, world empire and the blandish-ments of literature, of the best that has been thought and said in the world. This Christ censored incessant reading with scriptural comment. "However many books/Wise men have said are weari-some." He kept his balance on the dizzy pinnacle of the Temple. "Tempt not the Lord thy God, he said, and stood." Celia's students in the depressed English Midlands rejected John Milton. They would not suspend disbelief in his patriarchally predestined cosmology. They thought his characterization of Eve was sexist and his vocabulary élitist. Logocentric and phallocentric, the more sophisticated added for good measure. They had fed on the issues of social realist fiction, and would not hear his music. Here in the uniformly beige Press Centre the assembled oriental scholars listened quietly and politely. Their country, the guide book said, was Confucian, Buddhist, Catholic, residually shamanistic. The guide book was American, full of eclectic and egalitarian enthusiasm for all these cultural expressions. On the aeroplane Celia had learned their alphabet, an extraordinarily logical and lucid construction, devised in the Middle Ages of Europe by a scholarly ruler. It consisted of a series of discrete squares, in which the addition and subtraction of strokes and hooks represented a coherent system of sequential phonemes and dispositions of lip and tongue; plosive and susurrant. It was a language that would have delighted an artificial intelligence, or a less jealous divine artificer in the days of the Babel tower. It was reasonable. It represented, the guide book asserted, a series of sounds of which no other race was wholly capable, even after much practice. Did it, Celia wondered, proceed like Chinese dialects, in a versatile string of monosyllables? If it did, how did its speakers, its professors, hear Milton's transitions from Latinate complexity to Anglo-Saxon plain speech? She did not know who she was talking to. She quoted the confidently absolute Lady in *Comus*.

> Virtue can see to do what Virtue would
> By her own radiant light, though Sun and Moon
> Were in the flat sea sunk.

And in front a sea, a restricted sea of faces. Oriental faces, golden and clear-cut under fine black hair, thoughtful faces which were very simply inscrutable. Celia liked differences, large or minute. She could tell a Japanese face from a Chinese face and both from these faces, in general if not always in particular. No two faces are the same; this endless human diversity is one of the more hopeful things about the preponderant species on the planet. The human sciences predict, with varying accuracy, the behaviour of class, gender and money, as the biological sciences predict the chances of transmitting haemophilia, the self-destruction of lemmings and the heroic transatlantic crossings of certain butterflies. A psychologist had once told Celia that a man and a woman would have to engender eight hundred thousand children to have any statistical chance at all of producing identical offspring from different eggs. She had walked on the Great Wall of China on which, at any one time, one sixth of the workforce is likely to be taking exercise. All these men and women stroll calmly and busily in identical blue suits and peaked caps. All different. The uniformity of the black hair, to Western eyes, creates an illusion of greater similarity. Westerners must depend heavily on hair colour for their Gestalt of a stranger or an acquaintance. After the Chinese time, Celia found herself seeing her compatriots as unfinished monsters, pallid meat topped by kinky, lustreless, unreal hair.

Professor Sun rose at the back of the hall to address a question. There were at least three other Professors Sun in the lecture theatre, probably more. Names, the British Council had explained, are restricted in variety in the Far East. Westerners could not or did not learn the whole names of Easterners. Easterners patiently and courteously provided versions of their names which approximated to Western forms. So there were many Suns and many Moons also. This Professor Sun had considerable presence and a large, round, open-seeming face that it was tempting to read as good-humoured and amused.

"Yes," he said. "Yes. Well." He paused. His tone was censorious. All interventions began with this pause, and with a summary "Well" which sounded as though the lecturer had been judged and found more or less wanting. "You will have been told," the English had been assured, "that we are always very polite, that we never say what we think. We shall make a great effort not to be polite. We shall try to tell you very much what we think." What Professor Sun thought was that Celia's understanding of Milton's virtuous figures would have been considerably improved by greater understanding of the English Revolution and God's Englishman, of commonwealth and hierarchy in seventeenth-century England. He spoke fluently and well of these English-historical events, smiling engagingly but severely at Celia, not quite placatory. He quoted, not eloquently but accurately, from Milton. Milton's words were a field in which he travelled with ease, unlike Celia's students. He had authority. He was clearly a very senior professor. The English had been told that the senior professors would speak and the younger teachers keep silence, out of deference. When they spoke, all the women, and some of the men, held the right hand at a delicate angle, across the mouth, producing a boxed and hesitant sound which could have been read as embarrassment, or reluctance to communicate, or some extreme form of courtesy, protecting any interlocutor from breath itself. Professor Sun displayed this gesture at the beginning and end of his speaking. His compatriots displayed considerable approval of his erudition, or incisiveness, or grasp – nothing so indecorous as applause, but the faint pleasured hum and shifting of torsos which must be a lecture-room universal.

Celia's other lecture was about George Eliot. George Eliot, the idea of the large mind and long serious face, was modified even during those few days by the oriental attentiveness, by the everywhere-and-nowhere of Room 1840 with its sachet of bath fragrance, by the absence of English news in the paper that was pushed under Celia's door. George Eliot, Celia said, had believed in her time that human nature was governed by universal and discernible laws, in exactly the same way as the law of gravity governed the movement of the heavenly bodies. Celia spoke of George Eliot's skill in demonstrating the workings of these hypothetical laws in the minute particulars of individual lives. George Eliot did not lapse from the picture to the diagram. She said, "A human life, I think, should be well rooted in some spot of a native land, where it may get the love of a tender kinship for the face of the earth." Out of the high window a cold sun shone on the bald chalkiness which was all Celia had seen of this remote spot of the face of the earth, and which had given her no sense of it. Inside the room everything could have been anywhere, Japanese microphones, American-style presidential lectern, neon strip-lighting, Bauhaus-derived armchairs, modestly opulent. Always when she quoted this passage a kind of simplified image of flat, ploughed Warwickshire crossed her inner eye, a few hedges, a few elms, heavy Constable-dense clouds in a wet sky, a characterless particular space. Here the image persisted but was tiny, a miniature negative, at the end of a long optic tube. What did they see, those scholars of English, what spot of time or place represented those vanished brown fields?

They had drinks in the British Council's compound, housed behind a fortress-wall heavily patrolled by the military who, except always for their faces, resembled other militaries in other places, khaki and jungle camouflage, pistols and machine guns.

They sat in a bright evening on a lawn much sprinkled and dried by a hotter sun, amongst a herbaceous border of nameless flowers. The representative's wife became animated on finding that Celia knew exactly the corner of the northern English cathedral city she came from, could retrace her route along the rattling river and over the great bridge, knew the suburb of new bungalows where home was. She was an infant teacher and said she would recommend the books of Beatrix Potter to anyone. Mr MacGregor's garden, the bluebell-wood, Mrs Tiggywinkle's hillside. Unnamed black butterflies or moths swooped across the fairy lamps in that garden, when night came suddenly ultramarine and then inky. The visiting critical theorist, Dr Wharfedale, talked to the Council Grammarian and Professor Sun about Chomsky's transformational grammar and the hypothesis of a universal deep structure. The English language is a major growth area in our exports, said the Council-man. Of course Beatrix Potter uses rather long words, said the representative's wife, but the pictures are lovely. Wordsworth thought the real language of men was derived from the great and permanent forms of nature amongst which the lucky peasant naturally found himself. I wish I had seen the countryside here, Celia cried, I wish I knew what it was like, even a little. "We hardly know ourselves," said Professor Moon gently at her elbow. "Our city is terrible and without any character. If you would like it, we will take you to our Folk Village." He had a narrow, serious face, without the genial attack of Professor Sun. "I do not know how we let it happen, this city," he said. "But it is very solid, very durable."

That night there was a curfew. Celia, forewarned, sat in 1840 clutching the heavy rubber torch provided by the management, along with bath cap, miniature toothpaste, sterilized oriental men's slippers, the sayings of Buddha, the Gideon Bible, and a circle of shining miniature bottles of vodka, Bourbon, Scotch and gin. The building sighed and gave up the ghost. The digital clock-radio no longer glowed purple. The room seemed blackly elastic. The misnumbered lifts must also be stilled. She was darkly lifted up with no egress. She moved aside the heavy flutes of curtain on her box-wall and looked out. The tall towers, which had been disembodied pillars of lighted squares, became heavy canyons. The serpent of traffic became sluggish, moved sideways, lost its gloss and in two minutes was inert. The sky changed from hectic yellow ochre to darkness visible, in which the stars momentarily sprang to life before they were reaped by huge scissor-blades of white light. Through air-conditioning and soundproofing Celia heard the busy hum and rumble. Shadowy tanks, nose to tail, filled the clefts below. Helicopters clicked and whirred out of the dark, stooping down over the crawling monsters between the dark towers. Such alerts were frequent in this country. The enemy was just restrained beyond the border; it was rumoured that he had already tunnelled successfully several kilometres into the land, and could send advance troops and spies through the hidden portals of his passes, to infiltrate, to mingle, to destroy.

Penalties for breaking the curfew, for glimmering lights or roving pedestrians, were severe. Celia tried to read the Sayings of Buddha by the light of the rubber torch, and was shocked, when it rolled away, by her inability to retrieve it in the black. When it was over, the liquid purple figures confidently proclaimed a time unreal in this country, unrelated to dawn or dusk, and the radio, which had resonated with rattling and repetitive military instructions, sang out a soothing Viennese waltz.

There was trouble about the visit to the Folk Village because an edict had gone out that only cars bearing even registration numbers could travel on the highway that day, so as not to impede the manoeuvres. Professor Moon had obtained a dispensation. He and a second Professor Sun drove the English along motorways that could have been in Texas, or the valley of the Rhône, in Birmingham or Kalgoorlie, no doubt also in Saskatchewan and Outer Mongolia. They saw tarmac and a few foothills. The absence of a central crash barrier, said Professor Moon, meant that the highway could be instantly converted to a landing-strip in times of trouble. For jump-jets, for fighter planes, for helicopters. The sky whined from time to time with mechanical wings. They discussed the curfew. Professor Moon said he had enjoyed it. Our city is lit with an infernal glow, he said. Always. And polluted, very heavily. Last night I came out of doors as I used to do in childhood and looked at the Milky Way. Normally now it is invisible through the pollution. I used to study the stars, as a boy, he said. Celia felt it would be impolite to ask how old he was, what world he had grown up in. Instead she asked how immediate was the threat against which the military manoeuvres were directed. All is uncertain, said Professor Moon. We are always threatened, by nature of our geographical position. Our country is perpetually threatened with occupation, and has been perpetually occupied. For nearly a century a foreign power ruled here and prohibited even our language. We developed patience and a kind of cunning. Myself, I believe the manoeuvres are designed to conduce in us a sense of national unity. You had the spirit of the Blitz, did you not?

Celia thought of art as a work of rescue. These fragments, said T. S. Eliot, I have shored against my ruin, speaking of various electically framed morsels of Dante, Wagner, Middleton, the Upanishads, *Hamlet* and so on, having equally eclectically neglected to canonize others. Realist novelists are humbler magpies of significant things. Aunt Pullet's unworn silk bonnets, forever fair and still to be enjoyed, splendidly démodé in the 1830s seen in 1858. David Copperfield's carving knives, Emma Woodhouse's purchased lengths of ribbon. The Folk Village, seen from this point of view, was a work of art as well as a tourist attraction. Here was collected everything that was poised silently to vanish away, each excellent in its kind, country mansion, municipal gaol, funereal monument, working craftsmen, weavers and fanmakers, live hens in immemorial wicker hen runs, a female shaman with a sulky face sitting on a reconstituted verandah with her fortune-telling tools laid out before her. Every stone of these houses had been moved and re-erected, Professor Moon explained, every wooden slat and thatched roof. These were real houses, not ersatz, they had been lived in, they had their histories. Celia peered into spotless kitchens with huge storage jars standing darkly, with built-in boiling-pans and griddles, at floor level. Professor Moon explained the chimney. It could fill the whole kitchen-quarters with smoke on a wet or windy day. Not pleasant at all for the people in there. Only women were allowed into these quarters. No males, ever. Not even little boys? Celia asked. Only when they were very little, said Professor Moon. Was there an altar? Celia asked, thinking of something she was writing about lares and penates, about hearth spirits. The houses were graceful and bare. There were chests, carved, inlaid with mother-of-pearl, there were rolls of quilts, there were low tables and nothing else. They gave no clue to the thoughts or habits of their vanished inhabitants. Professor Moon chose not to answer Celia's question. He moved away, a little distance, and looked away, further. You do not realize, he said, that it was in houses like these that most of our people grew up. I myself grew up in such a house. Celia was aware that she had trespassed. She persisted, briefly. And were there parts of the house into which women could not go? she asked. Certainly, certain parts, said Professor Moon, vaguely. They were walking round the house, peering in at every aperture. He made no attempt to indicate which parts these might be. Outside folk-dancers danced in weaving circles, to the tune of two little hand-drums and a huge flow of flute-song relayed on a tannoy through feathery acacia-like tree boughs. They wore beautiful white linen clothes, tossing streamers of brilliantly coloured ribbons, daffodil, royal blue, puce, leaf-green. The people watching them wore blue jeans and sloganned tee shirts over boat-like plastic shoes. "Their clothes have no style," said Professor Moon, with forceful distaste. "Those horrible shoes are completely without grace or character." His English became more fluent, idiomatic and graceful as the afternoon went on. He bought them rice-wine cooled in an earthen flask and pillow-like white rice-cakes, mildly sweet, with a ghostly rice flavour and a weightless melting texture. He took them to the crafts' stall where the fans and rice-bowls, horseshoes and quilts made by the visibly displayed craftsmen were sold, priced in dollars and yen. Here he picked up a kind of hexagonal wooden cage on a long spindle, and asked, did they know what this was? "No," they said, and he told them. "This is for flying kites. When I was a boy, I was champion in our village. We competed ferociously."

He picked the object up, as an instrumentalist will pick up a violin or a clarinet he understands, which will in his hands sing, or as a good cook will weigh this knife or that.

"We kept glass dust, for smoothness, we dipped our hands in it," he said, miming this unimaginable gesture. Then he tossed the wooden cage into the air and caught it, turning the wooden spindle rapidly, rapidly, between elegant palms. Faster and faster it spun. He tossed and caught, faster and faster. His professorial face took on a new smile, not a polite smile, but a craftsman's smile of pleasure, a child's smile of surprise at skill. He smiled with closed lips and narrowed eyes, all the angular lines of his face slanting up to his composed eye corners. Celia felt delighted and excluded by his absorption. She tried to work out how a kite would be wound on this reel and failed. She summoned up an imaginary hillside full of small boys in white linen, all tossing and spinning, all smiling gravely, and above them dipping and hovering and swooping aerial fleets of dragons, suns and moons, all in the clear strong folk-colours. The visionary kites were Chinese, and the hill was Box Hill, where she flew kites with her small son. She fanned herself with her new fan, inked in soft blue on oiled creamy paper, spread on delicate wooden ribs, still smelling of the oil into which it had been dipped. She had been three days in the intermittent company of Professor Moon and knew nothing at all about him.

They were almost late, on their return from this cleanly festive ghost town, for the final banquet. Banquet is an odd word, suggesting perhaps to the English some municipal function in an industrial city where the New Left has not yet done away with robes and silver plate. The Chinese have adopted this word for their more convivial formal meals in their socialist state, where delicate flavours succeed each other with none of the brutality of paving-stone steaks and sickly chocolate-sauced pears. Milton's desert Christ, rejecting classical learning, rejected also the Tempter's proffered Banquet of Sense, a fantastic feast which had manifested itself from classical Mediterranean cultures through to this final Puritan flourish. The food for the symposium in English Literature was offered in an inner room in a restaurant, where the guests sat shoeless and cross-legged around a low, L-shaped table. Celia was here separated from Professor Moon who now had a shape in her mind, not of what she knew about him, but of what she was aware of not knowing, a form of absence, like a glass box under a clear light. The exhaustion of the strange came upon her, the sudden refusal of mind and senses to take in new faces, new words, new foods, new courtesies, or old ones whose meanings had shifted and become dangerous or void. Everyone smiled, there was warmth, food came and more food, long amber tentacles of salty jellyfish to be gathered delicately with fine stainless steel chopsticks whose slipperiness reminded her of childhood knitting-needles.

Her neighbour on her left was only half-visible as she concentrated on her chopsticks. He had a large round face like Professor Sun, but he was not Professor Sun, he was younger, gentler, more shy. "And what are you currently teaching?" she asked this man, gathering her forces. "English pastoral," he told her. "From the Elizabethans to the nineteenth century." He seemed mildly offended at the question, but Celia persisted. This was their *lingua franca*, Eng. Lit., pedagogy. She had not seen a student in this foreign land. She had stood in the murky sky on top of the Press Centre and had spoken, not knowing those to whom she presumed to speak. Any academic knows the hazard of verbal slippage in such situations. A slight shift in the tension of the mesh of discourse, an increase or decrease of perhaps fifty words in the selected technical vocabulary, a shift in the selection of what must be explained and what may be presumed to be understood, can wholly change the perception of the speaker – from the trenchant to the inane, from the illuminating to the *déjà-vu*. Now, belatedly, she sought orientation. They talked about Arcadia and the English Lakes, and the jellyfish was replaced by fiercely cold white cabbage in blood-red pepper sauce and vinegar. Across the table Professor Sun the second recounted his tearing desire for this dish, exiled in Buffalo, working on Joyce's Dublin, walking the streets in search of a compatriot or a non-existent ethnic restaurant with its own casks of pickle. Dr Wharfedale, a young and uninhibited truth-seeker, was finally clearing up points of anxiety. The tower, he enquired, in the middle of the city, the tower with the red numbers, what did that refer to? That, said Professor Moon, was a symbol of national pride. It displayed the number of days left to go before the city hosted the World Games. We are very keen on gymnastics, but we never win. Our bodies appear to be the wrong shape, our legs too short, our trunks comparatively heavy, but lately, since our nourishment has improved, since we have become richer with our economic miracle, this is changing. The young have longer legs and higher hopes.

Ah yes, the young, said Dr Wharfedale. I gather you have trouble with student protest on your campuses? This question, like Celia's question about altars, produced an eddy of silence. Then a series of disjunct answers. The country, one said, was threatened from outside, and economically unstable, expanding too fast, maybe. The culture was authoritarian and hierarchical, had always been so. Respect for ancestors and hierarchy was part of the national character. If now this was being questioned it was because the students were better fed and had high expectations. They also cannot remember, as we older folk can, the days of oppression, the days of colonial rule, the days when our language was forbidden and our works of art carried away to foreign museums. They do not value what we subversively fought to preserve. They wish to bring down. For the sake of bringing down. Like students everywhere, Dr Wharfedale pacifically said. The assembled professors considered him with suspicion, or so it seemed to Celia. I have noticed, Dr Wharfedale said, that when you speak, you always put your hands across your mouths, so. Is this a form of politeness? Or shyness, perhaps? It is because we believe it is very rude, very aggressive, to show anyone else our teeth, they answered. Very dangerous, it was once believed.

"Sometimes I think, to be quite truthful," said Celia's left-hand neighbour, "that I have wasted the whole of my life. It has all been very interesting, perhaps, all this Wordsworth and Milton and George Eliot, but I am not sure it has had any real value."

Celia, still thinking about the student will to reject, considering her neighbour's youth, hurried too rapidly to agree.

"I too have wondered what it is all for, in this world we live in. My students grumble that Milton has no right to ask them to know Virgil or Ovid or even the Bible, which to them is not particularly holy and which they haven't learned at school, as I did. I am not a Christian, why should I ask them to read *Paradise Lost*? But I am too old to change. These things are my roots."

"Well," said her neighbour. "Well, that is not exactly what I meant. Do you know what is meant by Third World literature?"

"Oh yes," said Celia, again too rapidly, for she did not know. She knew what the Third World was. It was an economic entity defined in relation to two prior worlds. And she had examined degrees in places where the only literature taught was written by women, or blacks, or homosexuals, voices contradicting or modifying a voice, now unheard, that had once claimed to be the best that was thought and said in the world. She did not like, as a woman, to be thus marginalized. She did not like all these separate differences to be lumped heterogeneously together in one anger. The Third World was not one, it was many. Except when it faced the First World, from which she came, as an enemy.

"I think perhaps we should be studying Third World Literature. We should think about imperialism. And economic imperialism."

There was a place in the city where it had been supposed she desired to go, where you were clutched by the arm from shack doors by fluent girls and eager grandmothers, come buy, come buy, Gucci bags, St Laurent battleblouses, Zeiss cameras, Sony Walkmen and Cabbage Patch dolls, the mimetic products of the miracle, indistinguishable from their platonic forms and a tenth of the price. You could buy a teeshirt with a tomato-pink and brassy Iron Lady, or one with mushroom-cloud and capering mutants proclaiming, "We've learned to live with the Bomb." Vanity Fair, Celia had self-righteously thought, and had corrected herself, no, economic growth.

She turned kindly to her radical young neighbour.

"Perhaps you should study it. Perhaps you should. I am told I should. But Milton and George Eliot are my roots, I do not want them to vanish from the world."

"Nor do I. But it may not be of great importance if they do."

She turned to him again and said, "I know how you feel."

He put his hand across his lower face. "I wonder if you do. No, I don't think you do."

It was then she made the mistake of asking his name. His face expressed, she could read it, baffled hurt succeeded by indignation and contempt. He brought from his pocket, wordlessly, the circular disc that had been pinned to his coat during their earlier deliberations and had been removed now, for they had all become friends, had exchanged ideas, they knew each other, did they not? He was not like Professor Sun, he *was* Professor Sun. Not to have known him was to annihilate everything that had been said or acted, to break the frail connections that had been made. She had failed to distinguish between oriental faces. You can't tell them apart, she might just as well have said. She had lost face absolutely. Her hand went up to her mouth. She told the truth.

"Tonight you look twenty years younger."

He said frostily, with his old attacking note. "I am forty-six. Young for a professor."

"You look twenty-six."

"Yes. Well."

All the way home, through the day-long dark of the perpetual night of flying, she brooded on this failure. She thought about the delicate process by which we recognize faces. Something in the brain constructs a face from circular elements, a visual equivalent of the hypothetical deep structure of language. Infants in their hospital cots are teased or titillated by perceptual research workers, who dangle over them paper suns or moons, adding eyes maybe, or a smiling mouth, sketched universals. And from there to the exact particular, how does the mind move? In the national

museum of that country hall after hall of Buddhas and Boddhisat-
tvas smile, unvarying and various. Their hands speak a language
Celia could not read, mudras that call power from the earth, or
evoke infinity. No two were the same, though they were all one.
The idea of England from the air was small, dense, disagreeable
and irrelevant, though to what it was irrelevant, she could not
exactly have said. It was required that one think in terms of the
whole world, and it was not possible. Later, in deference to
Professor Sun, she would read a book by a francophone West
African in which she found a curious key to the confused towers.
This black man was incensed by his compatriots' collusion at the
imposition of a deviant Western cosmography on the lively
animism of his people. Their poets and teachers, he said, kow-
towed to the miscalled universal values of Western literature
which were the product of ideology and superstition. Take the
shiny glass and steel skyscrapers erected on African soil by
Western bourgeois capitalism. These silly buildings omitted the
thirteenth floor in order to propitiate foreign ghosts, witches and
spirits. Dr Wharfedale had ascertained that their lecture tower
lacked a fourth floor in deference to antagonistic local powers.
Celia fancied that the world was perhaps after all ruled by
Milton's God, who walked among his subjects and observed
them building, with bricks and black bituminous gurge, an
ambitious tower of universal human speech, which might
obstruct heaven towers. So, in derision, he set a various spirit
upon them, who razed their native language from their tongues,
and replaced it with a jangling noise of words unknown.

Celia had always before been sorry for the amicable men of
Babel, who had surely desired a good thing? This jealous god was
only a local deity, Israelite and seventeenth-century Puritan. But
the dialect of the tribe was the human speech of particular men.
The universals haunted by the mocking various spirit were the
plate-glass tower, the machine gun, the deconstructive hubris of
grammatologists and the binary reasoning of machines. The
rational silver man-made wings hung fragile over the empty dark.

Somewhere briefly below, at some point, lay a plain, westward of Eden, where the builders had been frustrated in the days of Nimrod, where a group of nomads, who knew the place well, sat around an oasis, and looked up indifferently at its winking trajectory, a few communications satellites, and the indiscriminate bright flux of the Milky Way.

ON THE DAY THAT
E. M. FORSTER DIED

This is a story about writing. It is a story about a writer who believed, among other things, that time for writing about writing was past. "Our art", said T. S. Eliot, "is a substitute for religion and so is our religion." The writer in question, who, on the summer day in 1970 when this story takes place, was a middle-aged married woman with three small children, had been brought up on art about art which saw art also as salvation. *Portrait of the Artist as a Young Man, Death in Venice, À la Recherche du Temps Perdu.* Or, more English and moral, more didactic, D. H. Lawrence. "The novel is the highest form of human expression yet attained." "The novel is the one bright book of life." Mrs Smith was afraid of these books, and was also naturally sceptical. She did not believe that life aspired to the condition of art, or that art could save the world from most of the things that threatened it, endemically or at moments of crisis. She had written three brief and elegant black comedies about folly and misunderstanding in sexual relationships, she had sparred with and loved her husband, who was deeply interested in international politics and the world economy, and only intermittently interested in novels. She had three children, who were interested in the television, small animals, model armies, other small children, the sky, death and occasional narratives and paintings. She had a cleaning lady, who was interested in wife-battery and diabetes and had that morning opened a button-through dress to display to Mrs Smith a purple and chocolate and gold series of lumps and swellings across her breasts and belly. Mrs Smith's own life made no sense to her without art, but she was disinclined to believe in it as a cure, or a duty, or a general necessity. Nor did she see the achievement of the work of art as a paradigm for the struggle for life, or virtue.

She had somehow been inoculated with it, in the form of the novel, before she as a moral being had had anything to say to it. It was an addiction. The bright books of life were the shots in the arm, the warm tots of whisky which kept her alive and conscious and lively. Life itself was related in complicated ways to this addiction. She often asked herself, without receiving any satisfactory answer, why she needed it, and why this form of it? Her answers would have appeared to Joyce, or Mann, or Proust to be frivolous. It was because she had become sensuously excited in early childhood by Beatrix Potter's sentence structure, or Kipling's adjectives. It was because she was a voyeur and liked looking in through other people's windows on warmer, brighter worlds. It was because she was secretly deprived of power, and liked to construct other worlds in which things would be as she chose, lovely or horrid. When she took her art most seriously it was because it focused her curiosity about things that were not art; society, education, science, death. She did a lot of research for her little books, most of which never got written into them, but it satisfied her somehow. It gave a temporary coherence to her perception of things.

So this story, which takes place on the day when she decided to commit herself to a long and complicated novel, would not have pleased her. She never wrote about writers. Indeed, she wrote witty and indignant reviews of novels which took writing for a paradigm of life. She wrote about the metaphysical claustrophobia of the Shredded Wheat Box on the Shredded Wheat Box getting smaller ad infinitum. She liked things to happen. Stories, plots. History, facts. If I do not entirely share her views, I am much in sympathy with them. Nevertheless, it seems worth telling this story about writing, which is a story, and does have a plot, is indeed essentially plot, overloaded with plot, a paradigmatic plot which, I believe, takes it beyond the narcissistic consideration of the formation of the writer, or the aesthetic closure of the mirrored mirror.

On a summer day in 1970, then, Mrs Smith, as was her habit when her children were at school, was writing in the London Library. (She preferred to divide art and life. She liked to write surrounded by books, in a closed space where books were what mattered most. In her kitchen she thought about cooking and cleanliness, in her living room about the children's education and different temperaments, in bed about her husband, mostly.) She had various isolated ideas for things she might write about. There was a story which dealt with the private lives of various people at the time of the public events of the Suez landings and the Russian invasion of Hungary. There was a tragi-comedy about a maverick realist painter in a Fine Art department dedicated to hard-edge abstract work. There was a tale based, at a proper moral distance, on her husband's accounts, from his experience in his government department, of the distorting effects on love, marriage and the family, of the current complicated British immigration policy. There was a kind of parody of *The Lord of the Rings* which was designed to show why that epic meant so much to many and to wind its speech into incompatible "real" modern events. None of these enterprises attracted her quite enough. She sat on her not comfortable hard chair at the library table with its peeling leather top and looked from shelved dictionaries to crimson carpet to elegantly sleeping elderly gentlemen in leather armchairs to the long windows onto St James's Square. One of these framed a clean, large Union Jack, unfurled from a flagpole on a neighbouring building. The others were filled by the green tossing branches of the trees in the Square and the clear blue of the sky. (Her metabolism was different in summer. Her mind raced clearly. Oxygen made its way to her brain.)

It was suddenly clear to her that all her beginnings were considerably more interesting if they were part of the same work than if they were seen separately. The painter's aesthetic problem was more complicated in the same story as the civil servant's political problem, the Tolkien parody gained from being juxtaposed or interwoven with a cast of Hungarian refugees, intellectuals and Old Guard, National Servicemen at Suez and Angry Young Men. They *were* all part of the same thing. They were part of what she knew. She was a middle-aged woman who had led a certain, not very varied but perceptive, life, who had lived through enough time to write a narrative of it. She sat mute and motionless looking at the trees and the white paper, and a fantastically convoluted, improbably possible plot reared up before her like a snake out of a magic basket, like ticker-tape, or football results out of the television teleprinter.

It would have to be a very long book. Proust came to mind, his cork-lined room stuffed with the transformation of life into words, everything he knew, feathers on hats, Zeppelins, musical form, painting, vice, reading, snobbery, sudden death, slow death, food, love, indifference, the telephone, the table-napkin, the paving-stone, a lifetime.

Such moments are – if one allows oneself to know that they have happened – as terrible as falling in love at first sight, as the shock of a major physical injury, as gaining or losing huge sums of money. Mrs Smith was a woman who was capable, she believed, of not allowing herself to know that they had happened. She was a woman who could, and on occasion did, successfully ignore love at first sight, out of ambition before her marriage, out of moral terror after it. She sat there in the sunny library and watched the snake sway and the tape tick, and the snake-dance grew more, not less, delightful and powerful and complicated. She remembered Kékulé seeing the answer to a problem of solid state physics in a metaphysical vision of a snake eating its tail in the fire. Why does condensation of thought have such authority? Like warning, or imperative, dreams. Mrs Smith could have said at any time that of course all her ideas were part of a whole, they were all hers, limited by her history, sex, language, class, education, body and energy. But to experience this so sharply, and to experience it as intense pleasure, to know limitation as release and power, was outside Mrs Smith's pattern. She had probably been solicited by such aesthetic longings before. And rejected them. Why else be so afraid of the bright books?

She put pen to paper then, and noted the connections she saw between the disparate plots, the developments that seemed so naturally to come to all of them, branching and flowering like speeded film, seed to shoot to spring to summer from this new form. She wrote very hard, without looking up, for maybe an hour, doing more work in that time than in times of lethargy or distraction she did in a week. A week? A month. A year even, though work is of many kinds and she had the sense that this form was indeed a growth, a form of life, her life, its own life.

Then, having come full circle, having thought her way through the planning, from link to link back to the original perception of linking that had started it all, she got up, and went out of the Library, and walked. She was overexcited, there was too much adrenalin, she could not be still.

She went up and down Jermyn Street, through the dark doorway, the windowed umber quiet of St James's Piccadilly, out into the bright churchyard with its lettered stones smoothed and erased by the passage of feet. Along Piccadilly, past Fortnum and Mason's, more windows full of decorous conspicuous consumption, down an arcade bright with windowed riches like Aladdin's cave, out into Jermyn Street again. Everything was transformed. Everything was hers, by which phrase she meant, thinking fast in orderly language, that at that time she felt no doubt about being able to translate everything she saw into words, her own words, English words, English words in 1970, with their limited and meaningful and endlessly rich histories, theirs as hers was hers. This was not the same as Adam in Eden naming things, making nouns. It was not that she said nakedly as though for the first time, tree, stone, grass, sky, nor even, more particularly, omnibus, gas-lamp, culottes. It was mostly adjectives. Elephantine bark, eau-de-nil paint on Fortnum's walls, Nile-water green, a colour fashionable from Nelson's victories at the time when this street was formed, a colour for old drawing-rooms or, she noted in the chemist's window, for a new eyeshadow, Jeepers Peepers, Occidental Jade, what nonsense, what vitality, how lovely to know. Naming with nouns, she thought absurdly, is the language of poetry, There is a Tree, of many One. The Rainbow comes and goes. And Lovely is the Rose. Adjectives go with the particularity of long novels. They limit nouns. And at the same time give them energy. Dickens is full of them. And Balzac. And Proust.

Nothing now, she knew, whatever in the moral abstract she thought about the relative importance of writing and life, would matter to her more than writing. This illumination was a function of middle age. Novels – as opposed to lyrics, or mathematics – are essentially a middle-aged form. The long novel she meant to write acknowledged both the length and shortness of her time. It would not be History, nor even a history, nor certainly, perish the thought, her history. Autobiographies tell more lies than all but the most self-indulgent fiction. But it would be written in the knowledge that she had lived through and noticed a certain amount of history. A war, a welfare state, the rise (and fall) of the meritocracy, European unity, little England, equality of opportunity, comprehensive schooling, women's liberation, the death of the individual, the poverty of liberalism. How lovely to trace the particular human events that might chart the glories and inadequacies, the terrors and absurdities, the hopes and fears of those words. And biological history too. She had lived now through birth, puberty, illness, sex, love, marriage, other births, other kinds of love, family and kinship and local manifestations of these universals, Drs Spock, Bowlby, Winnicott, Flower Power, gentrification, the transformation of the adjective gay into a politicized noun. How extraordinary and interesting it all was, how adequate language turned out to be, if you thought in terms of long flows of writing, looping tightly and loosely round things, joining and knitting and dividing, or, to change the metaphor, a Pandora's box, an Aladdin's cave, a bottomless dark bag into which everything could be put and drawn out again, the same and not the same. She quoted to herself, in another language, "Nel mezzo del cammin di nostra vita." Another beginning in a middle. Mrs Smith momentarily Dante, in the middle of Jermyn Street.

Where is the plotting and over-plotting I wrote of? It is coming, it is proceeding up Lower Regent Street, it is stalking Mrs Smith, a terror by noonday. It is not, aesthetic pride compels me to add, a straying terrorist's bullet, or anything contrived by the IRA. Too many stories are curtailed by these things, in life and in literature.

In the interim, Mrs Smith read the newspaper placards. "Famous Novelist Dies." She bought an early paper and it turned out that it was E. M. Forster who was dead. He was, or had been, ninety-one. A long history. Which, since 1924, he had not recorded in fiction. "Only connect," he had said, "the prose and the passion." He had been defeated apparently by the attenuation of the world he knew, the deep countryside, life in families in homes, a certain social order. Forster, much more than Lawrence, corresponded to Mrs Smith's ideal of the English novel. He wrote civilized comedy about the value of the individual and his responsibilities: he was aware of the forces that threatened the individual, unreason, belief in causes, political fervour. He believed in tolerance, in the order of art, in recognizing the complicated energies of the world in which art didn't matter. In Cambridge, Mrs Smith had had a friend whose window had overlooked Forster's writing desk. She had watched him pass mildly to and fro, rearranging heaps of papers. Never writing. She honoured him.

She was surprised therefore to feel a kind of quick, delighted, automatic survivor's pleasure at the sight of the placards. "Now," she thought wordlessly, only later, because of the unusual speed and accuracy with which she was thinking, putting it into words, "Now I have room to move, now I can do as I please, now he can't overlook or reject me." Which was absurd, since he did not know she was there, would not have wished to overlook or reject her.

What she meant, she decided, pacing Jermyn Street, was that he was removed, in some important sense, by his death, as a measure. Some obligation she had felt, which tugged both ways, to try to do as well as he did, and yet to do differently from him, had been allayed. Because his work was now truly closed into the past it was now in some sense her own, more accessible to learn from, and formally finished off. She passed the church again, thinking of him, agnostic and scrupulous. She envied him his certainties. She enjoyed her own difference. She thought, "On the day that E. M. Forster died I decided to write a long novel." And heard in the churchyard a Biblical echo. "In the year that King Uzziah died I saw also the Lord . . ."

He had written, "The people I respect most behave as if they were immortal and society was eternal. Both assumptions are false: both of them must be accepted as true if we are to keep on eating and working and loving and are to keep open a few breathing holes for the spirit."

Mrs Smith was still exalted. A consuming passion streamlines everything, like stripes in a rolled ribbon, one weaving: newsprint, smudged black lines on the placard, Wren church, Famine Relief posters, the order of male living in Jermyn Street shop windows, shoes mirror-bright, embroidered velvet slippers, brightly coloured shirts, the cheese shop with its lively smell of decay, Floris the perfumer with the ghost of pot-pourri. And for the ear the organ, heard faintly, playing baroque music. A pocket of civilization or a consumers' display-area. She came to Grima the jeweller, a recent extravaganza, expensively primitive, huge, matt, random slabs of flint-like stone, bolted apparently randomly to the shop-frame, like a modern theatre-set for an ancient drama, black and heavy, *Oedipus*, *Lear*, *Macbeth*. And in the interstices of these louring slabs the bright tiny boxes of windows – lined with scarlet kid, crimson silk, vermilion velvet. The jewels were artfully random, not precision polished, but fretted, gold and silver, as stone or bone might be by the incessant action of the sea. And the stones – huge, glowing lumpen uneven pearls, a pear-shaped fiery opal, a fall of moonstones like water on gold mail – were both opulent and primitive, set in circlets or torques that might have come from the Sutton Hoo ship, a Pharaoh's tomb, the Museum of Modern Art. Windows, frames, Mrs Smith thought, making metaphors of everything, out of the library window I saw the national flag and summer trees, in here is the fairy cavern and all the sixties myths, and in the tailor was Forster's Edwardian world of handmade shirts and slippers. The windows order it. But it is not disorderly. Even the *names* – Turnbull and Asser, Floris, Grima – can work in a Tolkien-tale, a realist novel, or a modern fantasy. It is all *there*. There is time.

And then the man, who had turned the corner into Jermyn Street, plucked her by her sleeve, called her by her name, said how delighted he was to see her. She took time to recognize him: he had aged considerably since they last met. He was not a man she considered herself to know well, though at their rare meetings he behaved, as now, as if they were old and intimate friends. His history, which I shall now tell, was in most ways the opposite of Mrs Smith's, given that most histories of the university-educated English would appear very similar to a creature from another planet or even from Japan, Brazil or Turkey. Mrs Smith and Conrad had been to the same university, attended the same parties, had the same acquaintances and one or two friends in common in the worlds of education and the arts in London in 1970. Conrad had studied psychology whereas Mrs Smith had studied English literature. He had made passes at Mrs Smith, but he made passes at most people, and Mrs Smith did not see that as a token of intimacy. He had been, and remained, a friend of friends.

In Jermyn Street, as always before, he radiated boundless enthusiasm, as though there was no one he would rather have met at that moment, as though chance, or Providence, or God had answered his need, and hers almost certainly too, by bringing them haphazardly together. He leaped about on the pavement, a heavy man with a new, pear-shaped belly propped on his jeans like a very large egg on an inadequate egg-cup. He had a jean jacket over a cotton polo-neck through which rusty specks and wires of hair pierced here and there. He leaped with a boyish eagerness, although he was a middle-aged man with a bald brow and crown, and long, kinked, greasy fringes of hair over his collar. She particularly noticed the hair in the first moments. As an undergraduate he had had a leonine bush of it which gave him presence.

"Come and have a cup of coffee," he said, "I have so much to tell you. You are the ideal person."

In the past she would, out of fear, or distaste for being cornered and having her knee pressed or stroked, have refused this invitation. In the past, she had refused more of his invitations than she had accepted. There were resilient moods in which the writer in her was prepared to fend off the patting, stroking and breathing for the sake of information Conrad purveyed about things she knew too little about. Psychology, for instance. It was Conrad who had told her about the effects of experiments in total sensory deprivation, men suspended in lightless baths of warm liquid so that sight, and the sense of the body and then the sense of time and the self were annihilated. It was Conrad who had said that there were unrevealed numbers of volunteer students, whose personalities had disintegrated forever in this bodiless floating. Mrs Smith was curious about what held the personality together, what constituted the self. Conrad, whose life experience was varied, told her also, when she could bear to be told, about forms of bullying and torture, and about experiments on the readiness of ordinary men to inflict pain under orders. Mrs Smith was extensively curious but lacked the journalist's readiness to ask questions. Conrad's talkativeness was, in its way, a godsend.

But on that June day, she went to have coffee because of the music. She felt particularly warm to Conrad because of the music.

The story of the music was, is, a plot almost needing no character. All that need initially be known about Conrad to tell the story of the music is that he was a man of extraordinary nervous, physical and mental energy. He was not still, he did not stop, he was perpetually mobile. He bedded women with an extravagant greed and need which Mrs Smith found sensuously unattractive but interesting to be told about. He had married a rich and beautiful wife, very young, but all other women interested him. He liked activity: he had taken his academic psychological skills into the army, into the prison service, into commerce. He had an interest in advising television advertisers. As I said, he was to Mrs Smith a friend of friends, and in her early days of childbearing she had heard from friends tales of Conrad's restless activity. He had set out and joined in the Hungarian uprising. He had spent his honeymoon in the Ritz, three weeks without getting out of bed, he had been heard of as accompanying a filming expedition to Central New Guinea, to study cannibals, he had several children by actresses, au pair girls, students. He had been very busy. He had had a routine medical examination for a job with another film company working abroad and had been discovered to have tuberculosis. He had been sent to a sanatorium, and the friends had not seen him for several years. His wife had left him. All this filtered through friends to Mrs Smith, quietly running her house, feeding her children, reading George Eliot and Henry James.

In the sanatorium, Conrad had, in his enforced stillness, had a vision. He had seen that his life was finite, that it came only once, that a man must decide what was the most important thing to him and pursue that, and that only, with all his power. The most important thing in life to Conrad was, he decided, music. In the sanatorium that seemed clear to him. When he came out, gaunt and quiet, he had resigned all his lucrative work and had enrolled as a music student, a student of composition. He had married a second quiet wife. Meeting him at that time, a man submitted to a new discipline in middle age for the sake of an ideal vision, Mrs Smith had felt a mixture of envy and cautious scepticism. He was shining with certainty. The routine pass was couched almost as an invitation to a religious laying-on of hands. Mrs Smith rejected it, and went home to a flooded washing-machine, a threatening letter from a released anarchist drug-pusher to her husband, and the reflection that in the past much great art had been produced by the peculiar vitality and vision afforded by TB, which could now of course be cured, to our human gain and aesthetic loss.

She had seen Conrad once again between then and now, when he had knocked on her door and said she *must* come to lunch. The lunch had been expensive – mussels, turbot, zabaglione, wine. Mrs Smith had scrutinized Conrad, who ate and drank with passion. He ate all her new potatoes and all his, glistening with hollandaise sauce, and left an empty sauceboat. He wiped his lips with a damask napkin: his face also glistened with exertion and butter: his second wife, he said, had left him, taking the children. He was paying a lot of alimony. He had had a motet played at a Contemporary Music Festival in Leamington Spa. He was working for a cigarette company, devising ways of suggesting that cigarettes produced sexual pleasure, without this being apparent. The decline of lipstick-wearing amongst women made this harder. Once you could use a glamorous scarlet lip, wet-looking. Now it had to be clean and healthy. He wasn't happy about this; he had seen too much in the lung ward in the sanatorium. But there was the alimony. Did she know any good modern love poems he could set to music? He wanted to write for single voices, very plain. He had met an extraordinary Israeli singer. With an extraordinary range. Did women write love poems? Did she know women ate mussels because they reminded them of sex? Was it the marine smell, or the hint of the embryonic? Would she care for a brandy? An armagnac? A ticket for Stockhausen at the Festival Hall? The nature of our concept of musical sound, musical form, was being radically changed, as never before. He was engaged, too, in research about how to interest women in fortified wines. Of course, physiologically speaking, they couldn't take much. Up-market port and lemon. Class drink preferences were not wholly determined by money. Would she like a cigar? He rubbed her knee with his. Big and hot. She dodged efficiently.

All the same, there was the music. He had been *in extremis*, and had put music first.

They sat in front of cappucinos in an unassuming coffee bar. Now she was near him, she saw that he looked ill. There was thick beard stubble, his face was patterned by broken capillary tubes, his eyes were veined, his neck tendons stood out. His shoulders were sprinkled with dandruff and traced by fallen hairs.

"How's the music?" asked Mrs Smith.

"Marvellous. Wonderful. New. Never better. You look radiant. You look *so lovely*. It's *marvellous* to see you, looking so lovely. Not a day older – not a *day* – than when we walked along the Backs together and sat side by side in the University Library."

Mrs Smith did not recall that they had done either of these things. Perhaps her memory – which she must now trust to be so sharp – was at fault.

"I've just been thinking how pleasant it is to be middle-aged."

"You aren't middle-aged. You're as old as you feel. That's true, not just something to say. I'm young, you're young, we can do anything. I've never in my whole life felt so young, so healthy."

There were panels of sweat down his nose, in the crease of his chin, on his clammy brow. The ends of his fingers were dead white and his fingernails had dirt under them. He smelled. Across the new coffee smell he smelled of new sweat and old sweat under it, mortality.

"Tell me how the music is."

"I told you, it's fantastic. Every day, new discoveries. Revolutionary techniques. New machines. A new range of possibilities. I can't get over how *fresh* you look."

Mrs Smith knew that she had grey hairs, a marked fan of lines in her eye-corners, a neck better covered, a body loosened by childbearing. She did not attract wolf whistles. She was not generally considered to expect or hope that advances would be made.

"Don't say that, I'm thinking how happy I am to be irretrievably middle-aged. Because of time, because I'm *in time*. Listen – I've decided to write a long book – about my time, the time I've lived and won't have again."

It was the first time, possibly, she had volunteered a serious confidence in their acquaintance. It was because of the music.

"By the time we're middle-aged I can tell you they'll have discovered how to arrest the ageing process forever. They're working on it. It'll be quite possible soon to stop death, to stop death in most cases. I assure you, I've gone into it. You deprive the body of the signals – hormone decrease, loss of calcium, those things – that trigger off ageing. There's a political problem, they don't want everyone to know, naturally, they haven't solved the world population problem. But I have my sources of information. You trick your genes into working to perpetuate themselves in the body you've got, not a new one. It can be done. I had a vasectomy. No more kids, no more alimony, no more splurging my genes on other beings. Conserve. Perpetuate. Live. Don't talk about middle age."

"But I *like* it." She wanted him, for once, to hear. "I've just discovered I practise a middle-aged art. Spread over time. Time's of the essence."

"There's no such thing as time. Time's an illusion. The new music knows that. It's all in the present. Now. It isn't interested in the past, or in harmony, or in keeping time, in tempo, any of all that. We've broken the idea of time and sequence. We play with the random, the chaotic. Einstein destroyed the illusion of linear time."

"Not biological time," said Mrs Smith, bravely, having heard these arguments before, though not from Conrad.

"Instantaneous and disposable sounds," said Conrad, excited. "Always different, always now. Biological time's an illusion too. Only the more complicated organisms die. Simple cells are immortal. We can reverse that. We must make a better world to live in. That's what matters. We must survive. Can I trust you?"

Mrs Smith lowered her eyelids and said nothing. She expected a sexual confidence.

"I know I can trust you, that's why I met you. These things are not fortuitous. I was followed here. I'm in danger."

Mrs Smith did not know what to do with this introduction of espionage plotting. She continued to look non-committally intelligent, and to say nothing.

"There's a dark man across there, across the street, with an evil umbrella. Don't look now."

Paranoia, said Mrs Smith's mind. "Why?" said Mrs Smith, more neutrally.

"I am carrying", said Conrad, leaning forward across the formica table top, breathing stale smoke and sour fear in her face, "this folder of secret plans. It's a matter of life and death. I've got to get them to the Israeli embassy."

He laid a rubbed and filthy package before her, tied with various kinds of string, sprouting faded edges of xerox paper.

"This may prevent nuclear war. They have a Bomb, you know, they may be driven to let it off. Everyone's against them, fighting for survival, history conspiring . . ."

"I don't think . . ."

"You don't know. I worked for British Intelligence, you know. On some very hush-hush research. All those trips to eastern university conferences weren't what they seemed. I know my way around. In Israel everyone's in Intelligence. They have to be. I recognized it in Miriam immediately. I can't get her to trust me. I want the Israelis to accept this. In token of good faith. British good faith."

Mrs Smith was driven to ask, in a small voice, what "this" was, though not, she hoped, as though she really wanted to know. Across the road the man in a dark overcoat lit a cigarette, shifted his umbrella, looked through the café window, looked back at the gentlemen's shirts in their bold colours, scarlet stripes, roseate flowers, black and gold paisley. He did not look the sort of man to wear such shirts.

"The music department in this university has made an instrument – constructed a machine – that disintegrates solid bodies with sound waves. By shaking them. Sound broadcast by this instrument at certain frequencies disorientates people completely. Drives them round the bend. Arabs are peculiarly susceptible to sound. They hear a greater frequency range. I'm taking these plans to the Israeli embassy."

"How terrible," said Mrs Smith.

"Of course it's terrible. Life is terrible. Destroy or be destroyed. What I want you to do is keep the duplicate plans safe – just sit here and keep them safe – and if I'm not back in one hour take them to one of these people in the BBC Music Department. The BBC's full of spies. I know them. I have the list."

"Terrible I meant," said Mrs Smith, "to use the music. The *music* . . ."

He brushed this aside. "I'll give you £100. £500. Just for *half an hour*. As an insurance?"

"I don't want anything to do with it." Mrs Smith stood up. "I don't like it. I'm going."

"Oh no," said Conrad. "Oh no, you don't. You may be part of the plot, after all. You will stay here where I can see you."

He clasped Mrs Smith's wrist. The man on the opposite pavement looked at them again, pulled his hat over his eyes, became absorbed in the contemplation of a pair of black velvet slippers, embroidered with a pair of gold stags' heads. Mrs Smith thought of *The Thirty-Nine Steps*. Her desire to get out of this story, international incident, paranoid fantasy, became overmastering. She tried to pull away.

"I'm going, I'm afraid. I have work to do."

"You can't go out there. Those people have poison-darts in their umbrella-tips. Fatal. No known antidote."

"No, they don't," said Mrs Smith.

Mrs Smith pulled. "You have got to help." She raised her handbag and banged it against Conrad's bald head and red ear. He, breathing loudly, grabbed her crisp white shirt by the collar. Both pulled. The shirt came apart, leaving most of one sleeve and the left front portion in Conrad's hand. The restaurant proprietor, assuming rape, approached from behind the bar. Conrad's parcel fell under the table. As he bent towards it, Mrs Smith, her face scratched, one lace-covered breast exposed, ran out into Jermyn Street, attracting the brief, unsmiling attention of the window-watcher. When she was at the corner of Jermyn Street she heard Conrad's voice, plaintive and wild, "Come back, help me, help me."

Mrs Smith ran on, down Duke of York Street, along St James's Square, into the solid Victorian mahogany sanctuary of the London Library, which, at its inception, at the behest of Thomas Carlyle, historian and founder member, stocked the fiction of only one writer, George Eliot, who he believed had so deep an insight into the thought and nature of the times that her work was classified, by him, as philosophy.

In the mahogany ladies' room, with water from a Victorian brass tap, Mrs Smith mopped her face and wept for the music. She would have to borrow a cardigan to go home respectably. She had lost some virtue. (In the old sense of that word, from the Latin, *virtus*, manliness, worth, power; and in newer ones too.) She was shaken. She was a determined and practical woman and would go back to work, however her elation had been broken.

Conrad was mad. She would not inhabit his plot of deathly music-machines and lethal umbrellas.

How precarious it was, the sense of self in the dark bath of uncertainty, the moment of knowing, the certainty that music is the one thing needful.

"Death destroys a man," said Forster, the liberal humanist, the realist, who died on that day. "The idea of death saves him." It would take more than Conrad's local madness to deflect or deter Mrs Smith.

I have to record, however, that only two weeks later she went to see a surgeon in the Marylebone Road. She had a pain in her side, not much, not a bad pain, a small lump, a hernia.

She had a sort of growth, said the surgeon, a thickening of old scar tissue. He thought it would be better if he took it out.

"Not just now," said Mrs Smith. "I am busy, I have a lot of work to do, I work best in the summer, it's the school holidays. In the autumn."

"Next week," said the surgeon, and added in answer to her unspoken question; "it is certainly benign."

This is not what he said to Mr Smith, and indeed, how could he have said with such certainty, before the event, what it was, malignant or benign?

Mrs Smith, during the three weeks that in fact supervened before she entered the hospital, went as usual to the London Library. She stared a lot out of the window and tried to think of short tales, of compressed, rapid forms of writing, in case there was not much time.

THE CHANGELING

He wore a blazer of crushed-strawberry pink and cream and black stripes and a straw boater, about which he was not confident. He took it on and off, and turned it like a wheel in two hands in front of his flannels. "This time I have a real challenge for you," he said. Some of the garden-party guests had obeyed the injunction, "Edwardian dress", on their invitations, and some had not, so that leg o'mutton sleeves and silk parasols stood side by side with knee-length silk shirtwaisters and uncovered heads. Josephine Piper was wearing a long grey cotton skirt, a high-necked blouse, and an anachronistic straw hat of her own, not because she liked dressing-up, but because she always complied with requests, if possible, out of courtesy. She inclined her head to Max McKinley, whilst watching the polite little boys trot busily over the even and sunlit lawns, carrying sausage rolls, miniature pizzas, devils-on-horseback, made in the school kitchens. It was a progressive school: boys were taught cookery. "What sort of challenge?" she asked Max McKinley, smiling. She liked Max, not only because he liked and seemed to understand her writings, though that had been the beginning of the friendship and collaboration. Years ago, now, back in the 1960s when her son was the same size as these little ones, he had asked her, then relatively unknown, to come and talk to his boys about her work. And in due course Peter, her son, had come to the school.

Max said, "I want you to have a boy called Henry Smee for a few months. He's a brilliant boy, but not easy. He needs a warm, normal, intelligent house. I think" — Max leaned closer — "he needs you."

"Why?"

"I think — you'll see — I think Henry Smee *is* Simon Vowle in

The Boiler-Room. It is quite striking."

"How terrible," said Josephine, who had invented Simon Vowle, in a light enough voice. "How terrible for Henry Smee."

"It is terrible. I'm sure you can help him. I'm sure."

"You always ask the impossible," said Josephine, not displeased.

"He goes to Cambridge in the autumn. I've got him a summer job in a library. He needs a normal life and some understanding."

"I can try," said Josephine. "You'd better introduce us."

She was always very moved and enlivened by the energy of Max's care for his boys. He imagined every quiver, every spasm of young suffering: every boy was new and strange to him: he believed something could be done for all of them: he never gave up. In his place Josephine would long ago have retreated into impersonal efficiency, but she did not tell him that. She did not for a moment believe that Henry Smee had anything to do with Simon Vowle, except in Max's hyperactive imagination. Owing to a series of social activities and evasions she was unable to check on this before Henry Smee was delivered in person, to her house.

The house was a large Victorian house in South London, a well-proportioned, comfortable, rambling house, far too big for Josephine alone, and too big, even in the days of her household, which had briefly consisted of her husband and son, and then only of herself and Peter. After the stroke of luck which had been Max's invitation to speak at King Edmund's School, and Peter's acceptance there as a weekly boarder, she and Peter had tried to fill the bedrooms, surround the dining-table, with guests whom, when they were alone together, they called the Lost Boys. Orphaned boys who would otherwise have spent the school holidays in empty dormitories. Boys whose families were abroad, diplomatically or on business. A taciturn Zulu prince. A nervous, tearful vegetarian Indian from Mauritius. The boy who had been found stealing and selling transistors and calculators to pay for drugs. The boy who ran away to join a saffron-robed and shaven-headed sect and had come back capable only of intermittent attention and prolonged bouts of sleeping. Josephine and Peter talked over these boys, late at night, in their absence, sharing their knowledge of their fears, their secret hopes, their relations with the outside world. Peter told Josephine things which she never claimed to know, never referred to when talking to the boys, but delicately, she hoped, allowed for and adapted to. Peter was a very sharp observer of other people's fears. He observed with a concern more akin to Max McKinley's enthusiasm than to Josephine's cool and practical categorizing. For a year or two he had worshipped Max McKinley and then had inexplicably cooled. But by then much of Peter's behaviour was inexplicable or heart-breaking.

After Peter had gone, Josephine continued to accommodate temporary Lost Boys. She did not put them to sleep in Peter's room, which she kept brushed and dusted and ready for his possible return. They slept, as the earlier Lost Boys had slept, in cosy attics where they could play music without disturbing Josephine's silence. She swept out such an attic for Henry Smee and put a bunch of flowers from her garden on the desk, to welcome him.

Max brought him and stayed to supper. They had supper in the kitchen, a warm room, gleaming with russet and scarlet and copper, heated by a Swedish steel solid-fuel heater which was fed with wooden logs and smelled of bonfires. It was not, nevertheless, an imitation farmhouse kitchen, but urban and domestic, its walls hung with used and useful tools, its wooden shelves cleanly supporting scarlet plates and bowls of nuts and fruit. Throughout this first meal Max and Josephine talked somewhat feverishly, addressing more than half their remarks to Henry Smee who said nothing, nothing at all, did not even clear his throat.

Josephine had in fact been shocked when she saw Henry Smee. He did – and equally did not – look like Simon Vowle. You could have used, Josephine could have used, the same little groups of words indifferently to describe either. He was excessively thin and pale, with lank, colourless hair, moon-glasses and a long fragile head on hunched shoulders, the sharp bones standing out on cheek and chin. The words would have fitted, had been written by Josephine, but the image did not. An artist playing with a pencil could have reproduced immediately the down-pull of the mouth-corner, the side-wind of the thin neck, drawn back, fastidious, nervous. An invented face never has this wholeness or quiddity. If you write "moon-glasses" those you inwardly "see" and the chin is vague and unfocused. So also with the precise degree of colourless colour in fine hairs. It came to Josephine that Max, whenever he thought of Simon Vowle, now saw *this* face, as she herself had to struggle, thinking of Philip Marlowe, not to see Humphrey Bogart. The fact that this irritated her was the first intimation of the problem.

Max went home, and left Josephine alone with Henry Smee, who said he would go to bed, and went up, soundlessly, clinging to the banisters for support.

Over the next weeks they breakfasted together, Josephine and Henry, and met again for supper, on days when Josephine was in. She tried to talk to him, in spite of a reluctance which was partly an aspect of her own reticent nature, and partly inspired by a kind of force-field which emanated from Henry's tense and paradoxically limp figure. She talked to him about the university, where he would go, and about fine points of translation into and out of Latin, Greek and French, about which, in his small non-resonant voice, he could be very sharp. He never offered to help prepare these two meals, nor to clear a plate, nor to dry one. He held his knife and fork as if they were both too heavy and too crude for his purposes. He had a habit of stasis: if he got himself into a room he would then stand, every nerve, she could feel it, desperate to maintain his upright and immobile body. It was as though he was imprisoned in plate-glass, or fighting invisible streams of violent pressure. He had to be invited to move from door to chair, to sit, to stand, to bring his plate, which he held before him as a mechanical toy drummer holds his drum, on rigid arms between rigid fingers. Sometimes Josephine thought he was afraid of dropping her plates and sometimes that he felt it was not his place to have to touch them. He did not join in conversations she started in praise of the humanity of Max McKinley – he looked his look, which could be read as scornful or desperate, depending on her mood, rather than his. She had been told he was musical: she urged him to make use of the piano and of Peter's record-player. He replied that the piano was out of tune and that the quality of sound on the record-player was distressing to his ear. She imagined him in some fine aural torment and wished he could have smiled, looked self-deprecating as he spoke. She began to be afraid of him. She began to fear supper and to listen for his feet going up to his attic, and then to listen in fear for his door to open again, for him to begin his slow, deliberate, desperate-seeming descent.

The subject of Josephine's writings was fear. Rational fear, irrational fear, the huge-bulking fear of the young not at home in the world. Every writer, James says, discovers his or her subject matter early and spends a lifetime elaborating and exploring it. That may or may not be generally true, but it was certainly true of Josephine Piper. Her characteristic form was the long novella: her characteristic hero a boy, anywhere between infancy and late adolescence, threatened and in retreat. Some of these boys were actually mutilated or killed, driven away in cars with no inner door handles, rushed stumbling through urban jungles at knife-point, ritually tormented by gangs of other boys in public school dormitory or state school playground. If they were hurt it was always fast and unexpected: the subject was not violence but fear. Often they were not hurt: they suffered from a look, an exclusion, a crack in a windowpane, a swaggering bus conductor keeping order on the top deck because he himself was afraid for his life.

Josephine's work had been compared to Kafka as well as to Wilkie Collins and James himself. *The Boiler-Room*, whose central figure was Simon Vowle, was a surreal story of a boy in a boarding school who had built himself a Crusoe-like burrow or retreat in the dust behind the coiling pipe-system of the coke-boiler in the school basement and had finally moved in there completely, making forays for food and drink at night. It had a macabre end: Josephine Piper did not let her characters off. It had been described, with the usual hyperbole, as the last word on institutional terrors in schools. Josephine Piper could make an ordinary desk, a heap of football boots, a locked steel locker, tall and narrow, bristle with the horror of what man can do to man.

She recognized fear in Henry Smee, though she had no idea what he was afraid of, or whether his fears were real or phantasmagoric. She recognized something else too, from her own experience; the inconvenience, to the pathologically afraid, of an excessive gift of intellectual talent. Poor Henry could not but enjoy a grammatical dispute or the strict form of complex music: he perceived order and beauty, he remembered forms and patterns, he was doomed to think. He could not take up hiding as a way of life. She herself had been afraid as a child – where else could such knowledge have come from? – and had been so clever that it had had to be noticed, she could not hide it in silence and stammering, she had had to read and remember and in the end, as Henry was now doing, to go out at least temporarily into a world where these things mattered.

He developed an inconvenient habit. He would not speak, over breakfast or supper, and Josephine slowly ceased to persist in questionings that received monosyllabic or nodding answers. But he roamed the house at two, at three in the morning, in his pyjamas and dressing gown, and once or twice she came down, fearing intruders, to find him sitting in the kitchen, with a mug of Nescafé, staring at the stove. On these occasions, though he did

not confide in Josephine, he showed an extraordinary willingness
to talk. He would talk very quietly, so that she had to strain to
hear him, offering, she imagined, the flotsam and jetsam of his
thoughts, disconnected observations about the use of learning
Latin quantities, or the economy of Stravinsky, or a longish
disquisition on the Cambridge syllabus, with a parenthetical
remark that he hoped that he didn't have to share supervisions, he
found it hard to be in a room with more than one person at once.
This was the most personal thing he said, and yet, yawning and
low in blood-sugar, Josephone was aware that he was telling her
as best he could what or how he was. The trouble was that she did
not want to know. What she could face about what Henry was
telling her she already knew. And fear is infectious.

Fear is perhaps also hereditary. Josephine's mother had had a
mild and for others disagreeable case of agoraphobia, which had
worsened as she grew older, with what Josephine's father,
bewildered, socially embarrassed, lonely, called indulgence.
When Josephine was five or six her overwrapped mother would
take her overwrapped daughter as far as the local school and
had been known to go as far as the public library. By the time
Josephine was fourteen, at boarding school, Josephine's mother
rarely ventured outside her bedroom, and became giddy even in
the back garden. She had never said – Josephine had never
supposed it would be worth asking – *what* she feared, and her
daughter had been left to imagine. She remembered her mother
veering in agitation out of a bus queue in which they had been
standing side by side in uncompanionable silence, running up the
road, dropping books and paper bags of plums and carrots. What
was frightening about bus stops? It was more understandable
that the doorbell should arouse terror. Josephine, who had had to
negotiate the Kleen-e-ze man, the meter-readers, the doctor
himself, saw all these as menacing. How much more menacing
were the laughing large girls in the school dormitory, who threw
pillows, who launched themselves on each other's beds, who

ragged and mocked the thin child she was, shaking in her liberty
bodice? She had been saved, if she had been saved, by the solitary
and sensuous pleasure of writing out her fear. Already in the
boiler-room of St Clare's School she was writing clumsy tales of
justified terror, of bounding packs of girls who accidentally
squeezed the last breath out of their pathetic prey, of lost,
voiceless sufferers locked in cupboards and accidentally forgotten. The boiler-room had been thick with coal-dust: a scree of
coke sloped up to a closed and cobwebbed window under the
area and the pavement. If she opened the boiler door the flames
hissed and roared and the coke-dust glittered here and there. She
collected things: a blanket, a bicycle lamp, an old sweater, a
biscuit tin, a special box for pens, a folder that lived there. She
squeezed into her burrow, through pipe-gaps too narrow to take
a larger girl or member of staff. Sometimes she sacrificed bad
writing to the boiler, whose angry red turned briefly golden.
When she wrote about Simon Vowle the coke-smell came back in
its ancient fustiness and bitterness. Simon Vowle was an exor-
cism. The woman who could make and observe him was not
doomed to relive her mother's curious arrested life – *was not*?

Henry Smee and Josephine sat in front of the kitchen stove,
drinking powdered coffee. Henry was eating an apple, a Cox's
Orange Pippin, which Josephine had given him. He looked as
though the sound his teeth made, driving through the crackling
apple-flesh, distressed or embarrassed him in the silence. He sat
on a bench, his knees tight together, his thin ankles in his slippers
whitely together. When he was not eating he held his hands
together, pointing downwards, between his knees. Josephine
wanted to be in bed. She, like Henry, suffered from insomnia, but
she would rather have been reading. At three in the morning she
fended off fear with long narrative poems, at once difficult
verbally and offering another imagined world to enter. She asked
Henry how his work was going at the library and he replied that
their classification system was crazy and made a lot of unneces-

sary work: they think books are just things of a certain size, said Henry.

And then he said, "I read *The Boiler-Room*."

"Ah yes."

"Max told me to read it and I read it."

"Good."

"Simon Vowle." said Henry, and stopped. "Simon Vowle." It was a terrible effort for him. He was shaking. His coffee cup shook and he had to put it down. Josephine, who might have taken pleasure in writing about the pain it was for him to make any direct communication, nevertheless made no effort to help him.

"How do you *know* about Simon Vowle? He – he does little – intimate things – plays little games with himself – *you* know, naturally, why am I telling you? – that I thought only I knew about. I thought only I –"

Josephine was more than reluctant to embark on this conversation. She answered, flippantly for her, "I know by observation. It's not uncommon. People grow out of it."

"Oh no," said Henry Smee. His glasses were steamed up. He took them off and turned to her a blind, seeking, vulnerable face. "The world is more terrible than most people ever let themselves imagine. Isn't it?"

She should have asked him, what are you afraid of? She was afraid of him. She said, wilfully, "Surely not at St Edmund's, with people like Max? I sent my Peter there because it was such a friendly place."

"It isn't –" He twisted his useless hands in his dressing-gown. "It isn't – friendly to everyone. It isn't possible. They are impossible people."

"I'm very fond of Max," said Josephine's respectable voice.

"I wasn't happy."

"You will grow out of it. We all have to."

"Oh no. You don't – understand. No – you do – you wrote – You won't understand."

"I get tired at three in the morning."

"Of course. I'll go to bed. Of course."

He rose jerkily and made off, a shuffle, a tentative stepping. Max had sent him to her for help. She had not helped. She put his apple core in the bin and wiped and wiped her softly shining table top.

After this, she became continuously afraid of Henry Smee. When she was working she listened for his quiet tread in her house, when she was cooking she waited for him to slide round the door and stand uselessly erect just inside it, waiting for something or nothing defined. She felt above all threatened by his reading of Simon Vowle. Simon Vowle was herself, was Josephine Piper: there was no room for another. Writers are commonly asked what reader they imagine. There are writers, believe it, and Josephine Piper was one of them, who can only function by imagining no reader. Simon was her own fear, circumscribed and set up independently. Henry's presence in her house, reading Simon and, terrible phrase, but here for once peculiarly apposite, "identifying with" Simon, was a blow at her own carefully created, carefully worked, independent identity. She developed, for the first time in her busy life, a writer's block. All the people she invented had Henry Smee's face, his nervous mannerisms, his soft scornful-frightened voice. Her freedom had gone, the freedom with which she had imaginatively looked out from inside the other skull of Simon Vowle, seeing the other boiler-room, the different coke-heap, smelling through his nostrils the fustiness and bitterness.

Josephine was her own creation, as was separate Simon, as were the troop of other precursors and avatars of Simon. Josephine had made herself, with an effort of will, in opposition to her mother's fear, and what that might have made of her. She had said to herself, there *will* be a warm, friendly house, people *shall* come freely in and out, they will be made welcome amongst nice things. The warm and welcoming place, which now existed, was not, she knew, a true expression of herself. It was what she knew must be. What she was, was the obsessive hider in the boiler-room dust. Her husband, Peter's father, after five years of living in the warm place, eating the good food, had left her for a sillier, more slapdash woman, who did little or nothing with her time, who laughed a lot. People had asked each other, and had even asked Josephine, how he could do this. Josephine did not ask herself. She knew. He had found her out. She did not mind the loss of him too much. A strain had gone, as well as a motive for living. She had had Peter still. She made a home for Peter.

Peter had been so cheerful. So outgoing. Even as a little boy he ran fearlessly up to people on buses or railway stations. He brought friends home, one after the other, and seemed in no doubt that they would go home well-fed and well-entertained. She had had her guard up: had never let him see or sense her fear. She had talked to Peter, only ever really to Peter. He had become so involved in the selection and entertainment of the Lost Boys. She had perhaps not noticed that he had other fears. He did not have the uncompromising intellect of Josephine and Henry Smee. Exams were hard for him: he struggled to become qualified and went off to do a course, carefully selected by him and Josephine as "human", in Communications at a polytechnic in a southern port. It was not until it had been going on for some months that Josephine learned that he was attending no classes, and then not from him. He spent all his time helping a group who brought soup to ragged sleepers in parks and subways, who helped squatters to break into empty council flats or bourgeois houses, who were not above taking what they saw as necessities from supermarkets. Josephine went to see him once: he was living in a squat himself, long-bearded in layers of holed and smelly sweaters and cardigans. Josephine said "Why?" and Peter simply smiled pleasantly and told her he was happy enough. As though something was self-evident that to Josephine was not self-evident at all. He seemed unnaturally *easy* — easy-going, his body shambling and over-relaxed. Was this a new form of fear? Were the meths drinkers the logical culmination of the Lost Boys? Had he, later than his father, sensed that it was all made up, the warm firelight, the clean clothes, the open door, the smell of cooking? He smelled, her son, of old drains, of dirty wool, of damp ashes. Josephine blamed herself, but without her usual clarity about how and where precisely she had done wrong. Perhaps she had not done wrong. She simply was wrong.

Her bedroom was hers in a way the rest of the house was not. It was a small cell. She had moved calmly out of the conjugal master bedroom to what had been a servant's small box, next to what might have been the nursery, a place where a nurserymaid might have heard crying in the night and come. She had her old childhood bed, with cast iron head and foot, a small chest with a mirror over it, a table with a reading lamp, a peg rug on polished boards. She had not even a bookcase – books were brought in and out of this little place, but their soft colours brightened other walls. One night, perhaps a week after Henry Smee had brought himself to try to speak of Simon Vowle, and had been discouraged, she came home from a dinner and listened fearfully at the foot of the stair, as the mini-cab drove away, for Henry Smee's inexorable tentative tread. The kitchen was dark and empty, the stove cold. She went up, sighed, closed herself into her small room and began to scream. He was doing nothing very fearful: simply studying his own face, sitting on the end of her bed, in her square of mirror, in the light given by the street lamp. As she came in what she in fact saw was his reflected image staring at her out of the square of dark glass, lit up oddly by the light from the landing, through the door over her own shoulder. One of her drawers was slightly open, as though he might have been seeking out gloves or stockings, trying them on for fit, though this was entirely in her imagination, this trying-on, this appropriation. The only evidence was the open drawer, and she might have left that herself, in a hurry to leave. It was unlike her, particularly in here, but she might. His moon-face in the glass was distraught and glittering, eyeless because his glasses reflected reflection. His mouth was open in a great cry, but he made no sound. All the sound was her own screaming. He was white, and she thought again, he has taken my make-up: there was a faint smell of eau de Cologne and violets. But the white was surely his natural white-ness, the Simon Vowle paleness she had used to such good effect, lit up by the sodium lighting in the street.

"Get out," shrieked Josephine Piper, losing the self-control which, with the rhythm of her sentences, was what she most prized in herself, "get out, get out of my house, I can't bear any more of this, I can't bear your creeping, get out of my house now this minute or anyway tomorrow."

He closed his mouth, then, and smiled a small circumscribed and satisfied little smile.

"Of course," he said. "Now this minute or tomorrow, of course I'll get out."

"It was shock," said Josephine as he edged round her. "Only shock."

"Don't mention it," said Henry Smee.

He went, the next day. She did not try to stop him. In a month or two Max McKinley rang to break it to her, which he did with circumspection and tact, that Henry Smee was dead, that he had swallowed a bottle of aspirin, just before he was due to take up his place at university. For a moment Josephine's imagination presented Henry Smee to her, as though there still was a Henry Smee, the pale creeping, the compressed mouth, the thin legs in drooping trousers, the outside of Henry Smee whose inside was unknown and unimagined. Whose inside she had refused to imagine. But Josephine could not go on, quite apart from feeling that it was indecent to go on, to imagine the making of the decision, the number of aspirins, the waiting. Her imagination tidied Henry Smee into a mnemonic, a barely specified bed, a barely specified bottle, a form with one outflung arm. She said to Max McKinley, "I didn't know, I never got a sense of what drove him, he was so closed-in, how terrible." And Max said, "We failed him, we all failed him." And Josephine agreed.

But the writing-block went. The next day she was able to start again with nothing and no one between her and the present Simon Vowle, a writer at work, making a separate world, with no inconvenient reader or importunate character in the house. The ghost of those limp yet skilful hands, just that, attached itself to the form of the present Simon (whose name was in fact James) but not so that anyone would have noticed.

IN THE AIR

"The mean sea-level pressure at Brize Norton was one thousand and twelve millibars, steady. The outlook for Thursday; sun and showers, some of them heavy, with the chance of thundery outbreaks in places. Thank you for calling."

Mrs Sugden put down the telephone reluctantly. Today's voice was the reassuring good schoolmistress, her favourite. She preferred the female voices, which included also the breathy young thing in a hurry and a slightly doleful Midland bus-conductress type. The men included a military rasper, a stumbling student and a cheeky Liverpudlian who enjoyed frightening her with hail and gales, who livened up perceptibly with prophecies of disaster. Sometimes, shamefully, she listened to the schoolmistress twice, for company, although her memory was not failing and she had taken in all the information the first time. It was shaming in the way her increased television-watching was shaming. In her schoolteaching days she had always urged the children not to sit passively in front of the box. Make your own lives, she had said, see real friends, do real things, your things. Now she saw the insidious pleasure of the company, the voices in the room. She watched a brilliant ribbon of gardening and death-dealing, skating, Shakespeare and endless news. She drew the line at chat shows. She hated compères who smiled at her, sucking her into the front row of their perpetual stalls, or invading her private space with their horribly public intimacies and preening. Voices was one thing, false friends another. Those were the real fantasies.

Wolfgang came out of the kitchen, with rattling nails and serpentining, butt-waving body. After the weather-call, the walk. Wolfgang knew that. He opened his mouth in his paradoxical yawn of excitement, and a thin, tense creaking came out of his throat.

Mrs Sugden wondered whether this was good or bad weather for the man to come out in. His work – she thought of it as his work – must be much more pleasant in dry, clear weather. On the other hand, on that sort of day, there were more people about. The Common must be quite marshy after all the rain there'd been. Mrs Sugden had become a walking barometer. Her hip joints knew when the temperature or the pressure was about to drop. Her sinuses ached as the clouds closed, before the clouds closed. A kind of lightning-conductor ran down her thickened neck into the pads of her shoulders and down her upper arms. I have my health, that's the main thing, she told people, James and Alison when they telephoned, the Boot's pharmacist, the woman from the flat opposite, whom Mrs Sugden could not like, because she stank of tobacco, and, more shamingly, because she was London and raucous, which Mrs Sugden, though she had lived in London most of her sixty-three years, was not. But having one's health didn't mean that one didn't daily notice one's body more, as a nuisance, that was, as an impediment, not as the springing thing it had once been. There were things between it and the outer world, like the horny doors she had observed in childhood on hibernating snails. She didn't see so far or focus so fast. She noticed her hips, on the Common, and had to make a real moral effort to see the hooded crow, or the hovering kestrel.

"What do you think he'll do today?" she asked Wolfgang, who abased himself, grinning and pleading. "Where will he think is a good place?"

She reviewed the likely ones, as she did daily. The underpass smelled of recently stale urine and had dark puddles in it. A nasty place she'd keep out of, if she were him, but she wasn't him, that was the point, he might like the dark, or even the smell. There was the little wood by the pond, where every bush had its spiked decorations of crisp packets and cola tins and fading pastel tissues. That was a place she was sure he would like. There were also the earth works, and the rhododendrons round the pond.

Once, in the wood, someone who might have been the man had cycled very slowly past her. It might have been noon, on a good day: Wolfgang was foraging in brambles. He had cycled so slowly he had wobbled, and had looked straight at her, noticing, she thought, her fear. He was a huge man, in a singlet, and jeans, and working boots, with greying curly hair and a yellowish, yellow-clay skin. She had brought her whistle smartly out of her pocket and called Wolfgang. The whistle was a relic of playground duty: with it she had quelled gang-bashings and started netball matches. Its dried pea quavered tremulously in its throat and Wolfgang bounded up. The man went on, but was back, crossing her in the other direction, with a hard stare, before she was out of the wood. He knew she was afraid, and liked the knowledge. It went no further than that. She stumped slowly on in her zipped boots. The man did not acquire the features of the cyclist, but remained a shape-changer. He was black, he was white, he was brown, he was dirty grey, he was a thin youth with acne or an ageing bullet-headed stroller in leather jacket and trainers. He carried a briefcase, a plastic bag of junk from rubbish bins, a knife. He had all the time in the world, unlike Mrs Sugden, whose eventless days slipped into each other like nylon thread through a chain of enamelled television-beads. Every day she feared him a little more, every day the mental encounter took another step into the vividly realized. Mrs Sugden, a sensible woman, knew he was an obsession, but she did not know how to exorcize him. Yesterday's local paper carried an account of a rugger-tackled, abused female jogger (48) in the Park, and a raped teenager (15) in the concrete waste land behind the local supermarket. Why should he not wait for, or at the least, accidentally notice her too?

She was afraid to go out. Wolfgang could not understand her delays. She went round the flat, dusting already spotless books and silver teapot, watering the rubber plant. It was a nice flat, but small – one-bedroomed, with one living room and a ship's-galley-sized kitchen, in which were the washing machine and dryer

James and Alison had bought her as house-moving presents when the big house was sold up, when Brian died. The washing-machine was another source of wholly irrational shame. It was automatic, there was no work to it. She had always had one washday a week, sitting over her twin tub, lifting the clothes in and out of the steaming suds with wooden pincers, caring for them. She would rather have had visits from James and Alison, but James was in Saudi Arabia much of the time and Alison was busy teaching. And found her mother threatening, Mrs Sugden understood, for reasons neither of them had any control over, though they tried, at Christmas, sometimes at Easter, they tried for a day or two and then it broke down into fear and violent impatience over little things. Mrs Sugden hated her daughter for putting all the cutlery to drain streaky, and not drying it properly with a cloth. Alison hated Mrs Sugden coming in her kitchen, hated her offers of help with dishes or potatoes, saw them as criticism and threat. Both of them were schoolmistressy, used to having to appear to be unshakeably right.

Wolfgang whined. He was a standard or classic sheepdog, a working collie. He was black, white and tan, and very beautiful, with a deep glistening ruff, a curving white-tipped tail, intelligent amber eyes and an uncertain temper. He had bitten the postman's sock, once, and had nipped the buttock of a visiting policeman, who had congratulated Mrs Sugden on his effectiveness, with stolid magnanimity. Alison had said he shouldn't be cooped up in a flat, and so he shouldn't, Mrs Sugden knew. For this reason, because Wolfgang made her safe in her flat, she had to expose herself to the Common, the underpass, the wood, the sandy hollows and springy heather.

She knew it was irrational, though there was logic in it, to feel better indoors. There were women who had found men waiting for them in the dark when they came home, women who had been followed and then pushed quickly in from behind, women whose windows or barred doors had been contemptuously shattered. Mrs Sugden still felt safer within walls. Partly because of Wolfgang, who knew that this was his territory, who set up a whole orchestra of aggressive sound if anyone knocked, or stopped to stare, who howled and growled and pealed defiance and threat. In Brent – Mrs Sugden thought it was Brent, certainly somewhere like that – only two per cent of homes with dogs had been entered and seventy-five per cent of homes without. Inside her own walls she and Wolfgang had a chance. Outside was different. She knew other women might organize their fear differently, might be most afraid of being cornered, of having their own bed violated, their carpet smeared, their kitchen tools turned against them. In her own rooms, her heart ran evenly like her clocks, almost always, except when she was locking up, except when her hands were on cold glass with black night and whatever else just over the threshold. Fear seeped in through the warped lavatory window. But in general it was in open spaces that she expected the encounter. In open spaces her breath came short, her heart was larger and fleshier and beat in little spurts, she was webbed with dizziness. She could not have run for her life and knew it. This also was shaming. Fear and shame, these were what was left, were they? Mrs Sugden put on her coat, defying them as she defied them daily. Wolfgang circled and pranced in ecstasy. Mrs Sugden put on her woolly hat and gathered up his lead.

Her path took her along two roads of pleasant Victorian suburban houses, upwards towards the high ground. The roads debouched on a wide and whirling motorway junction which carved the common land, white and lethal. The underpass was the secret entry to the wild land beyond the concrete. Wolfgang rushed to and fro, lifting his leg on lampposts and parked cars, glistening with good health. A sudden car changed lanes as Mrs Sugden was looking over a hedge at some iris reticulata, and screeched to a halt beside her, facing the wrong way. Now? Out of a car, now? She looked at the driver's face, which was square, oriental, and expressionless. He was simply parking, he lived there, he had simply failed to signal. Mrs Sugden dropped her eyes and proceeded towards the underpass. The arch over this was adorned in shaky blood-red paint with the pacific slogan MEAT IS MURDER. The graffiti inside were mostly the work of a neat fanatic, with a spray-gun of white paint, who had surrounded the usual inscribed lists of names, pierced hearts, Julie, Lois, Sharon with tidy boxes and correctly spelled admonitions. "You are a whore." "You are an exhibitionist tramp." "You disgust me." Mrs Sugden would have given this moralist nine out of ten for handwriting, and ten for spelling. She imagined him in a shiny white raincoat to match his paintwork, staring fixedly from inside metal-rimmed glasses above well-polished shoes. He was certainly a manifestation of the man she feared: his work showed that his hand was steady and his intention clear. It might be that he preferred the young and the pretty, with whom he seemed to have a quarrel. He might not notice a thickened person with grey frizz under a woolly hat, plodding quietly through the puddles?

That was not certain. She had watched a whole television film on the subject, sitting on the sofa with a reluctant Wolfgang panting beside her. There had been an interview with one young convicted rapist who, silhouetted black against a bland turquoise ground, had said that he always chose ugly or unattractive women. Incredibly, he put his hand to his mouth and added, oh, I hope none of them are watching, I don't want to hurt their feelings. He explained. He did it out of a deep sense of inadequacy, a need to dominate. The civilized words tripped easily off his tongue, in this classroom discussion. He had been exposed to intensive group therapy. Pretty ones, he said, might have intimidated me, you know, I might have backed down. Hearing him say this, in his pleasant young voice, out of the black hole of his obscurity, Mrs Sugden had known that this voice was *his* voice, the man's voice, that she was listening to him speak. He was like boys she had taught, coming back to show off how they had got on in the world. Boys had liked her, as a teacher, in those younger days. She had liked boys. The cheeky youngster, the workman with his wolf-whistle from scaffolding, the teaching student grateful for being shown the ropes. It was the world that had changed and she with it.

At the further mouth of the underpass, on her way up into light, she encountered a solitary man, walking rapidly and frowning. He was tall, black-avised with a heavy growth of stubble on gaunt cheeks under a woollen cap pulled well down. Combat jacket, faded jeans, dirty trainers. Fear fogged Mrs Sugden's gaze. She went on walking, past him. He held his eyes averted, rigidly, as alarmed by her, apparently, as she by him. Or perhaps just English. Once there had been a time when people passed the time of day, surely there had, even if their polite greetings had been a formal indication that they posed no threat? Now, no one dared. She, for fear of provoking him, he, for fear of misapprehension. Or perhaps he was just sour. Perhaps he had not really seen her at all.

In the earlier days of her fear Mrs Sugden had tried to make herself think about other things. She had promised herself little rewards. If I get as far as the first copse, on the way to the pond, without thinking about him, there will be a letter from James. Or, more reliably, I will allow myself to buy a chocolate eclair. She had long ago given up this childish self-bribery with things she didn't really look forward to – she found it hard to look forward to anything much, except sleep. It had directly brought on the one mental battle which had caused her to turn tail before the copse, crying for Wolfgang in distress, battling her way home with bursting chest and wandering eyes. No, no, fear was better faced squarely. She could go out into his world if she was prepared for him, if she thought him out rationally, if she knew him and what might happen.

The question she asked herself, as she made her way along the track to the first copse, all silver birch and hazel catkins, quite like the country, if you ignored the solid background roar of motorway traffic on the other side of silence – the question was, was it always like this? Were little girls always violated and old women struck down in their thin blood, or is it more now, is it really more, and different? We are asked to think about it more, anyway, she answered herself, and if there was not more already, the thinking *makes* it more, it must be so. It is civilized that we can discuss these things openly and comfort the damaged, and not blame or shame them, but it all increases my fear, and not only my fear, but whatever he feels. For she knew that both she and he were fascinated by the hooded head, the solitary terror, powerlessness, no one coming to help. She knew he watched videos of cruelties he might not quite have thought of, as she nightly contemplated fates she had not yet imagined, as well as those she had. It was in the air.

The thing she was clear about, and wanted someone to be clear about too, was that her imagination of his being, of their meeting, was fuelled by fear, by fear pure and simple. Not by any kind of misplaced desire. She was not sure if he knew that, though she thought it was probably her fear he desired, and that he would have found desire, if she could ever have felt it, disgusting, to be punished in her. She had to turn off a Carry On film in which all the fat middle-aged harridans had enquired eagerly, at the sack of Rome, or Jhaipur, or somewhere else unreal and lunatic, when the raping was going to start. No. Desire was another thing. Desire in her had died long before Brian, who had died in his sleep and in hers, flinging out an unaccustomed arm across her breast in a brief, last, involuntary paroxysm. She remembered wanting Brian and the earlier, lively impatience of wanting or needing a man, men. Now she was like cold pudding, stiff and set. The house was quieter without Brian, and this was good, as well as lonely. His retirement, so brief, had been clutter and potter and constant small collisions of will and table-space and living-space. She was appalled for Brian, that he was not there, that his hopes and history and pleasure in food and views on Mrs Thatcher and delight in dahlias were gone, but for herself she was partly – how to put it coolly – satisfied?

No, it was nothing to do with desire, she thought, skirting the copse, coming on the ruffled pond. Here were an old man with a fat terrier bitch, two elegant track-suited young women with a dalmatian, and a group of little boys, cupping their faces over cigarettes, bunking off. He would never strike at the pondside, that she was sure. It was exposed, and heavily frequented. She could even, occasionally, ask a tweeded dog-walker to throw a stick into the water for Wolfgang. Her arthritis had finally put a stop to this game, this year. And Wolfgang was so young, he needed the resistance of the water, that tired him more thoroughly than running through air. She approached the little boys. "Would you throw my dog's stick for him? I'm not able to, myself." She caught the electric message between them: shall we be nice, shall we be nasty, is she to be classed as a silly old bag or a poor old thing in need of help, what will the group do? They were still quite little boys. Probably they already threatened other little boys. Perhaps they had their fears, too. One of them said, "Come on then," rough-friendly, and hurled Wolfgang's stick. Wolfgang sprang out onto the water, leaping and surging until he was out of his depth, then swimming purposefully and fast, his bushy white tail a luminous rudder in the translucent murk. Coming back, he shipped water and coughed at every stroke. The boys threw again and again. Wolfgang plunged. Beyond him were two Canada geese who'd never been seen there before. Lovely things, thought Mrs Sugden, with their stripy barrel bodies and their thin strong black necks. The male nudged the female and honked. Once Mrs Sugden would have remarked on their beauty to the boys, but now she held her peace. Some boys, not all, spoke jeering filth. One boy that size would hardly think of attacking anything as large as Mrs Sugden, let alone Wolfgang. But the whole bunch just might, if they egged each other on. Mrs Sugden knew boys. She knew that these boys knew things, they watched things on the screen she did not know or want to know. Men have fantasies, women don't, only love, which is a sort of fantasy, she thought. She had taught boys who might have been these boys' fathers. They had not known all that much. On icy dark days she had buttoned their stiff little flies with fingers clumsy-cold, tucking them in, tapping their innocence, telling them to run along now and keep clean. The lavatories, which were huge earth closets, were frozen solid, on bad days. Their little extremities were blue and waxy. They were not knowing little things, not like these, the cold air was different, whatever there had then been to fear, she herself had not been knowing enough to take account of.

In those days there had been both war and hanging. She stood there stolidly, watching the boys play with Wolfgang, and said to the man in her mind that it was easier to understand that it had nothing to do with desire if you thought of hanging. It depended how old he was, whether he would know what she meant, or need to have it explained. Hanging had frightened her more thoroughly and sickly than Hitler ever had. Perhaps this was a failure in her imagination but it was so. We were always going to win the war, she believed Churchill, but the hood and trap and condemned cell waited for every man. You see, she told him, I dreamed over and over I had to be hanged by mistake, although I hadn't done anything. I dreamed about being strapped up and blindfolded and dragged there. It was a sniff of pure evil, it was what men did to men, it was in the newspapers, in thrillers, in the air. You are him now, the hangman and the murderer. The one with power is foul, you see – the murderer became the victim in the dock. We stopped all that, we cleansed our minds of that horrible place. Now we think of women and little children in locked cars, in rubbish areas, in brambles on waste land. What I mean is, there can be simple fear, nothing to do with desire. You must not see my fear.

After Wolfgang's swim, they struck off into the copse. Wolfgang licked up filth and scrabbled in old leaves. The ground underfoot was sodden, under spongy sphagnum, with a dark peaty water that welled up, round the bright green tufts, like old blood. The things to be found here were always surprising. Once Wolfgang had turned up a pink high-heeled shoe. Once, Mrs Sugden had almost stepped on large Y-fronts, navy-blue piped in white, billowing slightly just under the liquid surface. They seemed to be almost new. Mrs Sugden did not disturb them. They gave her a little shock, not electric, but a sharp lapse in the supply of air to her lungs and brain.

She knew what it would feel like for everything to seize up with shock. She had precognitions of clamped arteries jerking her heart into boom and then flabby stillness. Inventing possible ways it might happen helped with the whelming of the fear. She invented someone stubble-bearded and smelly, veering away as Wolfgang bounded up, showing his teeth in his expectant grin. She imagined someone young and muscular and resourceful – moving the knife from beside her own jugular to catch Wolfgang's leap on it, contemptuously, as he sprang. She didn't know whether Wolfgang would spring or not, that was the truth. He was a cantankerous beast: he bit people for his own pleasure, not for her protection. In his youth he had frequently bitten other dogs. He liked dogs bigger and slower than himself, staid and portly dogs who presented a stable target. He had to be dragged off. His eyeballs at such times became suffused with blood, a clear poppy-scarlet. Last week Mrs Sugden had seen the same colour between the swollen eyelids of a mugged pensioner, televised in a powder blue shawl from her hospital bed. Every line of the grey and blooming-purple skin, of the spare yellow-white hair, of the dark threaded stitches across cheek and brow had stayed in Mrs Sugden's mind. But above all the scarlet eye-whites.

On the other side of the copse was a straight path. It was made plain and level with bitumen and asphalt for a certain distance, and then the surfacing abruptly gave way to sandy furrows. By the side of the straight path trotted, decorously, a cream Labrador bitch. Wolfgang knew this dog: it was one he liked to bounce at. Mrs Sugden knew it. It was a guide dog, enjoying a brief run on the loose. Its owner and charge walked steady and upright, looking neither to left nor right, along the smoothed track. She was a tall woman, in a straight tweed two-piece, with an impeccable knot of iron-grey hair gleaming above her collar.

She carried the dog's harness in one hand, and a handbag in the other. She advanced evenly, in sensible laced shoes. Mrs Sugden had spoken to her once, when Wolfgang had bounded up and tangled with the guide dog just as she was being re-harnessed. Mrs Sugden had apologized: the woman had said, in what Mrs Sugden labelled a cultivated voice, that it was nice for Elsie to have contact with other dogs. She had tried to pat Wolfgang and Mrs Sugden had counselled against it, saying his temper was uncertain. What was he like, the woman had asked, and Mrs Sugden had described him, enjoying it, his black, his white, his bright eyes, the sheen of good health. She had said how clever and well-trained Elsie must be. Elsie's owner said Elsie was too serious, a worrier, couldn't be persuaded to run off and play. It did her good to meet other dogs, she reiterated, unable to see Wolfgang's band of hackles, or the sneer where his lip lifted from his teeth at the side.

Mrs Sugden decided not to cross to that path, but to stay on the side where she was, in the shade of the trees. Wolfgang might upset dog or owner. Better safe than sorry. So she walked parallel, at a good distance, a bit behind. Watching, and thinking.

The blind walker had a follower. Not for the first time, even in Mrs Sugden's experience. She had seen him at least twice before, padding along the track behind the other woman and her dog. There was something indefinably wrong with him, even on these earlier occasions. He walked with exaggerated care, as though he were playing grandmother's footsteps. He was large, and thin, and young, or fairly young, and gangling. He had long blonde curls and a very bright blue track suit, piped in white, above rather frivolous training-shoes, rainbow-striped in girlish pastel shades. With rose-pink shoelaces. His movements were jerky and excessive: he put a hand to his ear and *hearkened* to a jay laugh, he stood with folded arms and legs grandly straddling and appeared to study early pussy-willow. Mrs Sugden had noticed before that he never passed the blind woman, but came along after, creeping and then jogging a little. Today he had changed his behaviour. He had always reminded Mrs Sugden of the television puppet Andy Pandy: today he had positively taken to capering, like a demented leprechaun, knees up and pointed toes down, in huge circles around the woman and dog. Mopping and mowing, said Mrs Sugden's fairy-tale vocabulary to her, as he bent lithely and sprang up again, mopping and mowing. She could barely see his face, but he appeared to be smiling. His arms gestured — a welcoming embrace, a kind of hand-over-hand imaginary rope-climbing. The blind woman must surely have heard him, but she appeared impassive, strode on, like a metronome, unvarying. The dog trotted beside her, marking the edge of the safe track. Mrs Sugden might have continued to observe from across the tufts of grass and heather if she had not noticed that the circles were diminishing. And that the hand at the end of the mobile arm flashed in the sun.

What she actually thought was superstitious, akin to the promise of James's unwritten letter, or the anticipated chocolate eclair. She thought, there's safety in numbers. She thought, if I don't go over there, there'll be no one at hand when it's my turn. She thought, Wolfgang's something, even if I'm a fat old biddy. She thought, I've got my whistle, I've got that. She was surprised how much thinking she was doing. She could hear her heart all right, but its thud was purposeful and even, not choking all over the place. She said, come on, to Wolfgang, who streaked ahead, tangling with Elsie just as the young puppet was crouching almost at the blind woman's side, peering up into her face.

"Good afternoon," said Mrs Sugden. "We've met before, I don't know if you remember, I described my dog to you, a black and white border collie, he seems to get on with yours."

"Oh yes," said the cool voice, from its distance in the dark. "Of course. Is he with you, your dog?"

He had his sharp nose buried between Elsie's buttocks.

"He's sniffing Elsie. You know."

"She's a bit timid of male dogs. She's not allowed to talk to them, of course, if she's working."

"Perhaps I could walk with you a little," said Mrs Sugden. "As we're going the same way."

He was now a little behind, sauntering. They were two, side by side, and he was behind, going slowly. The dogs stood nose to tail and smelled each other's natures.

"I go as far as the end of the asphalt. I'd be grateful if you'd tell me when we reach it. It is my limit."

"Of course."

They went out along the strip of asphalt at the blind woman's brisk pace. Mrs Sugden described things. Herself, to start with.

"My name is Sugden. Marjorie Sugden. A retired school-mistress."

"And mine is Eleanor Tillotson. A retired social worker."

He was still there. Did Miss or Mrs Tillotson have any idea of his presence, or its recurrence, or of his bizarre posturing? Mrs Sugden described things. The dogs. Now they're running along ever so nicely, side by side. Your dog is such a lovely colour.

"Like the froth on cappucino," Miss Tillotson said.

"A little bit creamier," said Mrs Sugden, judiciously. "A bit more buttery, less thin in colour."

If Miss Tillotson wanted a visual description, it had to be just.

"Not far to the end. I'll turn back with you."

"There's no need."

"I'm glad of the company. If you don't mind."

"On the contrary. Days in retirement are very long. One can go a whole day without speaking to anyone but Elsie. Of course, when I had my work, it was different. There was a lot of travelling, visiting homes and interviewing. I like to be occupied."

"Oh, so do, so did I. Time now goes so fast in one way, but it goes nowhere, nothing is achieved."

"You keep yourself healthy. And Wolfgang. I can tell."

* * *

The end of the asphalt was in sight. It was like the abrupt end of a pier, at the end of a harbour. Mrs Sugden thought of the blind woman and was astonished at her courage. She saw her striding out steadfast, treading this fine line between gales and invisible gulfs of infinitely worse fears than her own mean ones. Perhaps he would go on when they turned back together. Perhaps he would. If he did not, she would know what to think. What he did, was speak.

"Excuse me, but have either of you two ladies got the correct time?"

He stood in front of them as they turned, barring their way back. Gold curls, slightly damp or greasy, clustered on his forehead. His features were all exaggerated, like his movements. His mouth was large, and full of clefts and curves, firm though, not sagging, a violoncello of a mouth. His nose was full and snuffing, with curling nostrils and huge dark holes. The ledges were all strong and rounded – wide cheekbones, outstanding brows, long carved chin. His eyes were big, thick-lashed, pale blue. Miss Tillotson could not see any of this, she could not even know if he was black or white, only how tall he was, up there. It was she who told him the time, in her precise voice. Three forty-seven, she said. Mrs Sugden saw that she was reading this information with exact fingertips from a large watch without a glass.

"Thanks," he said. "I must be getting back. That's a fine dog you have. I've been watching you."

"I know," said Miss Tillotson.

"She looks after you very well."

"She does," said Miss Tillotson. She smiled. "She's over-conscientious. She won't leave me to run away and play."

"She'd attack anyone who tried to hurt you, though."

"Oh, I don't know," said Miss Tillotson, with foolhardy scrupulousness, it seemed to Mrs Sugden. "She's trained to guide me and stop me doing anything silly. She's got a nice nature."

"Wolfgang hasn't," said Mrs Sugden. "That's my dog. He's got an uncertain temper. Collies often have, I'm told."

He smiled at her, with all his face, as though he read her thoughts. She took Miss Tillotson's elbow, to reassure both of them. She felt Miss Tillotson stiffen with independence and then relax into acquiescence. He moved out of their way and fell into step beside Miss Tillotson, on the other side.

Mrs Sugden, even in her fear, had partly looked forward to having a talk with the other woman, now one was broached, now the social distance had been got over. It was amazing that annoyance at his intrusiveness should co-exist with consciousness of the way he had mopped and mowed, of the flash of his hand.

"I've often seen you," he said. "You always come this way."

"The path is even here. I can let Elsie run."

"Oh, *of course*. You come every day?"

"To let her have a run."

"Fantastic," he said. "Just fantastic."

"And you?" said Miss Tillotson. "Are you in training, or something? I hear you go up and down."

"I keep fit, yes," he said. "I'm unemployed, at the moment. I try to keep busy."

"I'm sorry to hear that."

"Oh, don't be. I'd go mad in a shop or an office. I'm fine, this way, I get out and about, in the air. There was only one job I wanted."

"And what was that?"

"I wanted to fly planes. I wanted to be up there. Always liked planes, from being ever such a small boy. But they won't have me."

"Oh dear. Why not?"

"Various reasons. Medical reasons. Nothing to worry about. They might change their mind. I was an air cadet, that was O.K. I'm working on them."

There was a silence. Miss Tillotson strode on, and Mrs Sugden trotted beside her, holding her elbow, and on the other side he padded, jogging on the spot more or less, slightly crab-like, his gaze fixed on Miss Tillotson.

Mrs Sugden talked about Elsie. She could hardly carry on, in his young presence, the interesting talk that had been started about lack of occupation. She felt it was indelicate to ask, with him galumphing there, all the questions she would have liked to ask about how Miss Tillotson managed things like cooking and buses, though she wanted to know, and felt that Miss Tillotson did not mind answering. Let alone ask whether Miss Tillotson was afraid, and if not, why not, how not? So she ascertained that Elsie had half a pound of fresh meat a day, and some Vitalin dog bran, and two hours' exercise as well as necessary journeys to the shops, and revealed that she felt she was not really fit to keep up with Wolfgang, but liked his company. She stopped short of saying she felt safe with him. It was their companion who raised safety.

"Don't you both worry," he said, "about being out on your own? With all the goings-on we hear about? Aren't you afraid?"

"I feel all right with Wolfgang," said Mrs Sugden miserably, wondering if she was condemning her bright dog, imagining a knife grating on his breast-bone.

"In my position," said Miss Tillotson, "you could be afraid of everything. Everything is hazardous, if you look at it in one way. So after a bit, it seems that you can only survive at all by not bothering about that sort of thing. So I don't. There isn't much I could do, if I was worried. Just live a little less, in a smaller circle. Which is the way my life could so easily have been contracted in any case. No, I'd rather come out in the air. So I do."

"I do admire you," he said, all liquid emphasis. "I think you're marvellous."

"Hardly," said Miss Tillotson. "Just trying to live with a considerable disability."

Mrs Sugden's mind was exercised about what would happen at the other end of the path, when the ways parted. She felt she should see Miss Tillotson home, to be sure, and that she wanted to be back within her own walls, and that he was teasing them both, smiling and concealing. She said, with more directness and warmth than she would have dared without this provocation, "I am very glad I spoke to you. It's been very pleasant to have company. The dogs are enjoying the company too. I hope we can go on – "

"Why don't you come back for tea?" said Miss Tillotson. "That is, if you have nothing better to do."

"I should be delighted."

"Good. I live just off the Common. Through the underpass. In Bellevue Mansions."

He had moved away slightly. He was running along the very edge of the asphalt promontory, arms wide-spread and aslant, torso veering from one side to the other, a huge boy-aeroplane. There was even a faint engine-hum between those extravagant lips. Mrs Sugden wanted to seize the moment to hiss a warning which should alert without alarming, but there was no time, he was back. He said, "I'll walk back with you. Just to make sure you're all right."

"There's no need. Mrs Sugden is coming to tea."

"I wish you'd ask *me* to tea."

"You said you must be getting back," said Mrs Sugden. "When you asked the time, you said you must."

"Back where to? Where've I got to go to?"

"You can come to tea, of course, if it would interest you," said Miss Tillotson.

"Oh, it would," he said. "It would. It'd be really great, I mean it."

Too much.

Mrs Sugden found time to marvel at the way Miss Tillotson managed the lift in her mansion block, call button, outer door, inner door, no hesitation, though they were all a little interlocked in the lift, eight dog-legs and his large splayed knees and swivelling shoulders. The flat was a surprise, very tastefully decorated with flame-coloured velvet chairs, reading lamps made of Chinese vases, glass-topped low tables on a dark Persian carpet, slightly hazed by cream dog hairs. There were mirrors in the hall and over the hearth in the drawing-room. There were pictures on the walls – a Chinese brush drawing of a cliff and waterfall, a print of Velasquez' "Las Meninas", with its complicated group of infantas and deformed dwarves, seen from behind the easel. There were bowls of spring flowers and a scented jasmine plant. Miss Tillotson switched on lights in the dark afternoon, and indicated chairs for them to sit in. Mrs Sugden wondered if she bothered to do this, in the dark alone. Or did she turn the light on for Elsie? There was a collection of silver-framed photographs on a little bureau.

"Are these your family?" said Mrs Sugden.

"Ah yes. The one in the wig is my barrister-brother, Clive. The two in gowns are my nieces, on graduation days. The baby is my grand-nephew, Maurice. The house is the family home in Somerset, where I grew up. Don't you think the one of Elsie is a good likeness?'

Over Mrs Sugden's shoulder he breathed his hot breath misting the legal and academic faces.

"It looks a recent one, of Elsie."

"Oh, no. You wouldn't believe it, but Elsie's nearly ten. She still looks girlish. I'll give her – and your Wolfgang – some water, and make us all some tea. Do you like China or Indian, Mrs Sugden – or Earl Grey? And – I'm afraid I don't know your name."

"Me name's Barry," he said. "Call me Barry. I'll have whatever you said last, Earl Grey I'll have. With two of sugar. Thanks."

Mrs Sugden offered to help in the kitchen, but felt unable to persist, in case that might appear rude, a questioning of Miss Tillotson's undoubted competence. So she sat where she had been told to sit, watching him roam amongst the pretty furniture in his incongruous shoes. One curious effect of Miss Tillotson's blindness was that Mrs Sugden came to feel that she herself was invisible. Miss Tillotson turned a polite blank face with great accuracy *almost* as it would have been if she could truly have met Mrs Sugden's eye, but not quite. Her sightless stare went somewhere to the side of Mrs Sugden's head, to the blank wall. Mrs Sugden found herself quickly wiping her face of dismay and distress, suddenly remembering that he could see her. He picked things up: an inkwell, a small lacquered box, a paperweight.

"She's got some pretty good stuff here, wouldn't you say? Some valuable knicknacks?"

"I don't know about value. It's very pleasant. Very well designed."

"Someone must do it for her," he said, Mrs Sugden thought brutally. "She can't pick chairs and curtains, hunh? She got help. Mebbe from that brother and his wife. Yah. Mebbe from them. She gets around pretty neatly, wouldn't you say? No nonsense. No feeling around. A bloody miracle."

"Oh yes," said Mrs Sugden, repressively.

Miss Tillotson returned with the teatray, which she placed accurately on a glass-topped low table. The teapot was ample and silver; the cups were very pretty, Crown Derby Mrs Sugden rather thought, and not entirely free of interior stains of stubborn tannin. Also the tray, a black Chinese lacquer, had been wiped in great visible streaks and smears. Miss Tillotson poured. She said, "Barry, would you be kind enough to give this to Mrs Sugden? Thank you. This is your own cup, with the two sugars. Help yourselves to biscuits."

She turned her dark questioning face to Barry. "Tell us about yourself. I used to have contacts, amongst employers. Maybe I can help."

Mrs Sugden was quite glad Miss Tillotson could not see what she herself categorized as the scornful leer that came over his face at this.

"I shouldn't think so. They don't want to know. And I don't want the sort of thing there is. You know, shifting packing cases, making trains of supermarket trolleys, YTS and all that crap."

"You can't want to be unemployed, either," said Miss Tillotson.

"I dunno. I get out in the fresh air a lot. I get time to think. I get to have tea with nice ladies like you."

The two dogs came importantly into the room from the kitchen. Elsie went to Miss Tillotson's side, and sat mildly pressed against her knee. Wolfgang prowled, uncertainly, investigating corners. Barry broke one of Miss Tillotson's biscuits in half and held it out to him.

"Here," he said. "Nice dog. Come over here. What did you say his name was?"

"Wolfgang."

"Sounds funny. Sort of fierce."

"It's German. It was Mozart's name. I don't know why I thought of it. He doesn't like biscuits."

"Oh no?" said Barry, as Wolfgang came up warily, and snatched. "Doesn't he just. You just don't indulge him. Good dog, old Wolfgang."

"People are always offering Elsie biscuits when I'm not looking," said Miss Tillotson. "They make her fat. Please don't give Elsie any biscuits, Barry."

"Of *course* not," he said, watching Wolfgang lick crumbs from the carpet.

It turned out to be a long teaparty. Most of the conversation was a dialogue between Barry and Miss Tillotson. He asked her all sorts of questions, very direct questions, questions Mrs Sugden would never have ventured on. He found out that Miss Tillotson had been blind since she was a small child, that she had worked with handicapped people most of her life, that she had studied Social Administration at London University. That she had a special little Braille machine for taking down notes of telephone conversations, that she lived alone, that Elsie was her fourth dog, that the death or retirement of a dog was something she dreaded.

"It's terrible, very frightening, the period of adjustment to a new dog," said Miss Tillotson. "I go away to a special centre, to get used to them, we walk the streets together. They can stop too soon, too far from the kerb, they can refuse to budge at all, they can do all sorts of things. They are nervous and over-conscientious and so am I. When we come home, it takes a long time to settle to old ways and routines. Routine is very important in my life."

"I think you are the most incredibly brave person I've ever met," he said, throbbing like a sincere guitarist, cocking his head on one side. Miss Tillotson did not answer this, but asked for the cups back and took out the teatray. They could hear her steps in the hall, her confident turn onto the kitchen linoleum, the sound of taps and water. Barry leaned forward and said to Mrs Sugden, "If you moved a few things – chairs, tables, that sort of thing, the kettle in the kitchen, I bet, or biscuit-tins, she'd be all over the place, wouldn't she, she wouldn't know what to do with herself?"

"Nobody would do such a thing."

"Oh they easily might, by accident. Easily. You could move that little table with the telephone, just to see what she'd do."

Mrs Sugden rejected various dangerous words: cruel, stupid, unkind, mean. She said, schoolmistressy, "That would be rather silly."

"Oh, I wouldn't do it for anything. I think she's fantastic. I was just thinking."

He looked at Mrs Sugden. "It was really nice of her to ask me to tea. Really nice. I bet *you* wouldn't."

Mrs Sugden had no answer. Her heart thumped.

"*You'd* be afraid to. Sensible, really. I might be any kind of maniac, how do you know, how does she? You ought to take care."

And as if to emphasize this, he put out his hand to Wolfgang, who sniffed his fingers and allowed his ears to be scratched.

After that, Mrs Sugden decided that she could not leave him alone with Miss Tillotson. They had to leave together, in which case she would herself be alone with him. It was like that puzzle about the fox and goat and the corn and the boat, or the similar one about cannibals and missionaries. She rose from her chair and said firmly, "Thank you for the tea, Miss Tillotson. I ought to be getting along, and I'm sure Barry ought too. I think we should go now. You must be busy."

As though she was. As though any of them were.

Miss Tillotson rose, too, graceful and isolated.

"It was very pleasant to have you. I hope you will come again. Can you find your own coat?"

He *lounged* in a velvet chair, his feet splayed amongst crumbs and dog hairs on the lovely carpet. The schoolmistress in Mrs Sugden spoke. "Come along, Barry. It's time to go home."

He was playing with the paperweight. Chunk, slap, from one hand to the other. Mrs Sugden was glad Miss Tillotson could not see him. She stopped short of saying, "Put that down, immediately, *exactly* where you found it." And yet he seemed to hear the thought, for he did put it down, he grinned and scrambled to his feet.

"All right, all right, just coming, Miss," he said, answering her tone.

Miss Tillotson hoped they would come again. Mrs Sugden said, "You must visit me," out of a dry mouth. Barry said, "Thanks, I'm really grateful, you've made my day."

Mrs Sugden had no idea what Miss Tillotson thought or sensed, or did not sense.

Out on the pavement, she clipped on Wolfgang's lead, and turned to Barry. She had decided her tactics. She asked him which way he went, already determined to set out in some quite opposite direction, even if it meant walking for a very long time to get home.

"Where do you go now, Barry?"

"Oh. I live over there. Westfield Park, you know."

"Wolfgang and I go this way."

"Of course. So you do. It's been nice meeting you. I really like talking to old ladies. It gives you an interest in life."

His hands were in his pockets. His jeans pocket bulged. He brought them out, and there was a large open knife, which he tossed smilingly from hand to hand, as he had earlier tossed the paperweight.

"Goodbye," croaked Mrs Sugden, watching the arc of the blade, uncertain if her legs were hers.

"Goodbye then. We'll see each other again, for sure. Up and down. I'm around a lot. I'll look out for you specially."

She turned away, tugging feebly at Wolfgang. He stood on the pavement, tossing the blade in the air, gawky and smiling.

"Be seeing you," he said, as she gathered speed. "Be seeing you."

PRECIPICE-ENCURLED

What's this then, which proves good yet seems untrue?
Is fiction, which makes fact alive, fact too?
The somehow may be thishow.

ROBERT BROWNING

I

The woman sits in the window. Beneath her is the stink of the canal and on the skyline is a steel-grey sheet of cloud and an unswallowed setting sun. She watches the long lines of dark green seaweed moving on the thick surface of the water, and the strong sweeping gulls, fugitives from storms in the Adriatic. She is a plump woman in a tea gown. She wears a pretty lace cap and pearls. These things are known, are highly probable. She has fine features fleshed – a compressed, drooping little mouth, a sharp nose, sad eyes, an indefinable air of disappointment, a double chin. This we can read from portraits, more than one, tallying, still in existence. She has spent the afternoon in bed; her health is poor, but she rallies for parties, for outings, for occasions. There she sits, or might be supposed to sit, any autumn day on any of several years at the end of the last century. She commands the devoted services of three gondoliers, a handyman, a cook, a maid and a kitchen-maid. Also an accountant-housekeeper. She has a daughter, young and marriageable, and a husband, mysteriously ill in Paris, from whom she is estranged but not divorced. Her daughter is out on a party of pleasure, perhaps, and has been adjured to take her new umbrella, the one with the prettily carved crickets and butterflies on its handle. She has an eye for the execution of delicate objects: it has been said of her that she would exchange a Tintoretto for a cabinet of tiny gilded glasses.

She has an eye for fashion: in this year where clothes are festooned with dead humming birds and more startling creatures, mice, moths, beetles and lizards, she will give a dance where everyone must wear flights of birds pasted on ribbons – "awfully chic" – or streamers of butterflies. The room in which she sits is full of mother-of-pearl cabinets full of intricate little artefacts. She is the author of an unpublished and authoritative history of Venetian naval architecture. Also of some completely undistinguished poems. She is the central character in no story, but peripheral in many, where she may appear reduced to two or three bold identifying marks. She has a passion for pug dogs and for miniature Chinese spaniels: at her feet, on this gloomy day, lie, shall we say, Contenta, Trolley, Yahabibi and Thisbe, snoring a little as such dogs do, replete. She also has a passion for peppermint creams; do the dogs enjoy these too, or are they disciplined? One account of her gives three characteristics only: plump, pug dogs, peppermint creams. Henry James, it is said, had the idea of making her the central character of a merely projected novel – did he mean to tackle the mysteriously absent husband, make of him one of those electric Jamesian force-fields of unspecific significance? He did, it is also said, write her into *The Aspern Papers*, in a purely subordinate and structural role, the type of the well-to-do American woman friend of the narrator, an authorial device, what James called a *ficelle*, economically connecting us, the readers, to the necessary people and the developing drama. She lent the narrator her gondola. She was a generous woman. She is an enthusiast: she collects locks of hair, snipped from great poetic temples, which she enshrines in lockets of onyx. She is waiting for Robert Browning. She has done and will do this in many years. She has supervised and will supervise the excellent provision of sheets and bathroom facilities for his Venetian visits. She chides him for not recognizing that servants know their place and are happy in it. She sends him quires of hand-made Venetian paper which he distributes to artists and poets of his acquaintance. She selects brass salvers for him. She records his considered and unconsidered responses to scenery and atmosphere. She looks at the gulls with interest he has instilled. "I do not know why I never see in descriptions of Venice any mention of the sea-gulls; to me they are even more interesting than the doves of St Mark." He said that, and she recorded it. She recorded that occasionally he would allow her daughter to give him a cup of tea "to our great delight". "As a rule, he abstained from what he considered a somewhat unhygienic beverage if taken before dinner."

II

Dear dead women, the scholar thinks, peering into the traces on the hooded green plane of the microfilm reader, or perhaps turning over browned packets of polite notes of gratitude, acceptance, anticipation, preserved perhaps in one of those fine boxes of which in her lifetime she had so many, containing delicate cigarettes on inlaid pearly octagonal tables, or precious fragments of verses copied out for autograph books. He has gleaned her words from Kansas and Cambridge, Florence, Venice and Oxford, he has read her essay on lace and her tributes to the condescension of genius, he has heard the flitting of young skirts at long-vanished festivities. He has stood, more or less, on the spot where she stood with the poet in Asolo in 1889, looking back to Browning's first contemplation of the place in 1838, looking back to the internecine passions of Guelphs and Ghibellines, listening to the chirrup of the contumacious grasshopper. He has seen her blood colour the cheeks of her noble Italian grand-daughter who has opened to him those houses where the poet dined, recited, conversed, teased, reminisced. He likes her, partly because he now knows her, has pieced her together. Resuscitated, Browning might have said, did say, roundly, of his Roman murderers and biassed lawyers, child-wife, wise moribund Pope and gallant priest he found or invented in his dead and lively Yellow Book. A good scholar may permissibly invent, he may have a hypothesis, but fiction is barred. This scholar believes, plausibly, that his assiduous and fragile subject is the hidden heroine of a love story, the inapprehensive object, at the age of fifty-four, of a dormant passion in a handsome seventy-seven-year-old poet. He records the physical vigour, the beautiful hands and fine white head of hair of his hero. He records the probable feelings of his heroine, which stop short at exalted hero-worship, the touch of talismanic mementos, not living flesh. He adduces a poem, "Inapprehensiveness", in which the poetic speaker reproves the inapprehensive stare of a companion intent on Ruskin's hypothetical observation of the waving form of certain weed-growths on a ravaged wall, who ignores "the dormant passion needing but a look To burst into immense life". The scholar's story combs the facts this way. They have a subtle, not too dramatic shape, lifelike in that. He scrutinizes the microfilm, the yellowing letters, for little bright nuggets and filaments of fact to add to his mosaic. In 1882 the poet was in the Alps, with a visit to Venice in prospect after a proposed visit to another English family in Italy. She waited for him. In terms of this story she waited in vain. An "incident" elsewhere, an "unfortunate accident" the scholar wrote, following his thread, coupled with torrential rain in Bologna, caused the poet to return to London. He was in danger of allowing the friendship to cool, the scholar writes, perhaps anxious on her behalf, perhaps on the poet's, perhaps on his own.

III

A man, he always thought, was more himself alone in an hotel room. Unless, of course, he vanished altogether without the support of others' consciousness of him, and the solidity of his taste and his history in his possessions. To be itinerant suited and sharpened him. He liked this room. It was quiet, on the second floor, the last in a long corridor, its balcony face to face with a great, bristling primeval glacier. The hotel, he wrote, sitting at the table listening to the silent snow and the fraternizing tinkle of unseen cattle, was "quite perfect, with every comfort desirable, and no drawback of any kind". The journey up had been rough – two hours carriage-drive, and then seven continued hours of clambering and crawling on mule-back. He wrote letters partly out of courtesy to his large circle of solicitous friends and admirers, but more in order to pick up the pen, to see the pothooks and spider-traces form, containing the world, the hotel, the mules, the paradise of coolness and quiet. The hotel was not absolutely perfect. "My very handwriting is affected by the lumpy ink and the skewery pen." Tomorrow he would walk. Four or five hours along the mountainside. Not bad for an old man, a hale old man. The mule-jolting had played havoc with his hips and the long muscles in his back. At my age, he thought, you listen to every small hurt as though it may be the beginning of the last and worst hurt, which will come. So the two things continued in his consciousness side by side, a solicitous attention to twinges, and the waiting to be reinvested by his private self. Which was like a cloak, a cloak of invisibility that fell into comfortable warm folds around him, or like a disturbed well, whose inky waters chopped and swayed and settled into blackly reflecting lucidity. Or like a brilliant baroque chapel at the centre of a decorous and unremarkable house.

He liked his public self well enough. He was surprised, to tell the truth, that he had one that worked so well, was so thoroughgoing, so at home in the world, so like other public selves. As a very young man, in strictly non-conformist South London, erudite and indulged within the four walls of a Camberwell bibliomaniac's home, he had supposed that this would be denied him, the dining-out, the gossip, the world. He wanted the world, because it was there, and he wanted everything. He had described his father, whom he loved, as a man of vast knowledge, reading and memory – totally ignorant of the world. (This ignorance had extended to his having had to leave England perpetually, as an aged widower, on account of a breach of promise action brought, with cause, against him.) His father had with consummate idealism freed him for art. My father wished me to do what I liked, he had explained, adding: I should not so bring up a son.

French novelists, he claimed, were ignorant of the habits of the English upper classes, who kept themselves to themselves. He had seen and noted them. "I seem to know a good many — for some reason or other. Perhaps because I never had any occupation." Nevertheless, he desired his son to have an occupation, and the boy, amiable and feckless, brooded over by his own irreducible large shadow, showed little sign of vocation or application. He amused himself as a matter of course in the world in which the father dined out and visited, so assiduously, with a perpetually renewed surprise at his own facility. He was aware that Elizabeth would have wished it otherwise. Elizabeth had been a great poet, a captive princess liberated and turned wife, a moral force, silly over some things, such as her growing boy's long curls and the flimsy promises and fake visions of the séance. She too had not known this world that was so important. *One* such intimate knowledge as I have had with many a person would have taught her, he confided once, unguarded, had she been inclined to learn. Though I doubt if she would have dirtied her hands for any scientific purpose. His public self had a scientific purpose, and if his hands were dirty, he could wash them clean in a minute before he saw her, as he trusted to do. He had his reasonable doubts about this event, too, though he wrote bravely of it, the step from this world to that other world, the fog in the throat, the mist in the face, the snows, the blasts, the pain and then the peace out of pain and the loving arms. It was not a time of certainties, however he might assert them from time to time. It was a time of doubt, doubt was a man's business. But it was also hard to imagine all this tenacious sense of self, all this complexity of knowledge and battling, force and curiosity becoming nothing. What is a man, what is a man's soul?

Descartes believed, he noted down, that the seat of the soul is the pineal gland. The reason for this is a pretty reason — all else in our apparatus for apprehending the world is double, *viz.* two ears, two eyes, etc. and two lobes of our brain moreover; Descartes requires that somewhere in our body all our diverse, our dual impressions must be unified before reaching the soul, which is one. He had thought often of writing a poem about Descartes, dreaming in his stove of sages and blasted churches, reducing all to the tenacity of the observing thinker, *cogito ergo sum*. A man can inhabit another man's mind, or body, or senses, or history, can jerk it into a kind of life, as galvanism moves frogs: a good poet could inhabit Descartes, the bric-à-brac of stove and ill-health and wooden bowls of onion soup, perhaps, and one of those pork knuckles, and the melon offered to the philosopher by the sage in his feverish dream, all this paraphernalia spinning round the naked cogito as the planets spin in an orrery. The best part of my life, he told himself, the life I have lived most intensely, has been the fitting, the infiltrating, the inventing the self of another man or woman, explored and sleekly filled out, as fingers swell a glove. I have been webbed Caliban lying in the primeval ooze, I have been madman and saint, murderer and sensual prelate, inspired David and the cringing medium, Sludge, to whom I gave David's name, with what compulsion of irony or equivocation, David Sludge? The rooms in which his solitary self sat buzzed with other selves, crying for blood as the shades cried at the pit dug by Odysseus in his need to interrogate, to revive the dead. His father's encyclopaedias were the banks of such blood-pits, bulging with paper lives and circumstances, no two the same, none insignificant. A set of views, a time-confined philosophy, a history of wounds and weaknesses, flowers, clothing, food and drink, light on Mont Blanc's horns of silver, fangs of crystal; these coalesce to make one self in one place. Then decompose. I catch them, he thought, I hold them together, I give them coherence and vitality, I. And what am I? Just such another concatenation, a language and its rhythms, a limited stock of learning, derived from my father's consumed books and a few experiments in life, my desires, my venture in dragon-slaying, my love, my loathings also, the peculiar colours of the world through my two eyes, the blind tenacity of the small, the single driving centre, soul or self.

What he had written down, with the scratchy pen, were one or two ideas for Descartes and his metaphorical orrery: meaningless scraps. And this writing brought to life in him a kind of joy in greed. He would procure, he would soak in, he would comb his way through the Discourse on Method, and the Passions of the Soul: he would investigate Flemish stoves. His private self was now roused from its dormant state to furious activity. He felt the white hairs lift on his neck and his breath quickened. A bounded man, he had once written, may so project his surplusage of soul in search of body, so add self to self ... so find, so fill full, so appropriate forms ... In such a state a man became pure curiosity, pure interest in whatever presented itself of the creation, lovely or freakish, pusillanimous, wise or vile. Those of his creatures he most loved or most approved moved with such delighted and indifferent interest through the world. There was the tragic Duchess, destroyed by the cold egotism of a Duke who could not bear her equable pleasure in everything, a sunset, a bough of cherries, a white mule, his favour at her breast. There was Karshish the Arab physician, the not-incurious in God's handiwork, who noticed lynx and blue-flowering borage and recorded the acts of the risen Lazarus. There was David, seeing the whole earth shine with significance after soothing the passionate self-doubt of Saul; there was Christopher Smart, whose mad work of genius, his Song to David, a baroque chapel in a dull house, had recorded the particularity of the world, the whale's bulk in the waste of brine, the feather-tufts of Wild Virgin's Bower, the habits of the polyanthus. There was the risen Lazarus himself, who had briefly been in the presence of God and inhabited eternity, and to whose resuscitated life he had been able to give no other characteristics than these, the lively, indifferent interest in everything, a mule with gourds, a child's death, the flowers of the field, some trifling fact at which he will gaze "rapt with stupor at its very littleness".

He felt for his idea of what was behind all this diversity, all this interest. *At the back* was an intricate and extravagantly prolific maker. Sometimes, listening to silence, alone with himself, he heard the irregular but endlessly repeated crash of waves on a pebbled shore. His body was a porcelain-fine arched shell, sculpted who knew how, containing this roar and plash. And the drag of the moon, and the elliptical course of the planets. More often, a madly ingenious inner eye magnified small motions of flesh and blood. The twinge had become a tugging and raking in what he now feared, prophetically it turned out, was his liver. Livers were used for augury, the shining liver, the smoking liver, the Babylonians thought, was the seat of the soul: his own lay athwart him and was intimately and mysteriously connected with the lumpy pothooks. And with the inner eye which might or might not be seated in that pineal gland where Descartes located the soul. A man has no more measured the mysteries of his internal whistlings and flowings, he thought, than he has measured the foundations of the earth or of the whirlwind. It was his covert principle to give true opinions to great liars, and to that other fraudulent resuscitator of dead souls, and filler of mobile gloves, David Sludge the Medium, he had given a vision of the minutiae of intelligence which was near enough his own. "We find great things are made of little things," he had made Sludge say, "And little things go lessening till at last Comes God behind them."

> "The Name comes close behind a stomach-cyst
> The simplest of creations, just a sac
> That's mouth, heart, legs and belly at once, yet lives
> And feels and could do neither, we conclude
> If simplified still further one degree."

"But go back and back, as you please, *at* the back, as Mr Sludge is made to insist," he had written, "you find (*my* faith is as constant) creative intelligence, acting as matter but not resulting from it. Once set the balls rolling and ball may hit ball and send any number in any direction over the table; but I believe in the cue pushed by a hand." All the world speaks the Name, as the true David truly saw: even the uneasy inflamed cells of my twinges. *At* the back, is something simple, undifferentiated, indifferently intelligent, live.

My best times are those when I approximate most closely to that state.

She put her hand on the knob of his door, and pushed it open without knocking. It was dark, a light, smoky dark; the window curtains were not drawn and the windows were a couple of vague, star-lighted apertures. She saw things, a rug thrown over a chair, a valise, a dim shape hunched and silver-topped, which turned out to be her brother, back towards her, at the writing-table. "Oh, if you're busy," she said, "I won't disturb you." And then, "You can't write in the dark, Robert, it is bad for your eyes." He shook himself, like a great seal coming up from the depths, and his eyes, dark spaces under craggy brows, turned unseeing in her direction. "I don't want to disturb you," she said again, patiently waiting for his return to the land of the living. "You don't," he said, "dear Sarianna. I was only thinking about Descartes. And it must be more than time for dinner." "There is a woman here," Sarianna confided, as they walked down the corridor, past a servant carrying candles, "with an aviary on her head, who is an admirer of your poems and wishes to join the Browning society." "Il me semble que ce genre de chose frise le ridicule," he said, growlingly, and she smiled to herself, for she knew that when he was introduced to the formidable Mrs Miller he would be everything that was agreeable and interested.

*   *   *

And the next day, on the hotel terrace, he was quite charming to his corseted and bustled admirer, who begged him to write in her birthday book, already graced by Lord Leighton and Thomas Trollope, who was indulgent when he professed not to remember on which of two days he had been born – was it May 7th or May 9th, he never could be certain, he said, appealing to Sarianna, who could. He had found some better ink, and copied out, as he occasionally did, in microscopic handwriting, "All that I know of a certain star", adding with a bluff smile, "I always end up writing the same thing; I vary only the size. I should be more inventive." Mrs Miller protested that his eyesight must be exquisitely fine, closing the scented leather over the hand-painted wreaths of pansies that encircled the precious script. Her hat was monumental, a circle of wings; the poet admired it, and asked detailed questions about its composition, owls, hawks, jays, swallows, encircling an entire dove. He showed considerable familiarity with Paris prints and the vagaries of modistes. His public self had its own version of the indiscriminate interest in everything which was the virtue of the last Duchess, Karshish, Lazarus and Smart. He could not know how much this trait was to irritate Henry James, who labelled it bourgeois, whose fictional alter ego confessed to feeling a despair at his "way of liking one subject – so far as I could tell – precisely as much as another". He addressed himself to women exactly as he addressed himself to men, this affronted narrator complained; he gossiped to all men alike, talking no better to clever folk than to dull. He was loud and cheerful and copious. His opinions were sound and second-rate, and of his perceptions it was too mystifying to think. He seemed quite happy in the company of the insistent Mrs Miller, telling her about the projected visit to the Fishwick family, who had a house in the Apennines. Mrs Miller nodded vigorously under the wings of the dove, and leapt into vibrant recitation. "What I love best in all the world Is a castle, precipice-encurled In a gash of the wind-grieved Apennines." "Exactly so," said the benign old man, sipping his port, looking at the distant mountains, watched by Sarianna, who knew that he was braced against the Apennines as a test, that he had never since her death ventured so near the city in which he had been happy with his wife, in which he was never to set foot again. The Fishwicks' villa was in a remote village unvisited in that earlier time. He meant to attempt that climb, as he had attempted this. He needed to be undaunted. It was his idea of himself that he was undaunted. And so he was, Sarianna thought, with love. "Then we may proceed to Venice," said the poet to the lady in the hat, "where we have very kind friends and many fond memories. I should not be averse to dying in Venice. When my time comes."

IV

"What will he make of us?" Miss Juliana Fishwick enquired, speaking of the imminent Robert Browning, and in fact more concerned with what her companion, Mr Joshua Riddell, did make of them, of the Fishwick family and way of life, of the Villa Colomba, perched in its coign of cliff, with its rough lawn and paved rooms and heavy ancient furnishings. She was perhaps the only person in the company to care greatly what anybody made of anybody; the others were all either too old and easygoing or too young and intent on their journeys of discovery and complicated games. Joshua Riddell replied truthfully that he found them all enchanting, and the place too, and was sure that Mr Browning would be enchanted. He was a friend of Juliana's brother, Tom. They were at Balliol College, reading Greats. Joshua's father was a Canon of St Paul's. Joshua lived a regular and circumspect life at home, where he was an only child, of whom much was expected. He expected very much of himself, too, though not in the line of his parents' hopes, the Bar, the House of Commons, the judiciary. He meant to be a great painter. He meant to do something quite new, which would have authority. He knew he should recognize this, when he had learned what it was, and how to do it. For the time being, living in its necessarily vague yet brilliant presence was both urgent and thwarting. He described it to no one; certainly not to Tom, with whom he was able, surprisingly, to share ordinary jokes and japes. He was entirely unused to the degree of playfulness and informality of Tom's family.

He was sketching Juliana. She was sitting, in her pink muslin, on the edge of the fountain basin. The fountain bubbled in an endless chuckling waterfall out of a cleft in the rockside. This was the lower fountain, furthest from the house, on a rough lawn on which stood an ancient stone table and chairs. Above the fountain someone had carved a round, sun-like face, flat and calmly beaming, with two uplifted, flat-palmed hands pushing through, or poised on, the rock face beside it. No one knew how old or new it was. In the upper garden, where there were flowerbeds and a slower, lead-piped fountain, was a pillar or herm surmounted with a head which, Solomon Fishwick had pointed out, was exactly the same as the heads on the covers of the hominiform Etruscan funerary urns. Joshua had made several drawings of these carvings. Juliana's living face, under her straw hat, was a different challenge. It was a face composed of softness and the smooth solid texture of young flesh, without pronounced bones, hard to capture. The blonde eyebrows did not stand out; the eyes were not emphasized by long lashes, only by a silver-white fringe which caught the sunlight here and there. The upper lip sloped upwards; the mouth was always slightly parted, the expression gently questioning, not insisting on an answer. It was an extremely pleasant face, with no salient characteristics. How to draw softness, and youth, and sheer *pleasantness*? Her arms should be full of an abundance of something; apples, rosebuds, a cascade of corn. She held her little hands awkwardly, clasping and unclasping them over her pink skirts.

Juliana was more used to looking than to being looked at. She supposed she was not pretty, though passable, not by any means grotesque. She had an unfortunate body for this year's narrow styles, which required height, an imposing bosom, a flat stomach, an upright carriage. She was round and short, though she had a good enough waist; corseting did violence to her, and in the summer heat in Italy was impossible. So she was conscious of rolls and half-moons and sausages of flesh which she would dearly have wished otherwise. She had pretty ankles and wrists, she knew, and had stockings of a lovely rose pink with butterfly-shells embroidered on them. Her elder sister, Annabel, visiting in Venice, was a beauty, much courted, much consulted about dashing little hats. Juliana supposed she might herself have trouble in finding a husband. She was not remarkable. She was afraid she might simply pass from being a shepherding elder sister to being a useful aunt. She was marvellous with the little ones. She played and tumbled and comforted and cleaned and sympathized, and wanted something of her own, some place, some thought, some silence that should be hers only. She did not expect to find it. She had a practical nature and liked comfort. She had been invaluable in helping to bestow the family goods and chattels in the two heavy carriages which had made their way up the hill, from the heat of Florence to this airy and sunny garden state. Everything had had to go in: baths and fish-kettles, bolsters and jelly-moulds, cats, dogs, birdcage and dolls' house. She had sat in the nursery carriage, with Nanny and Nurse and the restive little ones: Tom and Joshua had gone ahead with her parents and the household staff, English and Italian, had come behind. On the hot leather seat, she was impinged upon by Nurse's starched petticoats on one side, and the entwined, struggling limbs of Arthur and Gwendolen battling for space, for air on the other. When the climb became steep spare mules were attached, called *trapeli*, each with its attendant groom, groaning and coughing on the steeper and steeper turns, whilst the men went at strolling pace and the horses skidded and lay back in their collars leaving the toiling to the mules. She found their patient effort exemplary: she had given them all apples when they arrived.

She was in awe of Joshua, though not of Tom. Tom teased her, as he always had, amiably. Joshua spoke courteously to her as though she was as knowledgeable as Tom about Horace and Ruskin; this was probably because he had no experience of sisters and only a limited experience of young women. Her father had taught her a little Latin and Greek; her governess had taught her French, Italian, needlework, drawing and the use of the globes, accomplishments she was now imparting to Gwendolen, and Arthur and little Edith. They seemed useless, not because they were uninteresting but because they were like feathers stitched on to a hat, dead decorations, not life. They were life to Joshua; she could see that. His manner was fastidious and aloof, but he had been visibly shaken, before the peregrination to the Villa Colomba, by the outing they had made from Florence to Vallombrosa, with its sweeping inclines and steep declivities all clothed with the chestnut trees, dark green shades "high overarched indeed, exactly," Joshua had said, and had added, "You can see that these leaves, being deciduous, will strow the brooks, thickly, like the dead souls in Virgil and Milton's fallen angels." She had looked at the chestnut trees, suddenly seeing them, because he asked her to. They clothed the mountains here, too. The peasants lived off chestnuts: their cottages had chestnut-drying lofts, their women ground chestnut flour in stone mortars.

When they had first rushed into the Villa Colomba, chirruping children and pinch-mouthed, disapproving cook, and had found nothing but echoing, cool space between the thick walls with their barred slit windows, she had looked to Joshua in alarm, whilst the children cried out, "Where are the chairs and tables?" He had found an immense hour glass, in a niche over the huge cavernous hearth, and said, smilingly, "We are indeed in another time, a Saturnine time." Civilization, it turned out, existed upstairs, though cook complained mightily of ageing rusty iron pots and a ratcheted spit like a diabolical instrument of torture. Everything was massive and ancient: oak tables on a forest of oak pillars, huge leather-backed thrones, beds with heavy gilded hangings, chests ingeniously carved on clawed feet, too heavy to lift, tombs, Tom said, for curious girls. "A house for giants," Joshua said to Juliana, seeing her intrigue and anxiety both clearly. He drew her attention to the huge wrought-iron handles of the keys. "We are out of the nineteenth century entirely," he said. The walls of the *salone* were furnished with a series of portraits, silver-wigged and dark-eyed and rigid. Joshua's bedroom had a fearful and appalling painting of fruits and flowers so arranged as to form a kind of human form, bristling with pineapple spines, curvaceous with melons, staring through passion-flower eyes. "*That*," said Juliana, "is bound to appeal to Mr Browning, who is interested in the grotesque." Tom said he would not make much of the family portraits, which were so similar as to argue a significant want of skill in the painter. "Either that, or a striking family resemblance," said Joshua. "Or a painter whose efforts all turn out to resemble his own appearance. I have known one or two portraiture painters like that." Sitting now on the rim of the fountain trough, watching him frown over his drawing, look up, correct, frown and scribble, she wondered if by some extraordinary process her undistinguished features might be brought to resemble his keen and handsome ones. He was gipsyish in colouring, and well-groomed by habit, a kind of contradiction. Here in the mountains he wore a loose jacket and a silk scarf knotted at his neck, but knotted too neatly. He was smaller and thinner than Tom.

Joshua worked on the mouth corner. He had chosen a very soft, silvery pencil for this very soft skin: he did not want to draw a caricature in a few sparing lines, he wanted somehow to convey the nature of the solidity of the flesh of cheek and chin. He had mapped in the rounds and ovals, of the whole head and the hat brim, and the descending curve of the looped plait in the nape of Juliana's neck, and the spot where her ear came, and parts of the calm wide forehead. The shadow cast on the flesh by the circumference of the hat was another pleasant problem in tone and shading. He worked in little, circling movements, feeling out little clefts with the stub of his pencil, isolating tiny white patches of light that shone on the ledge of the lip or the point of the chin, leaving this untouched paper to glitter by contrast with his working. He filled out the plump underthroat with love; *so* it gave a little, *so* it was taut.

"I wish I could see," said Juliana, "what you are doing."

"When it is done."

It was almost as if he was touching the face, watching its grey shape swim into existence out of a spider web of marks. His hand hovered over where the nose would be, curled a nostril, dented its flare. If anywhere he put dark marks where light should be, it was ruined. No two artists' marks are the same, no more than their thumbprints. Behind Juliana's head he did the edge, no more, of the flat stony texture of the solar face.

Juliana kept still. Her anxieties about Mr Browning and the massive awkwardness of their temporary home were calmed. Joshua's tentative pencil began to explore the area of the eyes. The eyes were difficult. They must first be modelled – the life was conferred by the pinpoint of dark and the flecks of white light, and the exact distances between them. He had studied the amazing eyes created by Rembrandt van Rijn, a precise little bristling, fine, hair-like movement of the brush, a spot of crimson here, a thread of carmine there, a spider-web paste of colour out of which a soul suddenly stared. "Please look at me," he said to Juliana, "please look at me – yes, like that – and don't move." His pencil point hovered, thinking, and Juliana's pupils contracted in the greenish halo of the iris, as she looked into the light, and blinked, involuntarily. She did not want to stare at him; it was unnatural, though his considering gaze, measuring, drawing back, turning to one side and the other, seemed natural enough. A flood of colour moved darkly up her throat, along her chin, into the planes and convexities of her cheeks. Tears collected, unbidden, without cause. Joshua noted the deepening of colour, and then the glisten, and ceased to caress the paper with the pencil. Their eyes met. What a complicated thing is this meeting of eyes, which disturbs the air between two still faces, which has its effects on the heartbeat, the hair on the wrists, the flow of blood. You can understand, Joshua thought, why poets talk of arrows, or of hooks thrown. He said, "How odd it is to look at someone, after all, and to see their soul looking back again. How can a pencil catch that? How do we know we see each other?"

Juliana said nothing, only blushed, rosier and rosier, flooded by moving blood under her hat, and one large tear brimmed over the line of lower lashes, with their wet silkiness which Joshua had been trying to render.

"Ah, Juliana. There is no need to cry. Please, don't. I'll stop."

"No. I am being silly. I – I am not used to be looked at so intently."

"You are beautiful to look at," said Joshua, comparing the flowing colours with the placid silver-grey of his attempt to feel out her face. He put down his drawing, and touched at her cheek with a clean handkerchief. The garden hummed with insect song and bubbled with water; he was somehow inside it, as he was when he was drawing; he looked down and there, under the tight pink muslin, was the generous round of a breast. It was all the same, all alive, the warm stone, the water, the rough grass, the swirl of pink muslin, the troubled young face. He put his two hands round the little ones that turned in her lap, stilling them like trapped birds.

"I have alarmed you, Juliana. I didn't mean that. I'm sorry."

"I don't want you to be sorry." Small but clear.

"Look at me again." It was said for him; it was what came next; they no sooner looked but they loved, a voice told him; the trouble was delightful, compelling, alarming. "Please look at me, Juliana. How often do we really look at each other?"

She had looked at him before, when he was not looking. Now she could not. And so it seemed natural for him to put his arms along the soft round shoulders, to push his face, briefly, briefly, under the brim of the hat, to rest his warm lips on the mouth corner his pencil had touched in its distance. Juliana could hear the sea, or her own life, swirling.

"Juliana," he said, "Juliana, Juliana." And then, prompted by some little local daemon of the grass plot and the carved smiler, "Juliana is the name of the lady in one of the poems I most love. Do you know it? It is by Andrew Marvell; it is the complaint of the mower, Damon."

Juliana said she did not know it. She would like to hear it. He recited.

> "My mind was once the true survey
> Of all these meadows fresh and gay;
> And in the greenness of the grass
> Did see my thoughts as in a glass
> 'Til Juliana came, and she,
> What I do to the grass, did to my thoughts and me."

"She was not very kind," said Juliana.

"We do not know what she was," said Joshua. "Only the effect she had upon the Mower."

He gripped the little fingers. The fingers gripped back. And then the children came bursting down the pathway under the trees, announcing an expedition to the village.

Juliana was in no doubt about what had happened. It was love. Love had blossomed, or struck, like lightning, like a hawk, as it was clearly seen to do in novels and poems, as it took no time to do, voracious or sunny, in the stories she lived on, the scenes her imagination and more, her moral expectations, naturally inhabited. Love visited all who were not ridiculous or religious. Simply, she had always supposed her own, when it came, would be unrequited and lowering, was unprepared for kisses and poetry. She went to bed that night and turned on her dusty bolster among her coarse sheets, all vaguely aflame, diffusely desirous, terribly unused to violent personal happiness.

Joshua was less sure of what had happened. He too burned that night, less vaguely, more locally, making a turmoil of his coverings and tormented by aches and tensions. He recognized the old cherub for what he was, and gave him his true name, the name Juliana gave him, honourably, not wriggling into demeaning her or himself by thinking simply of lust. He went over and over every detail with reverent pleasure, the pink muslin, the trusting tear-filled eyes, the flutter of a pulse, the soft mouth, the revelations of his questing pencil. But, unlike Juliana, he was already under the rule of another daemon or cherub; he was used to accommodating his body and mind to the currents of the dictates of another imperative; he felt a responsibility also to the empty greenness that had existed in his primitive innocence, before. He wanted, he loved; but did he want enough, did he love enough? Had he inadvertently behaved dishonourably to this young creature, certainly tonight the dearest to him in the world, certainly haloed with light and warm with charm and promise of affection? He was twenty years old. He had no experience and was confused. He finally promised himself that tomorrow he would do as he had already promised himself he would do, set off early and alone up the mountain-side, to do some sketching – even painting. He would look at the land beyond habitation. He would explain to her: she would immediately understand all, since what he should say would be no more than the serious and honourable truth; that he must go away.

He rose very early, and went into the kitchen to beg sandwiches, and a flask of wine, from cook. Gianni was sent off to saddle his mule, to take him as far as the village, Lucchio, which could be seen clinging to the face of the mountain opposite. It was barely dawn, but Juliana was up, too; he encountered her in the dark corridor.

"I am going up the cliff, to paint," he said. "That was what I had intended to do, before."

"We must think a little," he said. "I must go up there, and think. You do understand? You will talk to me again – we will speak to each other – when I return?"

She could have said: it is nothing to me whether you go up the mountain or remain here. But she was honest.

"I shall look out for you coming back."

"Juliana," he said, "ah, Juliana."

The mule skidded on the stones. The road was paved, after a fashion, but the stones were upended, like rows of jagged teeth. Gianni walked stolidly and silently behind. The road circled the hill, under chestnuts, then out onto the craggier ascent. It twisted and the sun rose; the mule passed from cold shadow to whitish glare and back again. Hot stone was very hot, Joshua thought, and cold stone very cold. He could smell stone of both kinds, as well as the warm hairy sweating mule and the glossy rubbed ancient leather. He looked backwards and forwards, along the snaking line of the river that cut its way about and about between the great cones of the Apennines. The sky had a white clearness and emptiness, not yet gleaming, which was essentially Italian. He knew the mountains round: the Libro Aperto, or open book, the Prato Fiorito, velvety and enamelled with flowers, the Monte Pellegrino, covered with silvery edible thistles and inhabited, once, by hermits whose diet they were. He thought about the mountains, with reverence and curiosity, and his thoughts on the mountains, like those of many of his contemporaries, were in large part the thoughts of John Ruskin, who had seen them clearly, as no one else, it seemed, had ever seen them, and had declared that this clarity of vision was the essence of truth, virtue, and good art, which were, in this, one. Mountains are the bones of the earth, he had written. "But there is this difference between the action of the earth, and that of a living creature; that while the exerted limb marks its bones and tendons through the flesh, the excited earth casts off the flesh altogether, and its bones come out from beneath." Joshua thought about this, and looked at the working knobs of bone at the base of the mule-neck, under their thin layer of skin, and remembered, formally and then excitedly, the search for Juliana's bone under the round cheek. Ruskin was a geologist. His ideals of painting were founded on an intricate and analytical knowledge of how the movement of water shaped and unmade and shifted the eternal hills, of how clefts were formed, and precipices sheered. It had been a revelation to the young Joshua to read in *Modern Painters* how very young was man's interest in these ancient forms. The Greeks had seen them merely as threats or aids to the adventures of gods and heroes; mediaeval man had on the whole disliked anything wild or savage, preferring order and cultivation, trellised gardens and bowers to wild woods or louring cliffs. John Ruskin would have delighted in the mediaeval names of the hills through which he now travelled: the Open Book, the Flowery Meadow, the Pilgrim's Mount came straight out of Dante into the nineteenth century. Ruskin had characterized modern art, with some disparagement, as the "service of clouds". The mediaeval mind had taken pleasure in the steady, the definite, the luminous, but the moderns rejoiced in the dark, the sombre. Our time, Ruskin had said, and Joshua had joyfully learned, was the true Dark Ages, devoted to smokiness and burnt umber. Joshua had not understood about the necessity of brightness and colour until he came south this first time, until he saw the light, although intellectually he had been fired by Ruskin's diatribes against Victorian darkness and ugliness in all things, in dress, in manners, in machines and chimneys, in storm-clouds and grottoes.

Only, in Paris, he had seen something which changed, not the desire for brightness, but the ideas about the steady, the definite, the luminous. Something which should have helped him with the soft expanse of Juliana's pink dress, which he remembered, turning a corner and seeing the village again, clutching the cliff like thornbushes with half their roots in air. It was to do with the flesh and the muslin, the tones in common, the tones that were not shared, a blue in the pink cloth . . . you could pick up in the vein or the eyelid, the wrist, a shimmer, a thread . . . The hot saddle shifted beneath him: the mule sighed: the man sighed. Gianni said, "Lucchio, una mezz'ora." The white air was also blue and the blue white light.

When they got there, there was something alarming about this tenacious and vertiginous assembly of buildings, peacefully white in the mounting heat, chill in their dark aspects, all blindly shuttered, their dark life inside their doors. Houses stood where they were planted, where a level floor, or floors, could be found for them – often they were different heights on different sides. Many had tiny gardens fronting the empty air, and Gianni pointed out to Joshua, in two different instances, a toddling child, stiff-skirted, bonneted, tethered at the waist by a length of linen to a hook in the door posts. Even the church bells were grounded, caged in iron frames outside the church door, safe, Joshua could only suppose, from vibrating unstably against the overhanging rock-shelf.

Here Joshua parted from Gianni and the mules; they would meet again near the bells on the roadway, an hour or so from sunset. He took the path that curved up out of the village, which passed the ancient fountain where the girls came and went barefoot, carrying great copper vessels on their heads, swaying. At the fountain he replenished his water bottle, and moistened his face and neck. Then he went on up. Above the village was a ruined and much decayed castle, its thick outer wall continuous with the rock face, its courtyard littered with shattered building blocks. He thought of stopping here to draw the ancient masonry, but after reflection went on up. He had a need to study the wholly inhuman. His path, a branching, vertiginous sheep track, now wound between whitish sheer pillars of stone; his feet dislodged rubble and a powdery dust. He liked the feeling of the difficult going-up, and his step was springy. If he got far enough up and round he would have a downwards vantage point for sketching the improbable village. He thought alternately about Ruskin and about Juliana.

Ruskin disliked the Apennines: he found their limestone monotonous in hue, grey and toneless, utterly melancholy. He had expended several pages of exact lyrical prose on this gloomy colouring, pointing out that it was the colouring Dante gave to his Evil-pits in the Inferno, malignant grey, he gleefully recorded, akin to the robes of the purgatorial angel which were of the colour of ashes, or earth dug dry. Ashes, to an Italian mind, wrote Ruskin beside his London coals, necessarily meant *wood-ashes* — very pale — analogous to the hue seen on the sunny side of Italian hills, produced by the scorching of the ground, a dusty and lifeless whitish grey, utterly painful and oppressive. He preferred the strenuous, masculine, mossy and complicated Alps, awesome and sublime. Joshua had not really seen the Alps, but he found these smaller mountains beautiful, not oppressive, and their chalky paleness interesting, not dulling. Ruskin believed the great artists were those who had never despised anything, however small, of God's making. If he was prepared to treat the Apennine rocks as though they had been created perhaps only by a minor daemon or demiurge, Joshua, on Ruskin's own principles, was not. If he could find a means of recording the effects of these ashy whitenesses, of the reddish iron-stains in the stone, of the way one block stood against another, of the root-systems of the odd, wind-sculpted trees, he would be content. He would, if he could find his vantage, "do" the view of the village. He would also, for that love of the true forms of things desiderated by his master, do studies of the stones as they were, of the scrubby things that grew.

He found his perch, in time; a wideish ledge, in a cleft with a high triangular shadow bisecting it, diminishing as the sun climbed. He thought of it as his eyrie. From it he would see the village, a little lower, winding round the conical form of the mountain like a clinging wreath, crowned by a fantastic cluster of crags all sky-pointing like huge hot inverted icicles, white on the white-blue sky. These forms were paradoxical, strong yet aerial and delicate like needles, reminding him of the lightness of lace on the emptiness, yet stone of earth. He took out his sketching-glass and filled it, arranged his paints and his chalks and his pencils, became wholly involved in the conversion of estimated distances to perceived relative sizes and tones. The problem was to convey this blanched, bony world with shadows which should, by contrast, form and display its dazzle. He tried both with pencil and with washes of colour. Ruskin said: "Here we are, then, with white paper for our highest light, and visible illuminated surface for our deepest shadow, set to run the gauntlet against nature, with the sun for her light, and vacuity for her gloom." Joshua wrestled with these limitations, in a glare which made it hard for him to judge the brightness even of his own paper-surface. He was very miserable; his efforts took shape and solidified into failures of vision. He was supremely happy; unaware of himself and wholly aware of rock formations, sunlight and visible empty air, of which he became part, moment by moment and then timelessly, the notation of things seen being no more than the flow of his blood, necessary for continuance in this state.

At some point he became quite suddenly hungry, and took out of his knapsack his oily but agreeable packages of bread, meat, eggs, cheese. He devoured all, exhausted, as though his life was in danger, and put away his chicken bones and eggshells, for had not Ruskin himself complained that modern man came to the mountains not to fast but to feast, leaving glaciers covered with bones and eggshells. He had an idea of himself tearing at his food like a young bird on its ledge. Wiping his fingers, pouring more water for his work, he remembered Juliana, confusedly and from a distance, a softness in the corner of his consciousness, a warmth to which he would return when he returned to himself. He could never hurt Juliana, never. Behind the stone he had chosen for his seat were the bleached remains of some other creature's meal; skeletal pinions and claws, a triangular pointed skull, a few snail shells, wrecked and pierced. He made a quick water-colour sketch of these, interested in the different whites and creams and greys of bone, shell and stone. And shadow. He was particularly pleased with his rendering of a snail shell, the arch of its entrance intact, the dome of the cavern behind shattered to reveal the pearly interior involution. These small things occupied as much space on the paper as the mountains. Their shadows were as intricate, though different.

When he came to look out at the land again, the air had changed. Near, it danced; farther away, on the horizon, white cloud was piling itself up and throwing out long arms from peak to peak; under the arms were horizontal bars of black shadow which seemed impossible where the sky had been so bright, so even. He set himself to draw this advance, watching the cloud hang along the precipices, waiting to stoop, and then engulf them. A wind began to blow, fitfully, rattling his sketchbook. The river-bed darkened: sounds were stilled that he had hardly noticed, insect songs and the odd bird call.

The thing that he had seen in Paris, the thing that he knew would change his ideas about painting, was a large canvas by Monsieur Monet, a painting precisely of mist and fog, *Vétheuil in the Fog*. It had been rejected by its prospective purchaser because it had not enough paint on the canvas. It was not clear and definite. It was vague, it painted little more than the swirl and shimmer of light on the curtain of white water particles through which the shapes of the small town were barely visible, a slaty upright stroke here, a pearly faint triangle of possible roof or spire there. You could see, miraculously, that if you could see the town, which you could not, it would be reflected in the expanse of river at the foot of the canvas, which you could also not see. Monsieur Monet had found a solution to the problem posed by Ruskin, of how to paint light, with the small range of colours available: he had trapped light in his surface, light itself was his subject. His paint was light. He had painted, not the thing seen, but the act of seeing. So now, Joshua thought, as the first thin films of mist began to approach his eyrie, I want to note down these shifting, these vanishing veils. Through them, in the valley on the other side, he could see a perpendicular race of falling arrows dark and glistening, the hailstorm sweeping. The speed of its approach was beautiful. He made a kind of pattern on his paper of the verticals and the fleeciness, the different thickness and thinness of the vapour infiltrating his own ledge. He must be ready to pack up fast when it descended or his work would be ruined. When it came, it came in one fierce onslaught, a blast in his face, an impenetrable white darkness. He staggered a little, under the blows of the ice-bullets, put up an arm, took a false step, still thinking of Ruskin and Monet, and fell. And it was all over. Except for one or two unimaginable moments, a clutch at life, a gasp of useless air, a rush of adrenalin, a shattering of bone and brain, the vanishing between instants of all that warmth and intelligence and aspiration.

Down at the Villa Colomba they had been grateful for their thick walls and windows. The garden had been whipped and the flowers flattened, the white dark impenetrable. It lasted only ten minutes, maybe a quarter of an hour. Afterwards the children went out and came back crying that it was like Aladdin's palace. Everywhere, in the courtyard, was a glittering mass of green and shining stones, chestnut leaves bright with wet and shredded, hailstones as large as hazelnuts. Arthur and Gwendolen ran here and there gathering handfuls of these, tossing them, crying, "Look at my diamonds." The solid, the enduring, the familiar landscape smiled again in the washed sunlight. Juliana went out with the children, looked up at the still shrouded peaks, and filled her hands too with the jewels, cold, wet, gleaming, running away between her outstretched fingers.

Sarianna Browning received a letter, and wrote a letter. It took time for both these letters to reach their destinations, for the weather had deteriorated rapidly after those first storms, the mules could travel neither down from the Villa Colomba nor up to the paradise of coolness and quiet. Whips of rain flung themselves around the smiling tops; lightning cracked; tracks were rivers; Robert complained of the deep grinding of the pain that might be rheumatism and might be his liver. The envelope when she opened it was damp and pliant. Phrases stood out: "terrible accident . . . taken from us at the height of his powers . . . we trust, with his Maker . . . our terrible responsibility to his father and mother . . . Villa Colomba unbearable to us now . . . we trust you will understand, and accept our deepest apologies and regrets . . . we know Mr Browning would not probably desire to visit us in Florence, though of course . . ."

Sarianna wrote to Mrs Bronson. "Terrible accident . . . we trust, with his Maker . . . Robert not at his best . . . weather unsettled . . . hope to make our way now to Venice, since Florence is out of the question . . ."

The sky was like slate. The poet was trapped in the pleasant room. Sheets of water ran down his windows and collected on his balcony. He thought of other deaths. Five years ago he had been planning to ascend another mountain with another woman; going to rouse her, after his morning swim, full of life, he had come round her balcony and looked through her window to see her kneeling, composed and unnatural, head bowed to the ground. She had been still warm when he went in and released her from this posture. Remembering this, he went through the shock of her dead warmth again, and shuddered. He had gone up the mountain, all the same, alone, and had made a poem of it, a poem which clambered with difficulty around the topic of what if anything survived, of which hands, if any, moulded or received us. He had been half-ashamed of his assertion of his own liveliness and vigour, half-exalted by height and oxygen and achievement, as he had meant to be. This dead young man was unknown to him. For a moment his imagination reached after him, and imagined him, in his turn, as it was his nature to imagine, reaching after the unattainable, up there. Man's reach must exceed his grasp. Or what's a Heaven for? Perhaps the young man was a very conventional and unambitious young man: he did not know: it was his idea, that height went with reaching, even if defeated, as we all are, and must be. Over dinner, Mrs Miller asked him if he would write a poem on the tragedy; this might, she suggested, bring comfort to the bereaved parents. No, he said. No, he would not. And elaborated, for good manners' sake. Even the greatest tragedies in his life had rarely stirred him directly to composition. They left him mute. He should hate any mechanical attempt to do what would only acquire worth from being a spontaneous outflow. Poems arose like birds setting off from stray twigs of facts to flights of more or less distance, unpredictably and often after many years. This was not to say that this tragedy, any tragedy, did not affect his whole mind and have its influence, more or less remarkably, on what he wrote. As he explained, his attention elsewhere, what he had explained before and would explain again, say, when Miss Teena Rochfort set fire to her skirts with a spark in her sewing-basket, in 1883, he thought of the young painter, now dead, and of his son, whose nude sculptures had been objects of moral opprobrium to ladies like Mrs Miller, and of Mrs Miller's hat. There was a poem in that, in her stolid and disagreeable presence, bedizened with murdered innocents, and the naked life of art and love. Lines came into his head.

> What
> (Excuse the interruption) clings
> Half-savage-like around your hat?
> Ah, do they please you? Wild-bird wings . . .

Yes. "Clothed with murder." That would do. A black irritability was assuaged. He smiled with polite enthusiasm.

The lady sits in the window. The scholar, turning the browned pages, discovers the letter that she will receive. At first, in the story that he is reading and constructing this letter appears to be hopeful. The poet and his sister will not go further south. They will set their steps towards Venice. But it is not to be. Further letters are exchanged. Torrential rain in Bologna . . . Robert's pains worse . . . medical opinion advisable . . . roads impassable

... deeply regret disappointing you and even more our own disappointment ... return to London. An opportunity has been missed. A tentative love has not flowered. Next year, however, is better. The poet returns to Venice, meets in the lady's drawing-room the Pretender to the French and Spanish thrones, discusses with him the identity of the Man in the Iron Mask, exposes himself, undaunted, on the Lido, to sea-fret and Adriatic gust, reads tombstones, kisses hands, and remarks on the seagulls.

Aunt Juliana kept, pressed in the family Bible, a curious portrait of a young girl, who looked out of one live eye and one blank, unseeing one, oval like those of angels on monumental sculpture.

SUGAR

Vom Vater hab' ich die Statur
Des Lebens ernstes Führen;
Von Mütterchen die Frohnatur
Die Lust zu fabulieren.
Urahnherr war der Schönsten hold
Das spukt so hin und wieder;
Urahnfrau liebte Schmuck und Gold
Das zuckt wohl durch die Glieder.
Sind nun die Elemente nicht
Aus dem Complex zu trennen
Was ist denn an dem ganzen Wicht
Original zu nennen?

GOETHE

My mother had a respect for truth, but she was not a truthful woman. She once said to me, her lip trembling, her eyes sharp to detect my opinion, "Your father says I am a terrible liar. But I'm not a liar, am I? I'm not." Of course she was not, I agreed, colluding, as we all always did, for the sake of peace and of something else, a half-desire to help her, for things to be as she said they were. But she was. She lied in small matters, to tidy up embarrassments, and in larger matters, to avoid unpalatable truths. She lied floridly and beautifully, in her rare moments of relaxation, to make a story better. She was a breathless and breathtaking raconteur, not often, and sometimes over-insistently, but at her best reducing her audience to tears of helpless laughter. She also told other kinds of story, all the time latterly, all the time we were in her company, monotonous, malevolent, unstructured plaints, full of increasingly fabricated

215

evidence of non-existent wickedness. But that is another matter. I did not set out to write about that. I set out to write about my grandfather. About my paternal grandfather, whom I hardly knew, and about whom I know very little.

When my father was dying, I came into his hospital room once, and he sat up against his pillows and looked at me out of his father's face. I had never thought of them as being alike. My father was a handsome man, in a very English way, blue-eyed, fair-skinned, with fine red-gold hair that very slowly lost its fire and turned rusty and then white. He had quite a lot of it still left when he died, very lively silvery hair, floating. He had a wide, straight, decisive mouth. None of these words recall him. His father, my grandfather, never had any hair that I can remember, and had heavy cheeks and a fuller, more petulant mouth. It occurred to me for the first time, seeing his face in my father's, to wonder if his hair had been red. He had had six children, of whom my father was the youngest, all of whom had the fiery hair. My grandmother, I am fairly sure, was dark brown. I did not tell my father that I had seen this semblance, partly because it vanished when he spoke, partly because I thought of it as unflattering, having as a small child seen my grandfather as someone off-putting, stout and old. The old were old in my early childhood, in the war years: there was an absolute barrier. My father never came to seem old as my grandfather was, though he was seventy-seven when he died. At the time when I saw my grandfather in him he must have had about three months left to live. He was, by accident, in hospital in Amsterdam. It was a spotless and civilized hospital, full of seriously gentle doctors and nurses all of whom spoke an English more perfect than might have been found in any hospital at home. My father disliked his dependence and they made it decorous for him. Whilst he was there, which was several weeks, we all, my sisters and brother and I, visited him. The visiting hours were long, most of the afternoon and evening, and for most of this time on most of these days, he talked to us. All my life, I had held it against him that he never talked to us. He worked with steady concentration, long long hours, and was often away on circuit. During my early childhood, when his parents were alive, he had been away altogether, in the Air Force, in the Mediterranean, in the war. He was called back from the Nuremberg trials to his father's deathbed, or so my mother had always said. What exactly he was doing there, if indeed he was there, I have never heard and cannot imagine. In those weeks in Amsterdam he talked a great deal, about his father, about his mother, about his childhood, as he had never done. I don't know if he realized how very little he had ever said. He was a silent man but by no means a cold or distant man, not as you might think of a distant man, if you read that word, immediately.

He was a judge. When I say that of him, I do not think of him as sitting in judgment. I think of him as a man with an unwavering instilled respect for evidence, for truth, for justice. When he delivered moral opinions, you could see that he was of his generation, time and place, a good man, a Yorkshireman, ambitious to better himself, aware, largely from outside, of social discriminations and niceties of class, a late-convinced Quaker, a socialist-turned-social-democrat. I respected his moral opinions, I share most of them, I am his child. But more than these opinions I respect in him his wish to be exact, a kind of abstract need which is somehow the essence of virtue. You might say, love is the essence of virtue. We were very inhibited people. Even my mother, with her indisciplined rush of speech, fantasy, embarrassing candour, endless barbed outrage, even my mother was essentially inhibited in that sense. We didn't know how to talk about love. But truthfulness, yes. All those weeks, he kept looking at what was happening, with his respect for evidence. Once, towards the end, it faltered a little. He argued quite fiercely about the inexactness of the terms benign and malignant. All growths are malignant, he said, if they are hurting you, if they are engrossing themselves at your expense. I could see he knew what he was doing, playing with words; his eyes were not taking his speech seriously. His father died of cancer of the prostate, or so my mother said. During this curious excursus about these adjectives he said, as though I knew, which I didn't, that when he had had "that growth" removed from his own prostate some years ago it had been entered on his record as "benign". "What do they mean, benign?" he said cunningly, deliberately confusing himself, looking at me to see if I too could be confused. By the time of this conversation he was back in London. I think he had been told what his expectations were. They were then in fact a bare three weeks, though I believed, and he may have believed, that he still had many months, maybe a year. He was partly being kind to me too, confusing us both. He thought at that time a great deal about his father's death. He told me once, I am now almost sure that it was he who told me and not my mother, that his father's sufferings had been terrible. My father did not die of cancer of the prostate, nor even, as far as we can tell, of the wholly unsuspected voracious lymphoma whose cells the Dutch surgeons had discovered in the fluids drained from him in the coronary ward to which he was taken after collapsing in Schiphol airport from the heart disease which he knew very well he had. He did not suffer in his father's way.

It was his father's death that was one of the main points of dispute in his relations with my mother, during their last troubled years. I am nearly sure it was this dispute that gave rise to the direct accusation of lying which so distressed my mother. She had always maintained that she had been present at my grandfather's deathbed; she had been present, she led us to suppose, at the moment of his death. The events of my grandfather's passing, the family intrigues and stresses, the testamentary injustices only righted by the hurried return of my father, the lawyer, were one of my mother's best tales. They had become part of my own shaky sense of my origins, a kind of Dickensian melodrama of which my mother had been a brisk and humane witness and my father a practical hero. I had a vision of this scene derived largely from Victorian novels and a little from my infant memories of my grandfather's house, huge, bleak, dark, polished and gauntly uncomfortable. It all took place, in my imagination, in a kind of burnt umber light, thick and brown. Various surrounding persons wore frilled and starched caps and aprons over black stuff dresses. There was a carafe and a finely etched water glass on a bedside cupboard and my shrunk bald grandfather in a huge mound of feather pillows and mattresses, suffering an ultimate drowsiness of too much painkiller and mortal weakness. The brown light drifted like heavy dust. I do not know where this vision came from: not from my mother, though it was indissolubly connected to her eyewitness narrative. In his last years my father maintained more and more stubbornly and acrimoniously that this account was a fabrication, that only he himself had been present, that my mother had kept well away. He adduced her behaviour during other family disasters and crises, and the evidence was on his side. My mother had a terror of direct confrontation with grief and pain. She avoided her own mother's dying; she did not attend her grandson's funeral. Nor did she come to Amsterdam. She affected to believe that this crisis was temporary and inconvenient. I have no idea what she thought in her heart. In any case, my father's evidence seemed on all logical grounds almost wholly preferable. It was just that I discovered, during those weeks in Amsterdam, that I needed an idea of the past, of those long-dead grandparents, and that the idea I had, which was derived from my mother's accounts, was not to be trusted and bore no very clear relation to truth or reality. It was also clear that my father, during those last weeks, was trying to form a just and generous idea of his own father, whom he had fought, at a cost to both of them. So his account had also its bias.

Perhaps I should now set out the elements of the family myth derived from my mother's accounts of my father's family. These accounts are dyed with her own perpetual anxiety as to whether she herself was, in the last resort, acceptable or unacceptable to them. Also by her own most necessary, most comfortable myth that she herself had represented to my father a human normality, a domestic warmth, an ease of communion quite absent from the chill household and extravagant passions amongst which he had grown up. As a small girl I believed what I was told, including this myth, despite having lived for months with my querulous and cross maternal grandmother, despite daily exhibitions of my mother's frustration and rage.

The idea she gave me of the family in Conisborough is skeletal and discontinuous. She liked to tell the same few exemplary episodes over and over: the strange behaviour of my grandmother with the teapot, my own first wintry visit to the dark Blythe House, the never-quite-explained indifference or aloofness of my father's family to my parents' wedding. She faltered in telling this, and I think told differing versions, in some of which my paternal grandfather attended briefly and in some not at all. Something had hurt her badly, and when my mother was hurt to the quick the narrative power became disjunct, the odd sentence failed to reach its verb and died on a question mark. The hero of the wedding story was her own father, a red-whiskered, extravagantly open working man who had done her proud and had also in some way been hurt, or so I deduce. I remember that grandfather well, my only relation given to loud laughter, practical jokes and a dis-respect for reticence. He was kind and frightening, and ambitious for his daughters in a practical way, though admitting to a regret that he had no vigorous, mechanically minded son.

The central figure of the Conisboro' family was in one sense my grandfather, who is presented as a Victorian despot, purblind to the feelings of his wife and children, wholly devoted to his business which was the manufacture and sale of boiled sweets. He seems to have spent no time in the company of his six children, and to have had no thought for their future other than that they should be incorporated, in due course, into the family business, which was their life. My grandmother, a devout Methodist, was characterized, always, by both my parents, as "a saint". My mother went in considerable awe of her, though she would also utter witty and disparaging comments on her ungainly housekeeping, and imply that they had, in the end, come to love and respect each other. The eldest son, my uncle Barnet, was crippled at birth, and spent his twenty-nine years confined to a wheelchair. My grandmother, my mother said, had devoted herself wholly to this helpless son, "did everything for him herself", insisted on lifting and changing and pushing even when her strength was unequal to it. As a result, my mother implied, the other five were neglected, were, in her phrase, "left to drag themselves up as best they might." They were all, also, my mother claimed, extra-ordinarily gifted, intelligent, creative, vital, stunted, apart from my father, by my grandfather's incapacity to imagine that educa-tion conferred any benefits, or that any life other than the making of boiled sweets could possibly be desirable. They went to the local grammar school, where my mother indeed met my father, in the eleven-plus intake. From there they were removed as early as possible, given, in my mother's phrase, "any *material* thing they desired' and set to work for the sugar-boiling.

Barnet, Arthur, Gladys, Sylvia, Lucy and Freddie, who was my father. I met some of them, extremely briefly, though not Barnet and Sylvia. They are not part of my life, only of stories and sharp pictures, which, if they have anything in common, have the idea of furious energy, unmanaged passion, thwarted and gone to waste. The Arthur I saw I associate with thick carpets and golf clubs: the Arthur of the myth wanted to live dangerously, was a skilled pilot, a motor-cycle speedway racer in the Isle of Man, a volunteer rear-gunner in the First War. He flew, my mother said, round Conisborough Castle, a gloomy circular ruined tower, visible in my childish imagination from the upper windows of Blythe House. I see him roaring and dipping, looping the loop and circling, watched by the red-headed siblings envying the brief speed and freedom. The only other thing I know about Arthur is the manner of his death. This story is my father's, unusually. He had a heart attack from which he recovered, assumed, without evidence, that he had an undivulged cancer and a short life expectancy, and went out, belatedly, to live dangerously again, thus precipitating another heart attack and a fatal collision with the back of a stationary bus. "Wine, women and song," my father said darkly, partly shocked by his brother's failure to examine the evidence properly, partly envious of the extravagance. Arthur never left Conisboro' and the boiled sweets, however. I remember him red and solid and a little bluff. I remember a resemblance to his father.

Gladys married young, and briefly, because she had to, my mother said. She married a coalminer and divorced him with considerable firmness once the immediate need for respectability was past. My mother did not expatiate on Gladys, whom she clearly disliked. I can't remember how old I was when she first told me these few facts – old enough to have read some Lawrence as well as suffering *Jane Eyre*, old enough to imagine a romantic red-haired girl in a long serge skirt running through fields, hiding behind hedges, with courage and fear, to a place of secret and absolute emotion. I see always a dry stone wall and grey green, slightly sooty Yorkshire hill-grass. This imagination was daunted by my incapacity to connect this girl with the wild, ageing aunt who visited us briefly, in Sheffield, when I was thirteen, and presented us with two huge, pink-cheeked, rose-pouting, lace-frilled dolls in cellophane-covered boxes, and a diverse and lavish set of manicuring tools in a soft red leather case. My mother made this transient visitor most unwelcome and she never came again. My mother in fact hated any incursion by any guest into her fenced and indomitably comfortable domestic territory. I remember them sitting at tea, on two corners of the dining-table, my mother's mouth pinched with disapproval and distaste. My aunt was large and alarming. She wore an odd hat, which I have recreated as a bright purple silken turban, though I think that is my invention, and had a great unruly mass of wiry gingery hair and very pale sharp blue eyes, close to the sides of a prominent beaked nose. My mother poured tea, and waited very obviously for the visit to be over. My aunt began various jerky speeches which trailed away; her movements were abrupt and awkward.

After she had gone, my mother spoke with concentrated and sharply expressed distaste of the vulgarity and unnecessary extravagance of the silly presents. It was only this year that my younger sister told me that she had found the dolls magical and beautiful. Later, this aunt spent several years in a caravan perched on the North Yorkshire coast. I remember my father's alarm when the radio reported that part of these cliffs had been swept away, perhaps in the terrible storms of 1953. I remember him going north to sort out some trouble in which she had threatened a neighbour with a garden fork. She was, my mother said, "quite mad". Certainly she died after some years in a mental hospital. My father went to visit her, during her last years, and reported that she failed to recognize him. He never I think described her, or her acts, to me, except during those last null years, when he would say sadly that it made you wonder what it was all for. I found her story hopeful and exciting, against the evidence. What I was afraid of, in the days when I first learned about her, was the "normal", the respectable, the quotidian domesticity which my mother claimed to be happiness, suffered with savage resentment, and exacted payment for, from those she cared for.

My grandfather's two youngest children carried out acts of considered rebellion and escape. My mother's favourite tale, apart from the tale of the teapot perhaps, was the tale of my father's act of severance. She herself, a girl from the working class, from a back-to-back house with no inside plumbing, but supported by her father, had won unprecedented scholarships to Cambridge where she went in what I imagine as a frail tremor of intellectual will and unimaginable social terror to read English. Her Cambridge was the Earthly Paradise and the Queen of Hearts' garden of arbitrary obstacles and disgraces rolled into one. Until she died she went over and over moments of solecism she had too late detected in those years. She dreamed at least yearly, perhaps more often, that she was to be forced to resit her finals with no warning, and consequently to be exposed as a fraud. My father, who was, my mother acknowledged, the only student in her year who did better than she did in exams, had been briskly removed from school by his father to become a commercial traveller in boiled sweets. My mother said that this was a black time of his life, and that he became very ill, frightening his mother once or twice by fainting into the coal bucket. The "into" was part of her graphic style. As a little girl I had a clear vision of his pale limbs somehow telescoped and contracted into this dirty receptacle, like a discarded dead root, though I think now that he was probably trying to lift it, that the blood ran to his head. I knew exactly where this coal bucket stood in Blythe House. It stood on the threshold between the kitchen and the cellar, whose dark door led into a frightening blackness I remember stepping nervously back from. I must have been three. The coal bucket can never have been there, but I associate the two blacknesses, the fear of uncontrolled falling. My mother said my father would never afterwards talk about this time. In Amsterdam he did, a little, half apologizing to some unseen presence for the great trouble he had caused by his mixture of deviousness and distress. He had worked, my mother said, secretly and alone and late at night, unknown to his father, to take the Cambridge entrance exam, had saved and skimped every penny of what she called his "pocket money" and he later, in the hospital, called "my wages" and had finally won an exhibition to read law. So he had confronted his father, and had explained that he had saved, from this allowance, enough money for his first year's fees and lodging, and that he meant now to go to Cambridge, because that was what he wanted to do.

The end of this tale always puzzled my imagination. My grandfather, my mother said, had been filled with pride and delight at this announcement, and had "fallen upon your father's neck" – an unlikely motion, I always thought, in that portly and rigid trunk. I think now the phrase derives from the good father's reception of the Prodigal Son, but that is confusing, for my grandfather's hypothetical embrace welcomed revolt and prodigality. In any case, my mother said, Pa had immediately put

£1,000 into my father's bank, in order that he should live comfortably at Cambridge. No sentence of my grandfather's speech was recorded in my mother's account of this episode, which, although dramatically delightful, causes problems about his nature, and the true nature of his unreasonable rigidity and his children's incapacity to communicate with him. How could they have had no inkling that he would have been proud or pleased? Was he capricious? Stubborn? Easily enraged? Had his children ever tried to explain to him what they wanted or hoped for? Had they inherited from my saintly grandmother an expectation of self-denial and strict obedience which precluded any attempt at dialogue? Was he formidable, was he wrathful, was he stony, was he emotional? No one has told me, I do not know anything about him. My father said, "Pa tried to do the best for us according to his lights, but he couldn't conceive of things outside his business." Where did it all come from then, the drive, the ambition, the passions of his offspring? I associate him with Dombey, if only because I think my father did. He once said that Dickens's observation of Florence Dombey was a miracle, that a child neglected and passed over and denigrated does indeed become more and more self-critical, more anxious to please, to find authority reasonable. But he himself did not submit for long. He went to Cambridge, and did well, and had tea in punts with my pretty and fragile mother.

The story of Lucy parallels that of my father, in some ways. This again is my mother's version. At some point my grandfather had sent Lucy and Sylvia on a world cruise, for what reason my mother did not say, though she made it clear that in her view a world cruise was a poor substitute for higher education and some degree of financial independence. Lucy had been ravished by the open spaces and free life of Australia during this journey. It was an idea that at second-hand moved my father, too. When I was myself sitting Cambridge entrance and he a very successful junior barrister, or perhaps during the first slacker year after he took silk, he found time to write a thick, escapist novel, in which the

hero moved from the dark, dirty and dangerous world of Sheffield steel mills to a land of clear, clean deserts and great flocks of
wheeling, pearly parrakeets. He threatened occasionally to
emigrate. It was his generation's dream in the years of austerity
and the choking class structure and battle fatigue. Lucy did in fact
carry out this post-war dream, appearing one morning at breakfast in Blythe House to announce that she and a young woman
friend had passages booked to sail that very day. "That very day"
is my mother's contribution, and perhaps suspect, but the tale is
the same. My grandfather could only tolerably be dealt with by
faits accomplis. His reactions to this announcement are not
known to me. Lucy went to a life of violin-playing and the
breeding of Airedales. In the early years of his retirement my
father went out to see the deserts for himself and came back
troubled about the corruption of the aborigines by alcohol, and
perhaps a little lowered, as a man is whose dream vision has been
replaced by a solid and limited reality. I was glad he never
emigrated for I early developed a passion for languages, and
thus for Europe. My father died European, despite his vision of
deserts, as a direct consequence of a journey up the Rhine, which
he thought over, as he sat in his high Dutch hospital room, talking
to the Humanist visitor about the novels of Conrad and Charlotte
Brontë she brought him, and to a young surgeon about the kinds
of hawk planing over the roofs which were all he could see.
"It was civilized," he said with satisfaction, of his last painful
venture. He described cranes and herons and castles and the
moonlit water. And his own defeat by a brief climb from
mooring-place to town centre. He was also a good raconteur, not
like my mother, deliberate, weighing his words, judicious, telling
you some things and holding others back.

When did my mother first tell me the story of Sylvia? I must
have been too young to be told it, whenever it was, for I remember
it as my first absolute confirmation that my mother's myth was
untrue, that the hearth's warmth did not keep off the cold blast,
that there was no safety. Before, I thought there were two sorts of

people in the world, those to whom terrible things happened, as in books and the news, and those condemned to the protection of normality and the threat of boredom and custom. I believe my mother told me this story in the war itself, in Pontefract, where she kept house miserably whilst my father was away, except for a brief period of anxious and exalted activity when she taught English to grammar school boys. I loved her then. She talked to me about subjects and predicates, Tennyson and Browning, the Lady of Shalott, and not about household dirt and failures of attentiveness. I should already have known about uncertainty. I was a gloomy child and was in my secret soul certain that my father would never return from wherever he had abruptly vanished to, his red hair shorn, hung around with canvas buckets and kitbags under his ugly folded blue cap. There was a boy, too, at school, who died one night of diabetes. I remember being distressed that I couldn't really *know* he was dead, that everything went on just as if this wasn't so. Perhaps I only really learned about Sylvia later, but associate the learning with these other losses. Sylvia had fallen in love, on that fated world cruise, with someone whom my mother described as a "remittance man" in South Africa. They had married, and my grandfather had provided for them by offering them a workman's cottage he owned, in Conisboro'. There was a child, another Sylvia, who was, I believe, more or less my own age. They were very unhappy. The remittance man, according to my mother, was "very cold. Pa didn't understand. He came from a warm country. He was desperately cold." My saintly grandmother visited, furtively my mother managed to imply, with blankets and hot soup. She provided these also for the local poor. Quite what happened to the remittance man I never dared to ask. As a little girl I thought the word meant that he was somehow provisional and not to be considered. Perhaps he went home, to the hot sun and the gold mines and his life before the incursion of my tragic aunts. I have given him, in my imagination, the features of a South African novelist I know, thoughtful, considerate, secretive, withdrawn. When I was little I saw him as a Gilded Youth, in a boater.

At some point in her own history, and certainly when I was only just born, Sylvia killed both herself and her small daughter. I know this, because I inherited certain toys belonging to this destroyed cousin. There was a dog, or nightdress-case, zipped, furry, black and white and peaceably couchant, whom I loved for years before I discovered his provenance. And after. I remember with terrible courage shouting, when some clearance of out-grown toys was proposed, "You can't throw Wops away. He was Sylvia's." Knowing I did not know what this sentence meant to them, using it to save my dog, shamed. "Your father smoked terribly for two years after Sylvia died," my mother said once. This at least explained why he, who never smoked, owned a chased silver cigarette case. I could not imagine his feelings. My mother had reduced her accounts of Sylvia to various manageable dicta. Sylvia, she gave the impression, was the most gifted of the gifted gaggle. She could have done all sorts of things, my mother said, and always added, "It was like putting a racehorse to draw a milk-cart." She said also, scornfully, "She was no housewife, she had no idea." I imagined a hut-like house, stone-floored, coal-fired, with barely room to turn round in. There must, however, have been a gas-oven. I think I took Sylvia's fate as a warning against both brilliance and sexual passion. My father used to be partly amused, but ultimately more alarmed, by any evidence of extravagant passions in his daughters. He was a romantically-minded man, and believed that the first lover is always the most important. He was a virtuous man, and was, it seems clear, steadfastly faithful to my mother. He spoke of his brother Arthur, in Amsterdam, with a kind of mild envy. He felt he had always been too cautious. "When I come before my Maker," he said, sipping the glass of wine the doctors, despairing of cure, had permitted him, "which I do not expect will happen, I shall have to beg him to forgive me my virtues." My mother said he had learned from the others' disasters, he had learned to be careful and to value security and domestic peace.

My mother's accounts of my grandmother's selflessness were like pearls, or sugar-coated pills, grit and bitterness polished into roundness by comedy and my mother's worked-upon understanding of my grandmother's real meaning. Whilst I cannot remember any quoted instance of my grandfather's speech I can remember various sayings of my grandmother, including her welcome of my infant self, on my first visit. There she stood on the doorstep, my mother said, rigid and doubtful – I imagine it for some reason taking place on a snowy evening, in the early dark. She did not say, how lovely to see you, or let me see the baby, or come in and get warm, but "It hardly seems worth the trouble of all that packing just to come here. Babies are always best in their own house, I think." My mother would always add a long explanation of this ungraciousness – my grandmother .was genuinely self-deprecating, she was very well aware of the real trouble of transporting a baby with all her equipment, she was thanking my mother for having made the effort. The grit inside the pearly sugar-coating was a fear of rejection by both women, perhaps. "I nearly just turned round and went home," my mother always said, and always added, "but it was just her manner, she meant very well, really." And "she was really very fond of me, she came to see me as a daughter, I was a favourite." The famous teapot story is another such instance. It took place, I think, in the war, during petrol-rationing. My grandmother was driven over by the chauffeur, from Conisboro' to Sheffield, to take tea with my mother and to see another baby. She sat briefly, talking to my mother. But when offered tea, she stood up abruptly and said no, no thank you, she had stayed too long, she must get back to pour my grandfather's tea for him, he expected it. My mother's emphasis in this story was on the childish helplessness of my grandfather, who, with a houseful of servants, could not stretch out a hand and lift his own teapot. My grandmother's formidable manner and her excessive dutifulness were part of each other, in my mother's vision, a kind of folly of decorum in which the result was the rejection of my own mother's carefully prepared tea and cakes. "All that way, and the petrol, and the chauffeur's time, wasted just to pour a cup of tea," my mother would say scornfully and yet with fear. This story runs into the story of my grandmother's death. Even in her last illness, my mother would say, when she was weak and in great pain, my grandfather would not allow her to sleep alone in a spare bedroom. She gave the impression, my mother, of the elderly man howling like a lost child, "creating" on landings until my grandmother wearily "dragged herself" downstairs again, to his side. "He couldn't sleep without her," my mother said. And "he had no consideration." This inarticulate crying out is the only image of his speech I have. I see him pacing in an improbable nightshirt, beside himself. My mother's contempt for male helplessness was edged with savagery. This operated even during my father's last illness, which she persisted in seeing as a fantasy and a betrayal, which could have been better handled. Her original announcement of his collapse included the authoritative and unfounded assertion that he'd be perfectly all right in a day or two, there was no need for anyone to bother. Her account of my grandmother's death is riddled with doubt, but I have nothing else certain to hold, or imagine, my father never got round to telling his version of that story, so the enraged and frantically obtuse old man persists in my memory.

I had almost forgotten what was perhaps her favourite tale, the perfect example of the fecklessness and neglect to which my father, before he found her, had been subject. Two of the sisters — she was never quite sure which — Gladys and Sylvia, Sylvia and Lucy — had gone out into the fields to play, taking with them the baby, my father, whom they had put, for safety, into a horse-trough and had wholly forgotten, returning without him, remembering his whereabouts only when, many hours later, my grandmother asked where he was. The child had been discovered, my mother said, by searchers, lying half in and half out of the water in the stone trough, as the dark fell, quite abandoned. She always affected to find this story amusing, and always instilled into it a very understandable note of bitter indignation against everyone, the girls, the mother, the father, the state of affairs that could allow this to happen. When my father returned to it in Amsterdam it was with a kind of Arcadian pleasure. "We ran wild," he said with retrospective delight, "we had so few restrictions, we had each other and the fields and the stables – we had an amazingly free childhood, we ran wild." His little room in the Dutch hospital was warmly lit, for a hospital room. He had bad days when he huddled under the blankets and shivered with final cold. He had good days when he sat up and talked about the world of his childhood, the pony and trap, the taste of real fresh bread, the journeys they made in the ponytrap to the races and came back in the dusk singing all together, the poems they wrote, the amazing variety of wild flowers there then were. "I grew up before the motor-car," he said. "You won't really be able to imagine. It was a world of horses. Everything smelled, rather pleasantly, of horses. The milk was fresh and tasty. There were real apples and plums."

During those weeks, during that unaccustomed talking, which despite everything was pleasant and civilized, as he meant it to be, he did try to construct a tale, a myth, a satisfactory narrative of his life. He talked about what it was like to be part of a generation twice disrupted by world war; he talked about his own ambitions, and more generally about how he had noticed that it was harder for those who felt they had achieved nothing to die. He talked above all about his childhood and particularly, perhaps, though not illuminatingly, about his father. He talked of how his Aunt Flora's coffin had been refused houseroom, even for a night, by relatives who disapproved of her religious views. He knew he was dying. He had set out because he sensed he was very ill. But we were told before him, and more specifically, how fast and of what he was dying. He was surprised about the cancer. "I had no idea," he said to me, with a kind of grave amusement at having been caught out in ignorance, ignoring evidence. "It never occurred to me that that was what they were worried about."

And, on another occasion, casually, but with a certain natural rhetorical dignity that was part of him, "You mustn't think I mind. I've nothing to regret and I feel I've come to the end. Don't misunderstand me – no doubt in the near future there will be moments of panic and terror. But you mustn't think I mind." He said that for my sake, but he was a truthful man. He was already steeling himself against the panic and terror, which were in the event much briefer and more cramped than we then supposed.

He had often said before, though he didn't repeat it, at least to me, during those weeks, that a man's children are his true and only immortality. As a girl I had been made uncomfortable by that idea. I craved separation. "Each man is an island" was my version of a delightful if melancholy truth. I was like Auden's version of Prospero's rejecting brother, Antonio, "By choice myself alone". But during those extreme weeks in Amsterdam I thought about origins. I thought about my grandfather. I thought also about certain myths of origin which I had pieced together in childhood, to explain things that were important, my sense of northernness, my fear of art, the promised end. By a series of elaborate coincidences two of these had become inextricably involved in what was happening. The first was the Norse Ragnarök, and the second was Vincent Van Gogh.

We went to see the *Götterdämmerung*, in Covent Garden, on the last night of my father's doomed Rhine-journey. I had a bad cough, which embarrassed me. Now whenever I cough I see Gunter and Gutrune like proto-Nazis in their heavy palace beside the broad and glittering artificial water, and think as I thought then, as I always think, when I think of the 1930s, of my father in those first years of my life knowing and fearing what was coming, appalled by appeasement, volunteering for the RAF. When I was clearing his things I found a copy of the "Speech Delivered in the Reichstag, April 28th 1939, by Adolf Hitler, Führer and Chancellor". It was stored in a box of family photographs, the only thing in there that was not a photograph, as though it was an intimate part of our family history. At the time, because I was thinking about islands, I remember very clearly thinking about the similarities and dissimilarities between Prospero and Wotan. I thought, in the red dark, that the nineteenth-century Allfather, compared to the Renaissance rough magician, was enclosed in Victorian family claustrophobia, was essentially, by extension, a social being, though both had broken rods. When Fricka berated Wotan, I thought with pleasure of my father, proceeding slowly and freely along the great river.

My favourite book, the book which set my imagination working, as a small child in Pontefract in the early years of the war, was *Asgard and the Gods. Tales and Traditions of our Northern Ancestors*. 1880. It was illustrated with steel engravings, of Wodan's Wild Hunt, of Odin tied between two fires, his face threatening and beautiful, of Ragnarök, the Last Battle, with Surtur with his flaming head, come out of Muspelheim, the gaping Fenris Wolf about to destroy Odin himself, Thor thrusting his shield-arm into the maw of the risen sea-serpent Jörmungander. I remember the shock of reading about the Last Battle in which all the heroes, all the gods, were destroyed forever. It had not until then occurred to me that a story could end like that. Though I had suspected that real life might, my expectations were gloomy. I found it exciting. I knew *Asgard* backwards before my mother told me about Sylvia, that is certain. I remember sitting in church, listening to the story of Joseph and his coat of many colours and thinking that this story was no different from the stories in *Asgard* and less moving than they were. I remember going on to think that Ragnarök seemed "truer" than the Resurrection. After Ragnarök, a very tentative, new, vegetable world began a new cycle, washed clean of blood and fire and gold. I may, I see now, rereading the book as I still do, have been influenced in these childish steps in literary theory and the Higher Criticism by the tone of the authors of *Asgard*, who rationalize Balder and Hodur into summer and winter, who turn giants into mountain ranges and Odin's wrath to wild weather, and who talk about the superior truths illustrated by the beautiful Christian stories. They are not Frazer, equating all gods gleefully with trees, but they set you on course for him. I identified Our Northern Ancestors in my mind with my father's family, wild, extravagant, stony, large and frightening. They were something of which I was part. They were serious gods, as the Greeks, with their love-affairs and capriciousness, were not. The book was, however, not my father's, but my mother's, bought as a crib for the Ancient Icelandic and Old Norse which formed an obligatory part of her degree course. I can't remember if she gave it to me to read, or if I found it. I do remember that she fed the hunger for reading, there was always a book and another book and another. She never underestimated what we could take. She was not kind to her children as social beings, she screamed at invited friends, she felt and communicated extremes of nervous terror. But to readers she was generous and resourceful. I knew she had been the kind of child I was, speechless and a reader. I knew.

It was with my mother, on the other hand, that the Van Gogh myth originated. Her family name had a Dutch shape and sound to it. Her family came, in part, from the Potteries, from the Five Towns, and a myth had grown up with no foundation in evidence, that they were descended from Dutch Huguenots, who came here in the time of William the Silent, practical, warm, Protestant, hardworking craftsmen, with a buried and secret artistic strain. This Dutch quality was a kind of *Gemütlichkeit*, the quality with which my mother had hoped to warm and mitigate the wuthering and chill of my father's upbringing. In Sheffield, after the war, we had various reproductions of paintings by Vincent Van Gogh around our sitting room wall. There was one of the bridges at Arles, one of the sunnier ones, where the water is aquamarine and women are peacefully spreading washing. There were the boats on the beach at Les Saintes-Maries de la Mer, which I recognized with shock when I went there eight years later. There was a young man in a hat and yellow jacket whom I now know to have been the son of Roulin, the postman, and there was a Zouave in full oriental trousers and red fez, sitting on a bench on a floor whose perspective rose dizzily and improperly towards him. There were also two Japanese prints and what I think now must have been a print of Vermeer's Little Street in the Rijksmuseum, a housefront of great peace and steadiness, with a bending woman in a passageway on the left. I always, from the very earliest, associated these working women in Dutch streets with my mother. I associated the secret inwardness of the houses, de Hooch's houses even more than Vermeer's, with my mother's domestic myth, necessary tasks carried out in clear light, in their own confined but meaningful spaces. In my memory, I have superimposed a de Hooch on the Vermeer, for I remember in the picture a small blonde Dutch child, with a cap and serious expression, close to the woman's skirts, who is my small blonde self, gravely paying attention, as my mother would have liked. The Sheffield house, in whose sitting-room these images were deployed, was one of a pair of semi-detached houses purchased as a wedding present for my father by his father, who could never, clearly, do things by halves, who thought, rightly, it would be an investment. We left one of these houses for Pontefract, during the war, for fear of bombs, and came back to the other. At the period when I most clearly remember the Van Goghs and the Vermeer/ de Hooch the second house was in a state of renovation and redecoration. My grandfather had died, various large and digni-fied pieces of furniture had come to be fitted in, and there was money to spend on wallpapers and curtains. I remember one very domestic one, a kind of blush pink with regular cream dots on it, a sugar-sweet paper that my parents repeatedly expressed them-selves surprised to like, and about which I was never sure. In my memory, the Van Goghs hang tamed on this delicately suburban ground, but in fact they cannot have done so. I am almost sure that paper was in the dining-room, where my Aunt Gladys was flustered by my enraged and aproned mother. In any case my earliest acquaintance with the paintings was as pleasantly light decoration round a three-piece suite. This was part of what he meant his work to be, sensuous pleasure for everyone. When did I discover differently? Certainly before I myself went to Arles, before Cambridge, in the 1950s, and saw that tortured and aspiring cypresses were exact truths, of their kind. When my father collapsed at Schiphol I was writing a novel in which the idea of Van Gogh stalked in and out of a text about puritanical northern domesticity. There was nowhere I would rather have found myself than the Van Gogh museum in Amsterdam. I was reading and rereading his letters. He wrote about the Dutch painters and their capacity to paint darkness, to paint the bright-ness of black. He wrote about the hunger for light, and about how his "northern brains" in that clear, heavy, sulphur yellow southern light were oppressed by its power. He was not cautious, he lived dangerously. He felt his brains were electric and his vision too much for his body. Yet he remained steadily intelligent and analytic, mixing his colours, *thinking* about the nature of light, of one man's energy, of one man's death. He painted the oppression of his fellow-inmates in the hospital in St Rémy. He was a decorous and melancholic northerner turned absolute and wild. He observed and reobserved his own grim red-headed skull and muscles without gentleness, without self-love, without eva-sion. He was truthful and mad. In the mornings I went and looked at his paintings, and in the afternoons I took the tram out to my father's echoing hospital, carrying little parcels of delicacies, smoked fish, fruits, chocolates. In the afternoons and the evenings he talked. He talked, among other things, about the Van Gogh prints, which were obviously his own, his choice, nothing to do with my "Dutch" mother. He talked particularly about the portrait of the Zouave. That was on one of his good days. I had bought him some freesias and some dahlias. I had not realized, in all those years, that he was one of the rare people who cannot smell freesias. He claimed that on this occasion he could. "Just a ghost of a smell, just a hint, I *think* I can smell it . . ." he said. He helped me to mend one of the dahlias with sellotape, where I had bent its stem. "You can keep them alive," he said, "if you keep the water-channels open. I've often kept things alive successfully for surprisingly long periods, that way." He talked about Van Gogh's Zouave, the one of the family prints I had liked least, as a child, because the floor made me giddy and because the man was alien, both his clothes and his face. It was, said my father precisely, "a very powerful image of pure male sexuality. Absolutely straight-forward and simple. It was always my favourite."

He looked at me over the tops of his little gold half-glasses and smiled. "Van Gogh went to find the Zouaves in the brothel in Arles," I said. I was going to go on to say that Van Gogh believed that the expense of energy in sex was bad for his, or anyone's art. But he wasn't listening. He didn't really think I knew anything about Van Gogh. He had the idea that he might get well enough to go round the Rijksmuseum and see the Vermeers. He did. My sister took him, alarmingly unstable and determined. He wanted to hear music. He wanted to fit things in. Sometimes I think he meant to shorten his time by living well, so that he would die quickly. The Dutch doctors put life into him with nitro-glycerine drips and blood transfusions. He told me one day, making a story out of it, how he had walked to the lavatory, lurching along walls, creeping along corridors, gripping bed foot and door knob, only to find a queue of other frail pyjamaed men. He told this story with a detached, comic anger. He was saying, in effect, "this is what we come to." He was measuring his strength. On one of his better days he set out on the same journey quite gallantly. We had bought him some slippers. He was very troubled about the loss of his slippers and nailscissors, which had gone ahead of him, in the aeroplane he missed, to the home to which he never returned. My mother, who became obsessively angry about the taxi which had waited in vain for this aeroplane, was further enraged to receive someone else's suitcase, in the event. "With a dirty shirt, and someone else's dirty comb and used razor," she said. My mother drew back from all human dirt and muddle. My father sat on the edge of his hospital bed, scrupulously clipping his toenails. His ankle, between his pyjama and his new slippers, was white, and smooth, and somehow untouched, covered with young, unblemished skin. I looked at it and thought how alive it was.

In the mornings I walked along dark canals. I liked the city. I remembered that Camus had said that its concentric canals resembled the circles of Dante's Hell. I even bought a copy of *La Chute* to check the quotation, and carried it around with a paperback copy of Van Gogh's *Letters*, to read over my solitary lunches. Its hero calls himself a *juge-pénitent*. He recalls the wartime history of the city, with ironic detachment. He pleads (in the legal sense). Amsterdam is, he says, "au coeur des choses. Avez-vous remarqúe que les canaux concentriques d'Amsterdam ressemblent aux cercles de l'enfer? L'enfer bourgeois, naturellement peuplé de mauvais rêves." Despite my reason for being in the city, I didn't find it hellish, more reassuring in its persistent sea-fretted solidity. The people were kind and reasonable. The university teachers had agreed to take cuts in salary and working hours, in order to avoid redundancy. My father, who had not walked along the canals, nor studied the brick house fronts, sat in his concrete-walled cell and worked out the social background of everyone he met, the surgeon, the Humanist visitor, the nurses, the other patients. Unlike Camus, he did not suppose that to be bourgeois was to incline towards hell, bad dreams and bad faith. But, in his generation, he found places on the social scale infinitely fascinating and important. The surgeon owned sea-going yachts and an empty piece of Scotland where he fished salmon and shot grouse. My father, even in those weeks, was delighted by this discovery, by this contact with good breeding and success. He said to me of his own father, diagnostically and matter-of-fact, "I suppose we were lower-middle-class really. That was what we were." He was being ruthlessly exact. He would have wished it otherwise. He talked to the surgeon in his professional voice, from behind his professional mask, more openly smiling than what I think of as his true self, the reflective, solitary face I watched, as he thought out his past, and his future. If he would have to ask his Maker to forgive his virtues, he was sure that they were virtues, and that he had exercised them. When he came home, to the London hospital, there was a strike on, the surgeons wore smeared gowns and the ancillary staff were brusque and sloppy. Amsterdam seemed a fitter place for him, somehow. Its strangeness was in a way life-giving.

To me, too. I took pleasure, despite everything, in mastering the train system, in reading words in a new language, in making friends with the Humanist, who was distressed by the approaching death of a teenage German heroin addict. I stumbled across the flower market, on the canal bank, where I bought him the dahlias. I sat in a restaurant in the Leidseplein and ate a huge bowl of mussels with a glass of good white wine, in the dying October sunlight. The table was in a little glazed front parlour, half outdoors, half in, which reminded me of the covered porch in my grandfather's Bridlington house, where I had spent a holiday bedridden with measles. The windows were finely etched with floral and geometric patterns. These, too, I associate with my grandfather. I see as I write that the etched drinking glass and carafe that stand by his bed in my vision of his death are those that stood in fact by my bed, on the only overnight visit to Blythe House. I remember that we inherited these objects at his death. My father was allergic to shellfish. He had collapsed in court in Naples, in 1944, after eating lobster, and had developed huge hives on the bench in Hull, twelve years later, after a prawn cocktail. A police surgeon, examining him privily in a cell, had told him he must never eat shellfish again, and he never had, though he had taken intense pleasure in them. I did not feel bad about eating the mussels. There was too much else to feel bad about, and I would not have eaten them if he had been there, I think. I did feel bad about the paintings. I experienced my one moment of desolation during those weeks in the middle of the Rijksmuseum, among all the darkly ingenious still lifes, the heaps of dead books, *mementoes mori*, the weight of the varying sameness of past endeavour, the silence, my own incapacity to stop and feel curious.

The Van Goghs were different. I could not like, I could not respond to the very last paintings, the tortured and incompetent cornfield, with the black despairing birds crowding over the paths which lead nowhere. But the great paintings of Arles and St Rémy shone. The purple irises on gold. The perturbed bedroom. The solitary chair. The reaper, making his deathly way through white light in fields of shining corn. I knew what Vincent had said about this painting as the image of a cheerful death, a secular human image, of a man moving into the furnace of light. I stopped thoughts off. I thought of Vincent in front of Vincent's paintings. I brought postcards to my father for him to see, contained, faded diminutions of all this glory, and he painfully addressed them to my mother, her sister, his oldest friend, in trembling writing, saying that he was all right. We have all inherited his handwriting, which was cramped and nondescript. My mother's was generous and flowing and distinguished. We were all trained differently, yet we all write his small scrawl. How does that come about?

We talked about heredity during those long visits. He said my mother had come increasingly to resemble her mother, and that there was a lesson in that. We also talked about my mother's untruthfulness. My father felt that it was a failure in perfect good manners to complain about her narrative onslaughts on his own veracity. (This was complicated by a powerful fear they both had of failing memory, since accuracy meant so much to both of them, after all.) He said, not for the first time, anxious about the fact that it was not for the first time, that we had been over this ground, that she had claimed to have been at his father's death bed, where she had not been.

"I should know," he said. "He was my father. I was certainly there. How can I be wrong?"

It was then that I saw that much of my past might be her confection.

"Have you ever thought," I said, "how much of what we think we know is made out of her stories? One challenges the large errors, like that one. But there are all the other *little* trivial myths that turn into memories.'

He was struck by this, and produced an example, of how some flowers had died, and my mother had supposed that perhaps the cleaning-lady might have watered them too little, or perhaps too much – probably too much, and that that was why they had died, because Mrs Haines had overwatered them, and so hypothesis became the stuff of fact.

Earlier that year, when it had been she who was ill, we had had a similar conversation, and I had said, joking and serious, "It's all right for you. *You* didn't inherit those genes." Both of us, under stress, found this very funny, we laughed, in complicity. Later he told his housekeeper, over coffee, that I was the image of his mother, that I resembled that family, strikingly. But I don't think this is true, and the photographs I've seen don't bear it out. Now, in moments of fatigue, I feel my mother's face setting like a mask in or on my own. I have inherited much from her. I do make a profession out of fiction. I select and confect. What is all this, all this story so far, but a careful selection of things that can be told, things that can be arranged in the light of day? Alongside this fabrication are the long black shadows of the things left unsaid, because I don't want to say them, or dare not, or do not remember, or misunderstood or forgot or never knew. I left out, for instance, the tear gas. I wanted to write about Amsterdam as clean, and reasonable, and enduring, and so it was. But two of us came out of the airy space of the Van Gogh Museum into a cloud of drifting gas which burned our throats and scoured our lungs. There were black-armoured police and stone-throwing evicted squatters. Behind our hospital-headed tram was a smoking column of burning cars. For several nights we couldn't return to the hotel directly; it was cordoned by police and the paving-stones were torn up. My father could not begin to be interested in these manifestations. He was fighting his own private battle. To omit them is a minor sin, and easy to correct. But what of all the others? What is the truth? I do have a respect for truth.

I remember one particular day at Blythe House, when both my grandparents were alive. I remember this day clearly, though it is not my only memory, possibly because I wrote about it at the time. Now I try to calculate how old I was, I see that I am already confused. It was during the war, during my father's Mediterranean absence, perhaps 1943 or 1944, certainly a very sunlit day during what I remember as a succession of burning still summers, the beginning of my hunger for sunlight. I had stayed at Blythe House in winter. It had seemed stiff and frightening and huge, whether because I was then very little, or because it was so much bigger than our wartime house I don't know. I remember an enormous cold bathroom, with a deep bath standing portentously in the middle of a huge empty space. I remember a view of dirty snow, a children's playground with slide and circular roundabout and swings on loops of chain. I remember the cellar mouth and a dark, frowsty kitchen. I remember my mother's pervasive anxiety. But this summer visit was different. I noticed things. I was not wholly passive.

At the beginning and end of the visit my grandparents stood formally side by side in front of the house, on a gravel drive, and I looked up at them. My grandmother wore a straight black dress, crêpy and square-necked. Her hair was iron-grey and caught up, I think, in a tight bun or roll. Her expression I remember as severe, judicious, unsmiling. Her stockings were thick and her shoes button-barred and pointed. She was composed, I could say, she made no unnecessary movements, no conciliatory speeches, no attempt at affectionate embrace. (My other grandmother rushed and enveloped us, smacking her lips.) My grandfather's face was obscured because it was tilted slightly backwards. He had a large protuberant belly, across which was looped a gold watch-chain. I remember his belly most. He was not a fat man, nor a large man, but substantial. I thought – or if I did not think, I have since regularly thought, so that the ideas are bonded to this memory – both of Mr Brocklehurst, the tall black pillar of *Jane Eyre*, and of Mr Murdstone in *David Copperfield*. I did not expect my grandfather to do anything frightening or condemnatory, though I was afraid of committing a *faux pas*. He was identifiably a Victorian patriarch, that is all. Though in those days I had no idea of historical distance and supposed we were all threatened with Newgate prison for debt, and with Fagin's night in the condemned cell. I could tell, I think, that my grandfather was not very interested in me, and that he had nothing to say to me. But in some way I cannot now remember matters developed so that he escorted us to the works itself, to see the boiling of the sugar. On this journey we were accompanied by a tall man in a brown overall, with a lugubrious, respectful and friendly face, and by some other forgotten man, who lingers in my memory only as the owner of a cloth cap.

The works was gaunt and bare. The floor I remember as mere earth, though it cannot have been: it was certainly dark, not tiled, and dusty. It was all like an enormous version of the outdoor washhouses of the north, draughty and cold and echoing. On the left as we went in were large vessels I associated with the coppers my other grandmother boiled sheets in, stirring them with a huge wooden baton. I saw, or I remember, four of these. One was full of sulphurous yellow boiling sugar, one of a dark, cherry-red, one of bright green and one, which amazed me because it was an unusual colour for sugar, of a kind of pale inky colour, a molten sea of heaving, viscous blue glass. The colours and the surfaces were brilliant and enchanted. They undulated, they burst in thick, plopping bubbles, they swirled with curving streamers of trapped air like slivers of glass. There was a smell, not cloying but clear and appetizing, of browning sugar. We moved on and saw large buckets full of this gleaming fluid poured onto a huge metal table, or belt, which ran the length of the room. Smoking it hissed down and began to harden. Men with paddles manipulated and spread it, ever finer, more translucent, wider, like rolled pastry magnified numberless times, the colours paling so that magenta became clear peony-pink, so that indigo became dark sky-blue, so that topaz became straw-gold. And a kind of primitive mechanical tart-cutter descended and stamped these gleaming sheets, making rows of rounded discs. The process had things in common with glass-blowing, which then I had not seen, but which later, in Venice, in Biot, reminds me always of the urgent work with the hot sugar, before it cools. Humbugs ran not flat but in a long coiling serpent, thick as a man's trunk at one end, tapering to thumb-size, through an orifice which simultaneously gave it a half-twist and bit. The most miraculous moment was when my grandfather urged the man in the brown overall to show me how the stripes were made in humbugs. Now I have it, now, almost, I hear his voice. It was both hesitant and eager and wholly absorbed in its subject. I cannot remember the words, but I can remember his certainty that I would find this process, his work, as startling and satisfactory and amazing as he did himself. This is all I know about him at first hand, that his work fascinated and absorbed him. The humbug stripes were as extraordinary as he had promised. The humbug sugar lay, hot and soft in a huge mass at one end of the table. The overall man pulled off an armful of it, which he rolled roughly into a fat serpent coil, a heavy skein, like my mother's knitting-wool, on his two arms. We went out of the shed, into a yard, where a large hook protruded from the wall – very high up, it seemed to me, so that he had to reach up to it. But I was a very small child for my age, maybe it was not so high. The man hung the fat tube of brown sugar – dark, treacle-brown sugar – over this hook and began to whip it around, and around. I knew this motion, it was the regular turn of the playground skipping rope, twist and slap, twist and slap. And as I watched, the sugar lightened. From treacle to coffee, from coffee to a milky fawn, from fawn to a barley-sugar straw colour, and from there, through the gelatine colour of old dried egg-white to pure white, no longer translucent but streaked and streaked with infinitely fine needles of air. "It's the air that does it," my grandfather said. "Nothing but whipping in air. There's no difference between the two stripes in a humbug but air: the sugar's exactly the same." I remember him saying, "It's the air that does it." I think I remember that. We took the white rope back into the factory, and laid it on a dark one, and the two were wound round and round each other, spiralling and decreasing in girth, by skilled slapping hands, until the tapered point could be inserted into the snapping machine. I remember the noise it made, moving on the metal, a kind of crunching and crackling of dried sugar, and a thump and slap of the main body of it – this last noise a magnified version of school plasticine-rolling.

When it was over, my grandfather fetched out several conical paper bags and these were filled with the fragile slivers of sugar that fell away from the stamping machine. Those too I still remember. At first they were light and powdery and crystalline, palest of colours, rose, lemon, hyacinth, apple. Hot they tasted delectable, melting like sweet snowflakes in those days of sugar rationing. If rationed out and kept too long they settled, coagulated and became a rocky mass undifferentiated, paper-smeared, sweating drops of saccharine moisture.

I wrote about this, at East Hardwick School. It is the first piece of writing I remember clearly as mine, the first time I remember choosing words, fixing something. I remember, still, two words I chose. Both were from my reading. One was from a description of birds on a Christmas tree, in, I think, Frances Hodgson-Burnett's *Little Princess*. The birds were German, delicate, and made of very fine "spun-glass". The word had always delighted me, with its contradiction between the brittle and the flexible thread produced. I remember I used it for the fragments in our conical paper bags. I remember also casting about for a way of telling how violent, how powerful were the colours in the sugar vats. I wrote that the green was "emerald" and I know where I found that word, in the reading endlessly supplied by my mother. "And ice, mast-high, came floating by   As green as emerald." As green as emerald. Did I go on to other jewels? I don't remember. But I do remember that I took the pleasure in writing my account of the boiling sugar that I usually took only in reading. Words were there to be used.

Later, my grandfather encouraged me to pick his flowers. He had a conservatory, on one side of the grey house, with a mature vine, and huge bunches – I remember many huge bunches – of black grapes hanging from the roof and the twisting stems. He gathered one of these, and encouraged us to taste and eat. "More," he said, when we took a tentative couple of fruit. "They are there to be eaten." Grapes were unknown in those dark days. I remember dissecting mine, the different pleasures of the greenish flesh inside the purple bloom of the skin, the subtle taste, the surprise of the texture and the way the juice ran. I was taken out and told to pick flowers. I took a few dubious daisies from the lawn. "No, no," he said, "anything, anything at all, you help yourself and make a really nice bunch." He liked giving, that too I am sure of, from my own experience. I made a Victorian nosegay. Everything went right, it formed itself, circles of white, round circles of blue, circles of rose, a few blackeyed Susans. And a palisade of leaves to hold its tight, circular form together. I ran up and down, selecting, rejecting, rich. My mother described the early age at which I had distinguished the names, phlox, antir-rhinum, lupin. I don't remember her much that day; she must have been at ease. Or else I was. It was unusual for either of us to be at all settled, at all confident, at all happy. It was almost like my father's idea of his family life as Eden, though then I didn't know of that, knew only that these grandparents were to be regarded with awe. I don't think I saw them again. We did not go there often, and after a time my grandmother died, and then my grandfather, who could not, my mother said, live without her. "He was like a lost child. He was quite helpless, all the life gone out of him."

My mother only outlived my father for a little more than a year. She did not appear to grieve for him, going only so far as to remark that she missed having him around to agree with her about Mrs Thatcher's treatment of the miners. She was curiously despondent about the prospect of dying herself under a govern-ment for which she felt pure, instinctive loathing. Immediately after the war she had once told me that when it began she had thought through, imagined through, all the worst possible things that could happen, to England, to my father. "Then I put it behind me and simply didn't think of it any more," she said. "I had faced it." As a little girl, I found this exemplary and admirable. Action is possible if you stop off feeling. Some chill I had learned from my mother worked in Amsterdam when I stopped off the dangerous thoughts possible in the presence of Van Gogh's dying cornfields or his dark painting of his dead father's Bible. I could talk to my father about his father only by not loving him too much, not exactly at that moment, not thinking too precisely about his living ankle, cutting him off. My poor mother maybe – in part – cut him off too efficiently, too early, faced it all too absolutely and too soon. During the war, I have been told recently, the Air Force wrote to her relations begging them to influence her to desist from writing despairing letters to her husband in North Africa. Wives were asked to keep cheerful, to tell good news, not to distress the men. She faced his loss, I believe her, and then complained of her lot. She said when he had died, bewildered and uncertain, "I had got used to it already, you see, I had got used to him not being there, all the time he was in Amsterdam." She was explaining her apparent lack of feeling.

The day of his funeral was bitterly cold. It was just before Christmas. It was a Quaker cremation, attended mostly by non-Quakers, who did not break the tense silence. I felt nothing, I felt fear of feeling, I felt the rush of time. Outside my mother was pinched and tiny and stumbling. I said, "I remembered the day he came back from the war." "Yes," she said, very small and vague. He came back at midnight, or so my mother always said. He had sent a telegram which never arrived, so she had no idea. She went furiously to the door and burst out "It's too bad", thinking he was the air-raid warden complaining about chinks in the black-out. What did they say to each other? I remember being woken – how much later? I remember the light being put on, a raw, dim, ceiling light, not reaching the gloomy corners. I remember the figure in the doorway, the uniform, the red hair, a smile as surprised and huge and half-afraid as I imagine my own was. I remember him holding his officer's hat. Why hadn't he put it down? Or am I wrong? I remember even an overcoat, but I confuse the memory of his return hopelessly with his parting. The hair was less red, more gold than I'd remembered. He had a hairy ruddy-ginger Harris tweed jacket which my mother had always said exactly matched his hair, and which I still think of as "matching" it, though I saw differently and remember better. (And how to be sure with all the years of fading between then and that last cold day?) I sat up, scrambled to my feet and leaped an enormous leap, over my bed, over the gap, over the bed with my small sleeping sister. I don't remember the trajectory of this leap. I remember its beginning but not its end, not my safe arrival. I do remember – this is surely memory, and no accretion – a terror of happiness. I was afraid to feel. This event was a storied event, already lived over and over, in imagination and hope, in the invented future. The real thing, the true moment, is as inaccessible as any point along that frantic leap. More things come back as I write; the gold-winged buttons on his jacket, forgotten between then and now. None of these words, none of these things recall him. The gold-winged, fire-haired figure in the doorway is and was myth, though he did come back, he was there, at that time, and I did make that leap. After things have happened, when we have taken a breath and a look, we begin to know what they are and were, we begin to tell them to ourselves. Fast, fast these things took and take their place beside other markers, the teapot, the horse trough, real apples and plums, a white ankle, the coalscuttle, two dolls in cellophane, a gas oven, a black and white dog, gold-winged buttons, the melded and twisting hanks of brown and white sugar.